TILL DEATH DO US PART

For My Family

PROLOGUE

Who am I? I know who I used to think I was. An honest, loyal, thoughtful, hardworking, generous and reliable person. I was a good wife, daughter and friend. I was someone whom everyone liked. The first word most people would use to describe me was "nice."

Did I change? Or maybe those words never described who I truly was. Did I just pretend to be all those things? Play the role? Maybe I've always had a secret self that I kept hidden from everyone else because I didn't think the real me was someone people would like. I don't know why I care so much about what others think of me. To be honest, I never liked being referred to as "nice." I always thought it was just another word for "weak."

We all have secrets, a part of us that we don't want others to see. But I'm starting to realize that my hidden self may be a lot worse than most people's, and I don't know how much longer I can keep it concealed.

CHAPTER 1

On a scale of one to ten, I'm hovering near a one. It's 9:00 a.m. on a Sunday morning and my head is pounding, which isn't unusual for a weekend. I roll out of bed and stumble, bleary-eyed, into the bathroom and turn on the light. My eyes suddenly feel like they've been struck by lightning. I lower the dimmer halfway. Today's hangover is a real doozy. It feels like someone has lodged an axe in the back of my head.

As I lean over the sink, a wave of nausea washes over me. I shut my eyes for a few seconds until the spinning stops. Then I splash some cold water on my face. When I bring my head up, I catch sight of my red, puffy eyes reflected in the mirror. Not the glamour girl from last night.

I'm 37 years old, but most people think I'm in my early 30s. Today I'm looking closer to my age. My bright green eyes are a shade darker, and my eyeliner is smudged underneath them creating dark circles. My hair which was nicely styled last night, is now sticking out in various directions. I grab it and tie it back in a ponytail. No need to have that image burned into my mind. As I'm tying my hair back, I notice a large bruise on my lower right arm. I have no idea how *that* happened.

I think back to last night. I can't remember what time I got home. How did I even get home? As hard as I try, I can't remember. It's like the memory is there just beyond my reach, but I can't grasp it. I know I drove to my office in Yaletown intending to leave my car there and pick it up today. I'm sure I wouldn't have driven home after drinking, would I? The fact that I can't recall anything is making me uneasy.

My stomach tightens as I walk into the living room and look out the window at the driveway. My car isn't there. *Phew!* Next, I search the kitchen counter where I usually keep my purse. It's sitting there on its side with the zipper done up. I open it and start rifling through its contents. I find what I'm looking for at the bottom, underneath my wallet. A taxi receipt. I breathe a sigh of relief as I examine it.

It looks like I got home at 12:37 a.m. Not that late. It doesn't show the pick-up location. *Good.* A wave of guilt washes over me. I crumple up the receipt and push it to the bottom of the kitchen garbage where it will be hidden under the rest of the trash.

My throat is dry and sore and I can barely swallow. Last night seems to have sucked every ounce of fluid from my body. Opening the fridge, I grab a container

1

of filtered water, but it's empty. I must have drank it all last night when I got home. I refill it with some cold tap water and then pour myself a glass. As I gulp it down, I feel a refreshing chill run down my throat. When I'm finished, I pour myself another glass.

From the window, I see dark clouds forming in the sky. A light object catches my attention. A lone owl sitting on my railing about 12 feet away staring directly at me with large, yellow eyes. Its grey and white body sits perfectly still. I've never seen an owl in the wild before. It continues to gaze intently at me. I find it unnerving. The loud sound of a toilet flushing in the ensuite bathroom startles me out of my trance. My husband must be up. My heart begins to pound. The owl flies away.

I quickly walk over to the electric kettle to busy myself as Jon walks into the kitchen. My back is to him so that we won't make eye contact as I begin filling the kettle with water. He doesn't say good morning. This isn't unusual. After eight years of marriage, the social pleasantries have disappeared.

"What time did you get home last night?" he asks as he turns on the coffee maker.

I let out a slow, controlled breath. "Around 12:30," I say, trying to relax my body and sound casual. Good thing I looked at the taxi receipt. He probably knows when I got home but wants to see if I'll lie. I quickly glance at him to gauge his reaction. There's a tightness in his face.

"Did you stay at JJ's Bar & Grill all night?" His voice sounds accusatory.

I pause, not sure of what to say. "Yes. We just hung out at the restaurant," I respond.

He waits a minute, as if he's processing my response, then asks, "What's new with Shelley?"

Is he testing me? "Not much. She was just talking about Peter and a trip she's planning to Mexico in the winter."

Shelley is my best friend. She recently separated from her husband, Peter, who left her six months ago after seven years of marriage. She had gone to Hawaii with a friend for a one-week vacation and when she returned, she found that Peter had packed all his things and left. According to her, there were no signs that he was unhappy and there had been no conversations about divorce. He even took her out for a nice dinner before she left on her trip. She found out later that someone had anonymously informed him that she was cheating on him. She said it was just a short fling that meant nothing to her. She was devastated that it had cost her her marriage.

"Did you drink a lot?" Jon asks.

I pause to consider my answer. Jon criticizes the amount I drink, so I don't want to admit that I overdrank. But I can't even remember getting home last night so I'm not sure what he already knows. Judging by his tone, he's probably aware that I overindulged, but I don't wish to admit it.

"No. I only had three glasses of wine," I say, as I grab the milk from the fridge. "But I left my car at my office. I didn't want to chance being over the limit."

2

Silence.

I continue, "Maybe we can go for lunch in Yaletown later, and I can pick up my car?"

When I turn back, he's walking into the living room.

"Yeah. Maybe," he mumbles.

Then I hear the T.V. The conversation is over and I'm relieved. He'll probably sit there watching T.V. for hours. It seems like it's the only thing he enjoys doing these days. He wasn't always like that. He changed a lot over the last couple of years.

I think back to the first time Jon and I met. I was 27 years old and I was at a house party with two of my friends, Shelley and Christie. The party was being held by Christie's boyfriend, Sean. The three of us met at Shelley's place and drank a bottle of wine as we got ready. I was wearing a tight-fitting, short red dress and my blonde hair fell in loose curls over my shoulders. With my three-inch heels, I was feeling pretty sexy.

At that point, I hadn't had much luck with men. I'd dated a lot and had two long-term relationships, but both had ended badly. I tend to be attracted to the charismatic, bad-boy type. The sex is good, but there's always a major character flaw. My first serious boyfriend was an alcoholic who got abusive when he drank, and my second one cheated on me. I was at the age where I was getting tired of going to bars and parties. My biological clock was ticking and I wanted to have children. I knew that I needed to change the type of man I usually dated. I wanted to find someone who was stable and responsible, but also fun.

The party wasn't that exciting. I spent most of the night hanging out with Shelley because Christie was off with Sean and I didn't know anyone else. Shelley and I had been introduced to Sean's friends, but they were all taken. There were a number of single men at the party who chatted with us, but I wasn't attracted to any of them. I got the impression they were more interested in Shelley anyway. She was tall and slim with long auburn hair and blue eyes. The guys were always swooning over her. Men found me attractive as well, but I've always been a bit shy. Shelley, on the other hand, is flirtatious and outgoing.

It was around 11:00 p.m. when I walked into the kitchen to pour myself another glass of wine. Then I made my way to the washroom—and there he was, leaning against the wall outside the closed bathroom door. He was six feet tall with dark hair and a boyish look. His light denim jeans flattered his lean build. He looked hotter than the devil in a sweatsuit. I was instantly attracted to him. I still remember our first conversation.

"Are you in line?" I asked, hoping to start up a conversation with him.

"Yeah," he answered in a deep voice. "But you can go ahead if you want. I'm not in a rush."

I remember thinking how sweet he was to offer. "That's OK. I'm not in a rush either," I responded.

He smiled. "How do you know Sean?"

"He's dating my friend Christie," I replied. "How do you know him?"

"We work together."

"Oh. You're an accountant?"

"Yes. But don't mistake me for someone boring." He smiled again, and I chuckled.

"Accountants do seem to have that reputation," I said in a playful voice.

"Have you heard the joke about the interesting accountant?" he asked.

"Um. No," I responded.

"Me neither," he said with a mischievous smile.

I laughed. I knew then that I was interested in him. I love a guy with a sense of humour.

"Where do you work?" he asked.

"I'm a massage therapist. I own my own business."

"Impressive! My back has been killing me. Do you have a business card?"

I was pretty sure he was just trying to get my contact information, but I didn't mind. I reached into my purse and pulled out a business card and handed it to him. He looked at it. "Claire. Nice name. I'm Jon." He stretched his hand out toward me.

"Nice to meet you," I said as I grasped his hand. His handshake was firm and masculine.

"The pleasure is mine." He continued to hold my hand a bit longer than necessary as he gazed at me. The gentle, soothing green of his eyes was like a peaceful lullaby. Then the bathroom door flew open ruining the moment, and a drunk woman stumbled out. She bumped into Jon on her way past us and spilled his beer.

He looked at me with an amused look on his face and rolled his eyes. "Are you sure you don't want to go first?"

"No. You go ahead," I replied, smiling.

"OK. If you insist." He winked at me and entered the washroom.

My stomach flipped. He was flirting with me! I waited anxiously outside the door, wondering what to do next. I knew I'd need to use the washroom once he came out, but I wanted to keep talking to him.

Jon exited a few moments later. "Hey. Do you want to go for a walk? I mean, after you're finished in there." He tilted his head towards the washroom. "It's getting crowded in here and it's such a nice night."

I tried to control the excitement in my voice. "Yes. Sure. That would be nice."

Jon hadn't told me that he only lived about five blocks away. When we got to his place, he invited me in for a glass of wine. Thinking back, it probably wasn't that smart to go into a stranger's apartment, but I'd had a few drinks and he seemed harmless. As it turned out, he didn't even make a move on me. We sat in his living room drinking wine and talking until the early hours of the morning. Eventually, he called a taxi for me, and it wasn't until I was walking out the door that he kissed me. He definitely wasn't the bad-boy type that I was used to, but I was glad. I was finished with those days.

Sipping my tea, I glance over at Jon sitting on the couch in the living room, absorbed by the TV. *How things have changed.* It's amazing how time transforms relationships.

I walk down the hall to the bedroom where I find the clothes I was wearing last night piled on the floor beside the bed. I put my tea on the nightstand and bend down to pick them up. As I do, I feel a sharp pain in my right knee. When I pull my pajama bottoms down to take a look, I find a big bruise and a cut with dried blood under my kneecap. What the hell did I do to myself? I pick my jeans up off the floor. There's blood halfway up the pant leg where my knee must have bled. Great. I hope I can get that out. There's also a small rip in the knee area. Oh well. At least that's in style these days. I walk over to the closet and push my jeans to the bottom of the laundry basket where Jon won't see them.

CHAPTER 2

The next day I arrive at work at 8:00 a.m. and make a beeline for my office computer. I sit down before taking off my jacket, and as I do, I feel a throbbing pain in my knee. Ignoring the discomfort, I turn on my computer and log into my email account and immediately start drafting an email.

Good morning. Happy Monday! I enjoyed spending time with you on Saturday. It was a lot of fun, as usual. I think we had a few too many glasses of wine though. My memory is a bit foggy. But I do remember the important parts. All of them ;) Are we still meeting for lunch today?

I want to ask what happened to my arm and knee, but I don't want to admit that I can't remember. It's a bit embarrassing, and I'm worried I may have done something stupid. I hope I just tripped on my stairs when I was walking up to my doorstep. Any scenario that doesn't involve someone witnessing me fall or smash into something would be fine. I feel guilty about drinking so much. I've never blacked out before, and I'm starting to wonder if I have an alcohol problem. Next time I'll try to limit myself to three drinks.

After I push send, I take my jacket off and make myself a cup of tea. I'm glad to be back at work where I can keep busy and stop speculating on whether I made an ass of myself. I will have an answer soon anyway when I receive a response to my email.

I sip my tea while I get the treatment room ready for my first patient. She arrives 15 minutes later and I spend the next hour treating her. After she leaves, I sit back down at my desk, fingers hovering over my keyboard as I prepare to log back into my email account. As the page loads, I hold my breath in anticipation. *Please don't comment on how drunk I was.*

When I scan my inbox, my heart sinks. It's empty. No response. I slump back in my chair. That's unusual. Maybe something did happen. I feel a knot in my stomach. No. I'm sure I'd remember anything significant. But why no response? It's 9:30 a.m. It doesn't make sense. Maybe there is an email and it got lost in the digital abyss. I refresh the page, hoping that it will appear. But as the screen reloads, the empty inbox stares back at me, taunting me with its lack of content. With a frustrated sigh, I turn off my computer and try not to worry. I'll check again after my next patient.

An hour later I sit back down at my computer. It's just after 10:30 a.m. I should have a response by now. I log back into my email. A blank screen stares back at me. No messages. This isn't good. Am I overreacting? Should I try calling or texting? No. Bad idea. I stare at the screen for a minute longer before logging out again. I'll check one more time after my next patient leaves at around 11:30 a.m. If there's no response by then, something is definitely wrong. We were supposed to meet for lunch today.

I'm thoroughly distracted as I treat my next patient and I do a poor job. But she doesn't seem to notice. All I can think about is why I haven't received a response to my email. I try to divert my attention to other things by making small talk, but I have a bad feeling in the pit of my stomach.

As soon as my patient walks out the door, I rush back to my computer. I take a deep breath and log back into my email with nervous anticipation. The screen loads—and nothing. I feel physically sick. Not even the decency of a response? An explanation? I clench my fists. We had planned to meet today. It's rude not to at least send an email cancelling lunch. I close my eyes and think for a minute before composing another email.

Is something wrong? I thought we were meeting for lunch today. Are you upset with me for some reason? It would have been nice to at least let me know that you are no longer available to meet.

I click, "Request return receipt," before pushing send. I take one last look at my computer and decide that I'm not going to keep torturing myself by checking my email all day. Obviously, lunch is off. I'll check my messages once more before I leave work.

My stomach growls, and I realize that I'm starving. I apparently have no lunch plans so I walk down the street and grab myself a sandwich at a coffee shop and bring it back to my office to eat. I don't feel like being around other people.

As I sit at my desk with my sandwich, I try to think of something positive. It's early June and summer is just around the corner. Jon and I have planned a vacation to Barcelona in August. We've booked a hotel with a rooftop pool right in the downtown area. I've been researching all the sights we can see, and we've booked a couple of tours.

I decide to search the internet for things to do in Barcelona, but after perusing a couple of sites, I realize that I can't concentrate. My happy thoughts keep reverting back to Saturday night, and I keep playing it over and over again in my mind. I remember most of the evening and it was fun. I just can't remember the end of the night.

I'm relieved to see my next patient arrive. It's Steve and he loves to talk. I'm looking forward to the distraction. I've been treating Steve for the last eight months. He always has a different problem. At first, it was his back, then his knee, then his shoulder. There never seems to be anything wrong with him. I think he just enjoys massage therapy, and his employee health plan pays for it. He always talks about his personal life. He's divorced and has tried the dating scene, but he hasn't met the right woman yet. It often seems like he's flirting with me, but I

7

can't be sure. We're about the same age, and although he knows I'm married, he jokes around about finding someone similar to me. It's kind of flattering.

"Hi Steve. How are you?" I ask as he walks through the door.

"Not bad, apart from my shoulder. I think I've pulled something again." He rubs the back of his shoulder. "How are you doing?" As he asks this, he has a look of concern on his face. Or is that my imagination? Could he really read me that well?

"I'm good." I fake a smile, trying to look happy.

He doesn't respond, but nods slightly, staring at me for a second too long. "Did you have a good weekend?"

I feel a stab in my chest as my mind goes back to Saturday night. "Yes. It was nice. I'm glad we're finally getting some warm weather," I say, trying to divert my mind back to my conversation with Steve.

"Did you do anything interesting?" he asks.

Steve is acting weird. What is he getting at? "No, not really," I respond, "but it's always nice to have some time off. How about you?"

"Yes. Actually, I went to the Boat Show. I'm thinking of buying 19-foot Four Winns Horizon for the summer."

I smile. The awkwardness of the conversation was just Steve trying to lead up to this revelation. He wanted me to know he was buying a boat. "That's great!" I say enthusiastically. "I've always wanted a boat."

Steve seems satisfied with my reaction, and I lead him into the treatment room. We spend the next 45 minutes discussing boats and how Steve pulled his shoulder while playing tennis.

Somehow, I manage to make it through the day, distracting myself by chatting with my patients. It's finally 4:30 p.m., and it's time for me to go home. I look at my computer, and a wave of dread washes over me as I log back in. I don't think that whatever I see will make me happy. It will either be an upsetting email or nothing at all. I take a deep breath as I click on my email icon.

It's the same blank screen that has haunted me all day. I sit back in my chair feeling deflated. Tears well up in my eyes. I find it hurtful. I hate it when people ignore me. I'm the confrontational type. If I have an issue, I discuss it. To me, silence is the loudest insult. I turn my computer off and clean up before leaving. All I want to do is go home and crawl into bed. But I can't. Jon will be home, and I'll have to act like nothing is bothering me.

When I arrive home, I find Jon in front of the TV. His favourite spot. And he'll stay there expecting me to make dinner for him. It would be nice if he could have dinner ready for me when I get home, seeing as he gets home first. But the stars in the sky will burn out long before that ever happens.

I've always been jealous of my girlfriends who have husbands or boyfriends who like to cook. There are a surprising number of men out there who love making gourmet meals for their partners. But not my husband. His idea of making dinner is boiling some spaghetti and pouring a store-bought sauce on it.

8

I get changed and start to prepare our meal. I'm in a bad mood and consider pouring myself a glass of wine, but since alcohol seems to have caused my problems in the first place, I decide against it. I think I'll have a hot bath instead and then go to bed early.

As I'm chopping a green pepper for the salad I'm making, I can see the TV in the background and the image that pops up on the screen makes the blood drain from my face. It's him. Underneath his image are the words, "Man Missing Since Saturday Evening." I walk into the living room like a zombie while the reporter speaks into the camera.

A 42-year-old man last seen in Vancouver has gone missing, and police are asking for your help in finding him. The Vancouver Police Department say that Brad Carleton was last seen on Saturday, June 14th near Hornby and Beach Avenue at 5:00 p.m. when he left his apartment to meet some friends for dinner. His wife says he didn't arrive home that evening and he hasn't been seen since. His wallet containing his ID was located yesterday at May & Lorne Brown Park. Brad is described as 5'11, with dark brown hair and blue eyes. He was last seen wearing jeans, a black hoodie and dark running shoes. He was also carrying a grey backpack. If you have any information, you are asked to call 911.

"Oh my God." The words come out of my mouth before I can stop them.
Jon looks at me. "What's wrong?"
I can hardly breathe. "I know him. He's a patient of mine."
"Oh. I hope he's OK," Jon says. "I wonder what happened to him."
I feel like I might throw up. I stare at the TV screen, which has now switched to a different news story.
"Are you alright?" Jon asks, giving me a strange look.
"Yes. I'm fine. I just didn't know he was missing. I hope they find him."
I walk back into the kitchen in a daze. I feel like a boxer getting up off the floor after a knockout punch. I decide that I will have that glass of wine all.

9

CHAPTER 3

The wine helps to relax me a bit, and I manage to make it through dinner. Then I retreat to the bathroom for a bubble bath, where I can finally be alone. I'm shaking as I step into the hot water and lay back in the tub. What if something's happened to Brad? I thought it was strange that he wasn't answering my emails. He always responds. I run through all the possible scenarios in my mind. Could he have been hit by a car or gotten into a fight with someone? Did he have too much to drink and pass out on the street? Could he have been taken to the hospital? Probably not. The police likely checked already. But then again, he didn't have his ID. Apparently that was found in the park near his apartment. So perhaps he's unconscious and hasn't been identified yet.

I try to think of any other possible scenarios. Could he have gone to a friend's house? Maybe he'd been fighting with his wife. No. He'd never just not show up or call. He has a good relationship with his wife, and he didn't mention that anything was out of the ordinary at home.

Please let him be OK. I replay the events of that night over and over in my mind, searching for any clues of what could have happened. I try to think back to the last moment that I saw him on Saturday night. I wish I hadn't had so much to drink. It's all a blur. I can't remember if he said anything unusual or if he seemed upset in any way.

I think he was planning on walking home. It doesn't make sense that he'd stay out by himself. He said he told his wife that he'd be home by midnight at the latest. He wasn't that far from his apartment so he wouldn't have caught a taxi, unless my taxi driver dropped him off first before driving me home. That's a possibility because I don't think I would have left him to walk home by himself. On the other hand, he may have wanted the fresh air.

I want to email him again, but I only ever email him from my work computer. And I never call or text him. We made a rule that we'd only communicate by email from work, so neither of our spouses would ever be able to find a text, email or phone call on the devices we keep at home. I don't know what to do.

Then another thought strikes me. Are the police going to figure out Brad was with me that night? Who did he tell his wife he was going out with? I think he said that he told her he was going out with a few of the guys from work. The police are probably questioning all of his co-workers and realizing that he wasn't with any of them.

Brad used one of his credit cards to pay for the hotel. The police will likely be checking his credit card payments to figure out where he was on Saturday night.

A chill spreads throughout my body. There were security cameras in the hotel and I will be on them. We also went to a restaurant and used cash to pay, but the waiter might recognize Brad if he sees him on the news. And the restaurant probably had security cameras as well. Are the police going to play the security footage of me on the news and ask if anyone recognizes the woman in the video?

I start to panic. I need to do something. I have to try to contact Brad. If there's any chance he's able to check his messages, I need to try. I get out of the bath and take my phone into the bedroom to send him an email from my secret email account with the fake name SaraWilkinson99. This will be the first time I've done this from my phone, but I think the circumstances justify me breaking our rules. I can feel my heart thumping as I log into my email, irrationally hoping to find a response to the emails I already sent. But there is none. I type out another message.

Brad, are you OK? I'm really worried about you. I just saw you on the news and the police say you've been missing since Saturday night. If you read this, can you please respond? I love you.

I push send and put my phone away. I hope wherever he is, that someone finds him alive by tomorrow. I knew this affair was a mistake. Did it end up ruining both of our lives? Would Brad be home safe and sound if he hadn't been out with me? And now will our spouses find out about us?

I've never been a cheater. I've been faithful to every boyfriend I ever had. I'm the type of person who would leave a bar early if another guy was showing too much interest in me when I was in a relationship. In fact, I've always been against cheating. I thought it was only people with character flaws who were unfaithful. But that was when I was happy. And at the time I met Brad, about four months ago, I wasn't.

A couple years into our marriage, Jon and I started arguing. Not about anything serious, just little things, like he'd open the dishwasher and tell me I put my plate in wrong. Or we couldn't agree on what movie to watch. But I think that's normal for most marriages. If I had to pinpoint when things started going really wrong, I'd say it was when we began trying to get pregnant.

At first it was fine. I went off my birth control pills, and assumed I'd get pregnant right away. But after a year with no luck, we started timing when we'd have sex so that it would correspond with when I was ovulating. Our sex life became regimented. Jon would ask, "Aren't you supposed to be ovulating today? Have you taken your temperature? Isn't it time to have sex?"

And after six more months of trying, Jon started blaming me for not getting pregnant. When I'd pour myself a glass of wine, he'd look at me with disgust and say, "You know that drinking decreases your chance of getting pregnant, right?" Feeling guilty, I eventually quit drinking. When that didn't change anything, he said I was working out too much. So I stopped that too.

I began to feel resentful. It seemed like our whole life revolved around trying to make a baby. And every month when I'd get my period I felt like crying. We tried everything—ovulation kits, taking my body temperature, and herbal medicines that were supposed to increase my fertility. To make matters worse, at around the same time that we were desperately trying to get pregnant, several friends started having their own families, seemingly without any difficulties. It felt like we'd been left behind. Like we were standing at an airport with our tickets purchased and our bags packed, watching as everyone else boarded the plane and took off to some sunny destination. After two years of trying and no results, we both got checked out by a doctor. It turned out that I was perfectly fine, but Jon was sterile.

The next year was extremely difficult. After we found out about Jon's infertility, our sex life declined significantly. We had spent years having sex for the sole purpose of getting pregnant, and now there was no reason to have sex. Jon also went through a depression. He was embarrassed to tell our friends about his condition, saying it made him feel like less of a man. He became insecure and controlling. He started making comments every time I went out with my friends, like, "Weren't you just out with her last Friday?" or, "You're going out *again*?" I only saw my friends a couple times a month, but it didn't matter.

Jon also started criticizing the friends I hung out with saying that they were alcoholics or promiscuous. Shelley was his least favourite of all my friends, and was also the one I spent the most time with. I felt uneasy every time I told him I was going out with her because I knew he'd make some negative comment about it. He seemed to have this fear that I was going to go out and meet another man who I could have a child with. I was constantly reassuring him that I was fine with not having children. But our love began to fade.

I kept telling myself that sometimes the hand you are dealt is not the one you want to play, but you can't quit the game. You need to patiently wait for better cards. I guess I thought our relationship would fix itself, that it was just a phase that Jon was going through. I let go of the picture of what I thought married life would be like and was constantly trying to find happiness in what I had. But I knew I was fooling myself. I wasn't happy.

Then Brad entered my life and turned my world upside down. About six months ago, he came into my office to be treated for lower back problems. I still remember him walking through the door. He was wearing dark jeans and a stylish black jacket that was unzipped, showing a tight-fitting shirt over his muscular torso. He was tall with dark hair that was shaved short at the sides and longer at the top. His eyes were a gorgeous dark blue like two pools of sapphire, beckoning you to dive in. They had a certain spark in them like they were smiling at you.

When he walked through the door and announced his appointment, it took me a moment to respond. I couldn't pull my gaze away from those piercing blue eyes. I handed him some forms to fill out and he smiled as he took them from my me. As he did, our hands briefly touched and I felt a tingle throughout every nerve in my body. There was something about his eyes, his smile and his air of confidence. I've never had that kind of reaction to a stranger before. When Brad was finished with the forms, he handed them to me with an amused expression on his face. I think he knew I found him attractive. Most women probably did.

I asked about his lower back pain, and he told me he owned his own flooring company, but wasn't involved in any manual labour. He didn't take his eyes off of me throughout the entire conversation and I could feel my face flush. I eventually led him into the treatment room and asked him to get undressed and lie face down on the massage table. I could feel him watch me as I walked out of the room and shut the door behind me.

A few minutes later, I knocked and entered the treatment room. He was lying on the massage table, the sheet half way down his body revealing his tanned, muscular back. I pulled the sheet down a bit further and began the massage.

I've massaged thousands of people before and it's always been very professional. I don't have sexual thoughts when massaging attractive men. But there was something about this guy. When I touched him and started rubbing oil on his back, I couldn't help thinking a few inappropriate thoughts. I was glad he was facing downward so he couldn't tell what I was thinking.

Some patients lie quietly while I massage them, while others like to chat. Luckily, Brad was the chatty type. We talked throughout the whole massage, which took my mind off of his amazing body. He told me that he had moved to Vancouver from Montreal ten years earlier to be with his wife. He worked full time, but also had a number of hobbies and outside interests, like writing poetry and volunteering at an animal shelter. He was the perfect combination of manly yet sensitive. He also enjoyed the same outdoor activities that I did—hiking, biking and playing tennis.

Brad began coming in for treatments twice a week, and we continued our chats. I started to feel like I'd known him forever. After the third week, Brad asked if I'd like to play tennis one afternoon on our lunch break. We both owned our own businesses so we had pretty flexible schedules. We met up a few times for afternoon tennis matches. I didn't tell Jon. He was already too controlling, and I knew he wouldn't approve of me meeting up with another man, even if we were just friends.

Brad soon started scheduling his treatments for 11:30 a.m. After his treatment he'd ask if I wanted to join him for lunch. Our relationship developed slowly. We were attracted to each other, but managed to keep things on a friendship level for a couple of months. But the chemistry between us eventually became undeniable and during one of our lunches, after a couple glasses of wine, Brad leaned over and kissed me. A soft, slow kiss on the lips. It wasn't really a surprise. It felt natural. He suggested we book a hotel for our next meeting, and that we leave a bit of extra time in our afternoon schedules. After that, our afternoon meetings often included hotel visits. We had the most amazing connection. It was like we were soul mates.

I feel lost now, not knowing where Brad is. I'm so worried about him. Things don't look good. He's been missing for two days and his ID was found in the park. It's hard not to imagine the worst. I check my email several more times before going to bed, but there's still no response.

Not surprisingly, I can't sleep. When I close my eyes a tempest of thoughts, worries and fears unleash—a storm raging in my mind. I toss and turn trying to find a comfortable position, but it's as if my bed has become a battlefield where my mind and body fight a never-ending war. How long will it be before the police check Brad's credit cards and find out that he was at a hotel on Saturday night? Will I wake up to find images of me and Brad plastered all over the news.

CHAPTER 4

The next morning, I wake up feeling like I've emerged from a deep dark pit. My eyes are heavy and my head feels foggy. I sit up and look around, feeling a sense of disorientation. The room is still dark, but the faint light of dawn is creeping through the window, creating a pale glow. Jon is sleeping silently beside me.

I stumble out of bed, my legs weak and unsteady, and make my way to the washroom. My body feels sore and achy as if I've been running from something all night. I need to take a shower so that I can shake off the grogginess that clings to me like cobwebs. Last night I came up with a plan, and I will need a clear mind to execute it.

I arrive at work early and immediately log onto my computer and search for criminal defence lawyers. I find a firm, Duncan & Taylor, that has good reviews. When their office opens at 8:00 a.m., I call saying that I have an urgent matter and need to speak with a lawyer as soon as possible. I'm told that Cole Hayes is available at 3:00 p.m., so I book an appointment and move my last two afternoon massage patients to later in the week.

I arrive at Duncan & Taylor 15 minutes early and sit down in the waiting room. There's a pile of magazines on the table in front of me, so I grab one and start flipping through it. My eyes scan the images and words, but my mind is elsewhere. I try to focus, but it's no use. My thoughts are scattered like a deck of cards thrown in the air. Sighing, I close the magazine and put it back on the table.

A few minutes later, a tall, thin man in a dark suit approaches me.

"Claire?"

I stand up, feeling a bit unsteady. "Yes."

He reaches out his hand and I shake it.

"Cole Hayes," he says in a deep voice.

"Hi, Mr. Hayes," I say nervously.

"You can call me Cole. Follow me. We'll go chat in my office."

Cole leads me down a hallway and around the corner into a small office. A bookshelf filled with law books sits against the back wall, and a couple of boxes are stacked in the corner. His desk has files piled to one side.

"Have a seat." He gestures to the chair opposite him. I pull it out and sit down.

"So, what brings you here today?" he asks with a serious look on his face.

I don't really know where to begin. I'm embarrassed to admit my affair and I'm unsure about the rules of confidentiality.

"It's kind of a personal issue. I need to know that anything I say will remain confidential."

"Yes," he replies. "Anything you say to me is protected by solicitor-client privilege. I can't repeat it to anyone outside this firm without your permission unless you tell me that you intend to harm someone, but I'm sure that's not the case." He smiles warmly.

I try to smile, but it probably comes off more as an awkward grimace. My heart is pounding in my throat. "I'm not really sure where to begin," I say. "Have you heard about the man who went missing? Brad Carleton?"

I have Cole's attention. He leans forward in his chair, losing his previously relaxed posture. His eyes are wide and sparkling, a glint of excitement dancing within them. I imagine he spends most of his days dealing with petty crimes and misdemeanors.

"Yes. I saw that on the news." He fixes his gaze on me, as if eagerly waiting for me to continue.

"I was with him the night that he disappeared."

Cole's eyes narrow, like he is trying to figure out my role in Brad's disappearance.

"I was having an affair with him," I say, feeling my cheeks redden. Cole nods with a knowing look.

"Have you told the police?"

"No. I don't want my husband to find out." I pause. "Or Brad's wife." I look down at the floor. "I'm worried the police will check his credit card records and find out he was at a hotel. I'll be on the surveillance footage."

Cole nods. "There's a good chance that the police already have his financial records by now, and they will be checking the hotel's CCTV recordings."

I'm not surprised. Now for the purpose of my meeting. "I'm wondering if there is some way that I can tell the police that I was with him, but have the information remain private?" I ask.

Cole thinks about it for a minute. "I can talk to the police without revealing your identity, and advise that I have a client who has some information about what Mr. Carleton was doing on the night of his disappearance. I can see if I can come to an agreement that any information you provide will be kept from the media."

Hearing this, I immediately feel the tension leave my body. It's as if a gentle breeze has swept through me, blowing away all the stress and anxiety. "That would be great," I respond with a bit more confidence in my voice. "I haven't gotten much sleep since all of this happened. I'm so worried that something bad has happened to Brad."

I look at Cole for reassurance, and although his eyes soften as they meet mine, his mouth is etched in a frown and his forehead is creased with concern. It's clear he doesn't think Brad is OK. Changing the subject, I ask, "So what will you need from me?"

"I'm sure this must be a very nerve-racking experience," he responds. "I'm going to need you to tell me everything you remember about that night—what time you met up with Brad, what you did, where you went, and when you last saw him."

I tell Cole everything I remember about Saturday night, explaining that I started the evening by driving to my office and parking my car. Then I met Brad at 5:30 p.m. and we checked into the hotel. After that, we went for dinner at a nearby restaurant, Trattoria Verdi, where we had a delicious Italian meal and shared a bottle of wine. Next, we walked a few blocks down the road to a pub with live music and had a couple more glasses of wine. Then we went back to the hotel. I'm not sure what time it was. We had brought a bottle of wine to the hotel earlier, and we opened it but didn't drink it all. We made love and lay in bed talking for a bit. Then we both had showers and left. I caught a cab home. I only know this because I looked at my taxi receipt.

I don't remember if Brad got in the taxi with me or not. His apartment is about a 20-minute walk from the hotel. We didn't meet in the evening often, but when we did, he'd usually walk home because he wanted the fresh air. But if it was late and he was drunk, I probably would have told him to get in the cab with me so it could drop him off on the way. Judging from the time I got home, he was running late. He had told his wife he'd be home by midnight at the latest.

"So you don't remember getting home at all?" asks Cole.

"No." I pick at one of my fingernails. "I don't usually drink that much." I wonder if I should tell him about my bruised arm and the cut on my knee, but I decide it's not relevant and I'm already feeling embarrassed.

"So the last time you recall seeing Brad was in the hotel room?"

"Yes. I remember him checking out, but that's the last thing I remember."

"Alright. I'll contact the police department immediately and see if I can negotiate a confidentiality deal. But you should know that if something has happened to Brad and charges are laid, then any statement you give to the police will likely have to be disclosed to the person who is being charged. But I think it's worth coming to some agreement at this point to keep your affair away from the media."

"Yes, I agree," I say, feeling a sense of relief.

Cole stands up. "Great. I will get in touch after I speak with my contact at the police station." Then he adds, "Hopefully, Brad will turn up unharmed." But I notice that his eyes don't meet mine as he says this.

When I arrive home, Jon isn't there. Normally he's home by 4:20 p.m. *Strange.* He must be working late. I change into some sweats and a baggy T-shirt. I've been checking my secret email regularly but there is no response from Brad. I've also been searching the news to see if he's been found or if there is any further information on his disappearance, but there's nothing.

I notice the light is on in the ensuite bathroom. Jon always leaves it on. Shaking my head, I walk into the bathroom to switch it off. As I do, I see the work clothes that Jon was wearing this morning sitting on the bathroom counter. I guess he came home from work and left again. I consider calling him to see where he is, but I figure he'll message me if he's not going to be home by 5:00 p.m., which is the time I usually get home from work. Feeling exhausted, I lie down on the bed and shut my eyes.

I'm woken up twenty minutes later when I hear the front door slam shut. I quickly get out of bed, not wanting Jon to see that I was sleeping and get suspicious.

He walks into the bedroom. "You're home early." His voice sounds sharp.

"Yes. My last appointment was cancelled. Where were you?" I ask.

"Oh. I finished early today too. I just went to grab a coffee."

He doesn't look directly at me. Something seems off. Jon works from 8-4 p.m., so I don't understand how he got off early. Plus, he doesn't have a coffee cup in his hand, and I know he wouldn't have sat down in a coffee shop to drink it. He always just grabs something to go. Maybe he put it down when he walked in the door.

Jon passes by me and puts his phone and wallet down on the dresser. I walk down the hallway to the kitchen, and scan the counters, but don't see a coffee cup anywhere. I peek in the garbage. Nothing there either. I suppose he could have finished it in his car, but I'm not going to go outside and look. The lack of sleep seems to be making me paranoid.

Jon's loud voice behind me, causes me to jump. "Did you have a good day at work?"

I turn to look at him. "Yes. It was fine. How was your day?"

"Good," he says, walking toward the refrigerator. "Did you hear anything more about that patient of yours who went missing?"

The question takes me by surprise and I can feel the adrenaline rush through my body as the room begins to shrink around me. I can't let him see any emotion.

"No. I haven't heard anything. I believe he's still missing," I say, but because I am worried about my voice wavering, I overcorrect and the words end up sounding harsh like I am angry.

Jon looks over at me and furrows his eyebrows slightly. "That's too bad," he says as he grabs a snack from the fridge and then sits down in front of the TV.

Way to go Claire. That was smooth.

Jon remains in front of the TV until I finish making dinner, which is the usual state of affairs in our household. I don't know if it's because of all the stress and anxiety I've been going through, but today it really bothers me.

I spend 45 minutes barbequing some steaks and making mashed potatoes and corn on the cob. Jon eats the dinner but doesn't compliment me on it, which is also not unusual. After dinner, he puts his dirty dishes in the sink and seats himself back down in the living room with his tablet. All of the dishes used to make the dinner remain on the counter and in the sink.

I walk into the living room.

"I guess I'll clean up," I say staring at him.

Jon looks up from his tablet. "Great!"

I know he got the hint but is purposely ignoring it. "It would be nice if you would do the dishes since I made the dinner," I say, trying to keep my voice calm.

"OK. Just leave them there. I'll do them later," he responds, his eyes not leaving his tablet.

"I don't want dirty dishes lying all over the kitchen. Can you just do them now?" I ask. "It's not like it takes that long to put them in the dishwasher."

"I'm tired," he says, jaw clenched. "I just want to relax for a little bit. I'll do them later." Then he looks over at me. "What's the big deal?"

"I don't like dirty dishes sitting around the house," I reply. I want to add that Jon will probably leave them there until tomorrow, but decide not to.

"Who cares?" he asks, the words dripping with annoyance.

"I do!" My voice is now shaking with anger. "I worked all day too, and I'm also tired and want to relax. But instead, I spent 45 minutes making you a nice dinner, which you didn't even comment on, and now I ask for you to help with the cleanup which will probably only take five minutes, and you refuse."

"I didn't refuse. But fine. I'll clean up the dishes," he slams his tablet shut, and starts to get up off the couch.

"Forget it," I say. "I'll just do them myself."

"OK. So you don't want me to do them?" he sits back down.

"I wanted you to do them without me having to ask," I respond. "I wanted you to recognize that I spent 45 minutes making a nice dinner after a long day at work and offer to help with the cleanup."

"I just offered," he snaps.

"No. You didn't. I had to ask."

"Wow, Claire. You need to calm down. What's wrong with you?"

Jon always knows how to push my buttons, and he's doing a great job of it now. "I am calm," I say loudly and recognize that I don't sound it.

"Why are you getting so upset about the dishes?" I know he's trying to get me going, and I should just ignore it, but I can't.

"It's not about the dishes," I say, letting out a heavy sigh.

"Well, that's what we're talking about." He rolls his eyes and shakes his head as if to suggest that I'm stupid.

"I'm just saying it would be nice if you did things without me having to ask," I reply, trying to keep my emotions in check.

"Look," he says, glaring at me. "I've had a hard day at work, and I just want to relax for a bit before doing the dishes. You're always harassing me."

"What? I don't harass you!" I reply, my voice loud.

"Yes, you do! 'Your bathroom's disgusting Jon.' 'Put your clothes away, Jon.' 'Why are you home early Jon?' You get upset at everything I do!"

"That ludicrous!" I yell. Then I add, "And at least I talk to you. You're always staring at the TV. The only conversation I get around here is with Siri."

He glares at me. "Yes. Your conversations about housework are so riveting. In fact, I'd be hard-pressed to think of a more interesting conversation." He shakes his head. "You're a real piece of work, Claire." Then he adds, almost under his breath, "And I don't mean art."

"Fuck you!" I yell, and then instantly regret that I've let him get to me. Still, I can feel the anger seething through my body as I turn and stomp back into the kitchen. His assessment of what he does around the house is completely at odds with reality. I clean up the dishes myself, making sure to bang them around loudly so Jon knows how mad I am. Then I walk heavily down the hall to the bedroom, slam the door behind me and stay there for the rest of the evening.

CHAPTER 5

The next morning, I get up early and leave for work before Jon gets up. I'm still upset about last night and I don't feel like dealing with him this morning. As I step outside and walk down our driveway, I look through the window of his car to see if there's a takeaway coffee cup. There isn't. I don't know why it bothers me so much, but it does. I just don't believe that he went out for a coffee yesterday and I'm wondering why he'd lie. I suppose I could have just asked him why he got off work early and where he went, but I didn't want him to question me along those same lines so I dropped it. Oh well. It's probably nothing. I have much bigger things to worry about.

When I arrive at work, I play my phone messages. There aren't any from Cole, but there are two from Shelley. She's the only person I told about Brad. She met him on one occasion, so she knows what he looks like and she's obviously seen the news reports that he's now missing. She knew better than to call me on my cell phone and take the risk of Jon overhearing our conversation, so she's been texting and leaving messages at my work.

With all the stress, I didn't feel like explaining what had happened, so I ignored her calls and texts. But now I feel like I need someone to talk to. I had previously booked two hours off work for lunch today so that I could meet Brad, and I don't want to spend that time alone. I send Shelley a quick text.

Do you want to meet at Carley's Café for lunch today? Noon?

Carley's is a little hole-in-the-wall restaurant where we can chat without the risk of anyone overhearing our conversation. She texts back almost immediately.

I'll be there. I hope everything's OK.

I'm looking forward to seeing Shelley. It's been difficult dealing with Brad's disappearance on my own, and it will be nice to have someone to talk to. There are still no developments regarding his disappearance and with each passing day, I start to lose hope. The uncertainty of not knowing where he is or what has happened to him has been unbearable. I've been trying to hold on to the belief that he will be found, but it becomes harder and harder as time goes on.

I need something to distract my mind. My first patient, Karen, will be arriving shortly. She's a 32-year-old petite Asian lady, who is one of my chattier patients. She's a housewife and talks a lot about her husband, who apparently spends a great deal of time at work. Karen doesn't have many friends and she seems lonely. I get the feeling that she's a bit neglected at home.

I suggested once that Karen get a dog to keep her company, but she says her husband doesn't like them, which seems odd. I could understand not having the time or not wanting to take on the responsibility of owning a dog, but I've never understood why someone wouldn't *like* dogs. They are the embodiment of loyalty and love. From the wagging tail to big slobbery kisses, they always seem to know when you need a friend. Jon and I discussed getting one, but we both work full-time, so we decided it wouldn't be fair to leave a dog home alone all day.

My phone rings while I'm setting up the treatment room and I miss the call. When I walk back out to check my messages, I find that it was Karen cancelling her appointment last minute. She apologizes but leaves no explanation. I feel somewhat relieved as I wasn't in the mood for her today. I don't mind patients talking about their personal lives, but she asks a lot about mine, which makes me uncomfortable—especially now.

When it's close to noon, I make my way to Carley's Cafe and find a quiet table near the back. Shelley arrives 15 minutes later. She spots me and waves, and when she reaches my table, she gives me a long hug.

"I've been trying to get a hold of you for days. Are you OK?" She pulls back and looks directly at me. "I saw the news. What happened? Weren't you with Brad on Saturday night?"

She knows I was because I asked her to be my alibi. I had to tell Jon I was out with her. I hate asking Shelley to lie for me. I know it isn't fair to involve her in my affair, but I rarely see Brad in the evening and I knew she would agree to do this for me. She's my best friend and I witnessed many indiscretions on her part when she was married, so I know she won't judge.

"Yes. I was, but I don't know what happened," I respond.

Shelley sits down across from me. "When did you last see him?"

"We were together until maybe midnight and then I went home. I don't know what he did after that." I feel tears welling up in my eyes.

"It's OK hon," Shelley says as she reaches across the table and rubs my arm. "So, what was he doing when you last saw him?"

I feel a tightness in my chest. "I'm not sure. We were at a hotel and I caught a cab home, but I don't know if he got in the cab or not. I had a lot to drink. I can't remember."

"You don't usually get *that* drunk. You can't remember anything?" Her eyes meet mine and her gaze is intense and penetrating as if trying to read my thoughts.

"No. I can't remember anything past leaving the hotel. It's weird. I've never blacked out before."

Shelley regards me for a moment. Then says, "I'm so sorry. What do you think could have happened?"

"I don't know. But it doesn't look good, does it?" I swallow and blink back tears. I don't want to cry in public.

Shelley's expression takes on a look of concern. Her forehead furrows as she asks, "Is there anything I can do?"

"No." I shake my head. "I'm worried that I might show up on the hotel security camera. And I'm sure the police will be checking Brad's credit cards and they'll see where he was."

Shelley nods as she takes in what I've said. "What hotel were you at?"

"The Blue Lagoon," I respond. As I say it, her eyes flicker with a hint of emotion, like a spark in the darkness. It's subtle, but I'm sure I saw it.

The waitress comes by and takes our orders. When she leaves, I say, "I hired a lawyer."

Shelley's eyes widen. "What? Why?"

I tell her what I discussed with Cole. Shelley seems speechless. I can see she thinks I made a mistake.

"Are you sure that was a good idea? I mean, won't the police investigate you now since you were the last person to see him?"

"I don't think so," I say. "I caught a cab home. It would be much worse if there was a news broadcast of me and Brad checking into the hotel. I can't risk having our spouses see that. Plus, someone would recognize me and the police would find me anyway."

"You're right," she says. "It was smart to contact a lawyer. It makes sense." Shelley takes a sip of her water, then asks, "But what do you think happened to him?"

"I wish I knew," I reply.

Just then my phone rings, and Duncan & Taylor appears on my call display. I look at Shelley. "It's the lawyer." She gestures for me to answer.

"Hello?"

"Hi, Claire. It's Cole. Did I catch you at a good time?"

"Yes. I'm just having lunch, but I can talk."

"Great. We have a deal. The police have agreed that if you come in and provide a statement, they will protect your identity. They will have a contract drafted up. They'd like to meet with you right away. I know you're working today, but are you free at 5 p.m.?"

That will be difficult, but I need to give my statement as soon as possible before the media gets a hold of any information. "Yes. I can be available then," I respond.

"Great. I'll take a look at the contract before we meet. Can you be outside the Cambie Street Station at say 4:30 p.m.?" he asks.

"Yes. I think so," I say, "as long as there are no traffic problems."

"I'll give you my cell phone number, and if you're running late you can let me know."

"OK. Do you know how long it will take?"

"I'm not sure," Cole replies. "Probably an hour or two."

This means I won't be home for dinner, but I'll have to make it work. I finish my call with Cole while Shelley watches intently.

"So?" she asks when I hang up.

"So, it looks like I have a deal," I say. "I'm going to meet with the police after work."

"That's fantastic! Such a relief. I've been so worried about you." She smiles warmly. "Do you want me to come with you for support?"

"No. My lawyer will be there so it will be fine, but thanks for offering." The waitress places our meals on the table. "I do need a favour though."

"Sure. Anything," she says and then sticks a forkful of spaghetti in her mouth.

"I need to tell Jon that I'm meeting you after work. I'll tell him we're meeting here for dinner."

"No problem," she says with a smile. "You know I'm always here for you."

When Shelley and I finish our lunch, I go back to my office and send Jon a quick text before setting up for my next patient.

Shelley asked to meet for a bite to eat after work. I hope that's alright. I should be home before 7.

I know Jon won't be happy for two reasons. It is the second time I am out with Shelley in one week and he'll have to make his own dinner. I send another text.

There are leftovers in the fridge.

It feels like forever before I'm finally finished treating my last patient. I look at my watch. It's time to leave to meet Cole. As I grab my car keys, I notice my hands are shaking. I really hope this goes well. I'll feel much better when the agreement is finalized.

As I walk out the door, it occurs to me that I might be able to get some information about how the investigation into Brad's disappearance is going. I hope they've found some clue as to what may have happened.

Traffic is light and I arrive a few minutes before I'm scheduled to meet Cole. As I sit in my car looking at the police station through the windshield, I can feel the fear in my chest, like a grenade that's ready to explode. I force myself to open the door and get out. Then I take a deep breath and try to calm my mind. I've practiced what I want to say many times. Everything should go smoothly.

Walking toward the entrance, I spot Cole standing outside the doors. Seeing him relaxes me a bit. It will be good to have him here with me.

"Hi Claire," he says with a smile. "How are you?"

He's wearing a navy-blue business suit with a purple and blue striped tie. I feel a bit underdressed in my jeans, T-shirt and cardigan. Oh well. I'm sure no one cares how I look.

"I'm fine," I respond. "A bit nervous."

"That's understandable," he says with a reassuring smile. "I thought we could go over the agreement before we meet with the police. Do you want to talk out here?"

24

"Sure," I say, wondering if I will even be able to concentrate on what he's saying.

"So basically, you are agreeing to provide the police with a statement in exchange for their agreement to keep your identity hidden."

"Yes. But I also don't want the fact that Brad was having an affair to go public," I respond.

"Right. And you'll see in the contract that your relationship will be kept confidential unless there is some clear evidence of foul play in Brad's disappearance, in which case the police may need to disclose the information you provide in order to further their investigation. If that happens, they may need to reveal the affair to another person, but they won't reveal your identity unless absolutely necessary."

I look at Cole, not completely understanding.

"For example, if Mr. Carleton were to turn up dead, and his wife was a suspect, the police may need to question her on whether she was aware of his affair because it could be a potential motive."

"OK," I say. It seems safe enough. The scenario only has his wife finding out if Brad's dead and she's a suspect.

"Also, if you were to become a suspect in his disappearance, the police would have the right to reveal your identity and the information you provide."

Me a suspect? I can feel bile creeping up my throat.

"Are the police going to investigate me?" I ask, my voice shaky.

"At this point, there is no indication of that. They likely would have figured out your identity on their own in any event, and if that happened the media might have found out about you as well. I think you made the right decision to come forward and voluntarily provide your statement. I believe this is the best we can negotiate in terms of confidentiality."

Cole looks at his watch. "Our meeting is in five minutes. Why don't you come in and read over the contract while we're waiting and let me know if you have any questions." He looks at me, his gaze soft and empathetic. "Don't worry. Everything will be fine."

We walk through the entrance to the police station and Cole tells the lady at the front sitting behind the glass shield that we have an appointment. We are asked to sit in the waiting room, which is surprisingly empty. I've never been to a police station, but I expected it to be more hectic, like the emergency department at a hospital.

I sit with my legs crossed, bouncing my knee up and down. For some reason, being at a police station makes me feel like I'm guilty of something. Cole passes me the contract to read over. It's only a couple of pages, but I'm having trouble concentrating, so I have to read some sentences more than once. I hand it back to him when I'm finished. I don't have any questions.

Cole tells me what I can expect to happen at the interview. I try to focus on what he's saying, but my mind keeps going back to his comment about being a suspect. I just want to get this over with.

A few moments later, a man in a police uniform enters the waiting room and looks at me. "Claire Johnson?"

"Yes." I stand up at the same time as Cole does.

"Hi. I'm Constable José Lopez." He extends his hand and I shake it. He looks to be in his late 30s. His dark hair is cut short, almost completely shaven. His stance is that of a marine.

José turns to Cole. "And you must be Cole Hayes?" Cole nods and shakes his hand. "We're ready for you. Please follow me."

José turns and heads back toward the door he came out of. We follow him through it and then down a long hallway into a small room with a table in the center. There's an Asian lady with shoulder-length dark hair sitting at it with a file in front of her. A water jug with glasses sits to the side.

"Please have a seat." José motions to the two chairs on the opposite side of the table from the lady. "This is Constable Dianna Chiu."

I sit down at the opposite side of the table from Dianna, my hands shaking as I clutch my purse tightly in my lap. José seats himself beside her, and Cole sits beside me.

Dianna looks at me but doesn't smile. "Thanks for coming in Claire. I understand Mr. Hayes has gone over the confidentiality agreement with you?"

"Yes," Cole answers for me.

"Great. Here is our signed copy." She passes it across the table to me. "If you can sign down on the bottom of the third page and have Mr. Hayes witness it, we can get started."

My mouth feels dry, so I pour myself a glass of water while Cole takes a quick read of the contract to make sure it's the same as his copy. Then I sign it and pass it back to Dianna, who slips it into the file folder in front of her.

Dianna begins by asking me some background questions—my age, address, employment and marital status. After that, she asks about my relationship with Brad—how and when we first met, where and how often we would meet, whether he mentioned any problems in his marital relationship, or if I knew of anyone who might be holding a grudge against him. Then she starts questioning me about the night Brad disappeared. I tell her everything I can remember, but the time frame is hazy. José sits beside Dianna taking notes throughout the interview.

"So you can't remember anything past leaving the hotel?"

"No."

"And you have no recollection of what time it was when you left?" Dianna's eyes are fixed intently on my face.

"No. But my taxi receipt says I got home at 12:37 a.m.," I reply.

"Right. And you threw that away?"

"Yes."

"But you're sure the receipt was from Greenline Taxis."

"Yes."

"Did you know that Brad turned his phone off at around 9:30 p.m.?"

The question catches me by surprise. Dianna's stern gaze is upon me, her pen twitching in her hand as she waits for my answer.

"I knew he would turn it off sometimes because he was worried that his wife might be able to track his location through his cell phone. He might have turned it off when we went into the hotel. I'm not sure."

"And did you also turn your phone off?"

"Yes. I think I did. It was off when I checked it in the morning."

Dianna looks at me for several seconds before nodding her head. "We took a look at the CCTV footage from the Blue Lagoon."

I feel a prickling sensation shoot up my spine. I take another sip of my water.

"It shows you and Brad leaving the hotel at 10:52 p.m."

I stare at her, mouth open. How is that possible? I didn't get home until 12:37 a.m., and my house is about a 25-minute drive from the hotel.

"Do you know where you went after you left the hotel?"

I glance at Cole. He looks at me with a quizzical look. He obviously wasn't expecting this question. I try to speak, but my mouth feels dry, and my throat tight. I clear my throat.

"I—I don't know. I thought I went home. I—" My mind is racing. "I don't know. Maybe I was trying to find a taxi." I know that's a lie. It wouldn't have taken that long to find a cab.

Dianna looks at me with a hard, skeptical expression. I can tell she doesn't believe me. Then she takes some notes. The room is as quiet as a tomb, other than the sound of Dianna's pen on her paper. As I sit there, I can feel my frustration and fear rising.

After what feels like an eternity, Dianna finishes her notes. Then she launches in asking more questions. My mind is a jumbled mess of fear and confusion and the rest of the interview is a blur. When it's finally over, we are asked to wait while José drafts up a statement for me to sign.

Sitting silently at the table, I suddenly feel hot and overwhelmed with nausea.

"Where's the washroom?" I ask, voice trembling.

José tells me it's down the hall and to the right. I stand up slowly on wobbly legs and walk in a trance down the hallway to the washroom. It is a single stall, so I shut the door behind me and lock it. Leaning over the sink, I splash some water on my burning face. Then I breathe in deeply, trying to relax.

Taking off my cardigan, I tie it around my waist. *Where did I go at 11 o'clock? What happened that night? Why can't I remember anything?* I feel my stomach churn. *Get a grip, Claire.* I refuse to believe I played any part in Brad's disappearance. I'm not violent. I know I would never hurt him.

Looking up into the mirror's unforgiving honesty, I can hardly recognize my face. My once bright eyes are now dull and tired, my skin pale and sallow. I grab a paper towel and dry my face. Then I apply some makeup before walking back down the hallway to the interview room.

Cole looks at me and quietly asks how I'm doing. I tell him I'm fine and sit down beside him. No one speaks as we wait for José to complete my statement.

When he's finished, he hands it to me to read over. It seems accurate, so I quickly sign it after Cole approves it. I want to get out of the police station as soon as possible.

As I pass the statement back to Dianna, I see that she is looking at my arm, rather than my face.

"That's quite a bruise you have on your arm. Where did you get that?"

I had completely forgotten about it, and the question takes me by surprise. I try to think of something to say, but nothing comes to me.

"Did that happen on Saturday night?" she asks, her expression cold and unyielding.

"I'm—I'm not sure," I respond. "I think so." I can feel a pain in the back of my throat and I know the tears are about to come. I hold them back, refusing to cry in front of her. I don't want to look guilty.

"You don't remember? That's quite a large bruise," Dianna says, her voice laced with doubt.

"No. I don't remember," I respond, and realize that this doesn't sound good. I follow it up with, "I bruise easily." I try to smile, but Dianna doesn't smile back.

"When did you first notice it?" Her face is inscrutable.

Hold it together Claire. "I think Sunday morning." I should have lied, but it's too late now.

"I see. Do you mind if we take a quick picture of that?" she asks in a frigid tone.

Great. Now it probably looks like I was fighting with Brad on Saturday night. But I don't want to refuse the photo, and I don't hear Cole speaking up and objecting. I think it's best if I cooperate.

"Sure. No problem," I say, trying to sound casual as my heart thumps in my throat. José leaves to get a camera and returns a few minutes later.

After the photo of my arm is taken, Cole walks me out to my car. As soon as we are out of earshot from everyone, he asks, "Do you know how you got that bruise?"

"No," I respond. "I was drunk on Saturday and I probably bumped into something."

"OK., he says with a nod. Then he adds, "I didn't know that they'd looked at the CCTV footage. Do you have any idea where you could have gone after leaving the hotel?"

"No," I reply. "That's the last thing I remember. I just assumed I went home."

"That's what I thought," Cole says with a reassuring look. "But let me know if you remember anything further."

It's 6:45 p.m. as I shut the door to my car to begin my drive home. I told Jon I'd be back by 7:00 p.m. and I don't want him to be suspicious, so I will need to hurry. As I start to drive, I realize that I forgot to ask José or Dianna whether there had been any developments in the investigation. The interview wasn't as conversational as I had anticipated. In any event, it appears that the only development was me on a security camera leaving the hotel much earlier than I believed. A shiver runs through my body as I try to push that thought out of my mind. I'd like to forget the whole experience.

Thankfully there's no traffic and I make it home just past 7:00 p.m. When I walk through the door, I find Jon watching TV with a dirty plate on the coffee table in front of him. Passing by the living room, I enter the kitchen and pour myself a glass of wine. I'm sure he will disapprove since he thinks I've already been out with Shelley, but I don't care. I need something to take the edge off.

Looking at Jon sitting innocently in front of the TV with the remains of his leftover dinner makes me feel guilty. What did I get myself involved in? He has no idea what I've done, all the lies and deceit. And now what if I become a suspect in Brad's disappearance? He'd hate me if he knew the truth, and he'd have every right to. I sit down beside him and he looks at me with surprise.

"How was your dinner with Shelley?" he asks.

"It was OK. She met a new guy and she wanted my opinion on him." I'm so tired of lying. Lately, the lies just roll off my tongue, one after another. "I would rather have stayed home, to be honest," I add. This, at least, is the truth.

He smiles. But then I see him glance at my wine. "I only had one glass with Shelley. I had to drive. Do you want a glass? Maybe we could watch a show together tonight," I suggest.

Jon takes a few seconds to respond. I think he's in between feeling suspicious, but also happy that I want to spend some time with him. "Sure. Let's choose a show." He passes me the remote and picks up his plate from the coffee table as he goes into the kitchen and puts it in the dishwasher. "I think I'll have a beer instead of the wine though."

CHAPTER 6

The next morning, I wake up feeling less anxious. Jon and I spent a nice evening together, and for once I don't have to worry about my face being broadcast all over the news. While Jon is in the shower, I lay in bed and check my secret email. It's become a morning ritual, even though I don't expect to find anything.

As I log on through my phone, I feel a sense of dread. It's the same feeling I always have when I check this email account. But as suspected, there's nothing there. I can't help feeling disappointed, even though I was sure I wouldn't find anything.

The second part of my morning ritual is to check the news. With a tightness in my chest, I search Brad's name on the internet to see if there are any new developments in his disappearance. But there's nothing, just a picture of his handsome, smiling face staring back at me. My heart still skips a beat every time I see his photo. But then I remember that he's missing, and all I can feel is a sharp stabbing pain.

I have a busy day at work so I get out of bed and turn the shower on. After I get undressed, I realize there are no towels. I walk down the hallway toward the linen closet, my bare feet gliding silently over the polished hardwood floor. As I open the door and reach for a towel, a soft murmur coming from the bedroom catches my attention and my hands pause mid-air. It's Jon talking in a low voice, barely audible. My curiosity piqued, I instinctively wrap a towel around me and tiptoe closer to the bedroom door. My ears strain to make out what Jon is saying.

"I've got to go," he whispers. "OK. Yeah. I've got to go." His words carry a sense of urgency that sends a shiver down my spine.

With a mix of trepidation and anticipation, my fingers tighten around the doorknob. As I enter the bedroom, I see Jon quickly place his phone on the nightstand. Then he starts making the bed, something he rarely does. He seems to be pretending that he wasn't just talking on the phone. When he looks up at me, I can see a flicker of guilt in his eyes. I consider asking him who he was talking to, but it will make me sound like I'm accusing him of something and I don't want to be *that* person. So I grab some clothes from my dresser drawer to make it look like I had a reason for being in the bedroom. Then I go back into the washroom and have my shower.

Jon has been acting strange lately. This isn't the first time I've heard him talking in a low voice on his phone and then getting off the call when he hears me coming. I wonder who he's talking to. It doesn't sound like a work call. Why would he have to whisper?

Shaking my head, I tell myself I'm being silly. I've heard that people who lie think that everyone else is lying too. It's ironic that I'm checking up on Jon when I'm the one being deceptive. I don't think he's cheating, but he does seem to be hiding something from me.

When I get to work, I check my appointment book. Steve is the first person booked. I'm glad. He's always chipper and chatty. He will take my mind off all the negative things happening in my life. After boiling the kettle for my morning tea, I sit down at my computer. Normally I'd be excited to log on and check my email from Brad, but today I feel lost. I will have to busy myself with work to keep my mind off of him because I know if I start thinking about him, the tears will come. I will need to let the sadness out at some point or it will poison me. But I can't right now.

Steve arrives 20 minutes later, right on time.

"Morning Steve."

"Morning."

"How are you?"

"Good thanks. You?"

"Good."

"You can go on ahead into the treatment room and get changed," I say. But Steve just stands there looking at me. There's an awkward silence. It seems like he wants to say something, but all he eventually says is, "Thanks Claire," and then he walks past me.

A few minutes later, I start the treatment. Something seems off with Steve. I try to start up a conversation.

"So are you going to buy the boat you saw at the boat show?" I ask.

"No. I'm still shopping around." Steve is definitely quieter than usual. He says nothing for a few minutes, but then he starts the conversation I think he's been wanting to have.

"I saw one of your patients on the news. The man that's missing, Brad."

How does he know that Brad was coming here? I don't know what to say. "Yes," I respond. "I saw that. I hope he's OK."

"He's a friend of yours, isn't he?"

I freeze. It takes me a second to process what he's just said. How does he know that Brad and I were *friends?* "Sorry?" My voice sounds squeaky. *Get it together Claire.*

"I've seen him here before. He drives a black Audi sports car, right?"

Should I admit I know what type of car Brad drives? "Um, I think so."

"I saw you with him a couple of times at the park playing tennis. I go jogging on the track there."

Crap. He saw us together. "Right. Yeah. We played tennis a couple of times," I admit.

"I saw on the news that he went out on Saturday night and never came home. I guess someone found his ID in a park. Pretty scary."

31

"Yes. It is. I don't know what could have happened." I want him to stop talking about Brad.

"His wife must be very worried about him."

I swallow hard. *Why is he mentioning her? Does he think I don't know he's married?* "Yes," I respond. "I can't imagine what she must be going through."

Steve doesn't say anything for a minute or so and I think the conversation is over. Then he continues. "I think I saw her a few weeks ago. I was at JJ's for a drink after work, and she was having dinner with Brad. She's quite attractive—tall, slim, long red hair."

Now I think I'm going to vomit. I don't know what she looks like. I never asked, and Brad never showed me a photo. We didn't really talk about our spouses much when we were together. Hearing how attractive she is makes me feel jealous. I know the feeling is inappropriate. I should feel bad for her, that her husband is missing and that he was cheating on her. Why is Steve telling me all of this anyway? Does he know about my relationship with Brad? Also, it seems odd that he's run into Brad so many times. Very odd. I'm starting to feel really uncomfortable. I need this conversation to end.

"Hopefully she has some family and friends to support her," I say and then I pause for a moment before asking, "So what boats are you looking at?" I hope the subject change isn't too abrupt. But I can't talk about Brad any longer.

The change of topic works. Steve seems happy to chat about the different types of boats that he's interested in and the pros and cons of buying one. Brad's name doesn't come up again in our conversation.

After Steve leaves, I sit down at my desk and close my eyes for a moment. So much for Steve taking my mind off Brad. Was that conversation really as weird as I thought it was? How could Steve have just happened to be in the same place as Brad so many times? I guess it's conceivable that he could have seen Brad here if their appointments were back-to-back. It's also not that unrealistic that he'd have seen us playing tennis. He mentioned that he lives near the park. Still, something about Steve's tone seemed off. I get the feeling he knows more than he's saying.

My next patient walks in early and I get up to prepare the treatment room. I'm distracted throughout the massage. My conversation with Steve plays over and over in my mind. I'm trying to remember my tennis games with Brad. Were we affectionate in public at the tennis court? I'm pretty sure we were. We often held hands and hugged or kissed.

We never saw anyone we knew on the tennis courts, and I didn't think there would be anyone in the park who would see us and recognize us. I guess I should have been more careful. But maybe Steve just saw us playing tennis like he said. I need to stop being paranoid. Worst case scenario, he saw us being affectionate and he tells the police he saw us together. They already know, so it really doesn't matter. I don't think he'd do that anyway.

By lunchtime, I've managed to push my conversation with Steve out of my mind. I am about to go grab myself a sandwich when I notice the message light flashing on my work phone. I play it.

"Hi, Claire. It's Cole Hayes calling. There's been a new development in Brad's disappearance. Could you call me as soon as you get this? I need to talk to you right away."

A shot of adrenaline rushes through my body. I immediately hang up and begin to pace back and forth as I type Cole's number into my phone. *Did they find Brad?*

"Hello?" He answers on the second ring.

"Cole? It's Claire." My voice cracks.

"Hi, Claire. Constable Lopez contacted me today. He says they found Brad's cell phone."

"Oh." I'm unable to hide my disappointment. I'm glad that there has been a development, but I had hoped that they found Brad. "Where did they find it?"

"That's the thing. Someone found it in the alleyway behind your office."

"Behind *my* office?"

"Yes. The police also found a towel with some blood on it in one of the dumpsters. They're going to send the towel in to the lab to see if the blood matches Brad's, but they'd also like to come by your office now and take a look around. They apparently dropped by earlier but your door was locked. I guess you were treating a patient."

"They want to come by right now? Why do they want to look in my office?"

"I'm not sure. They might want to see if you have towels that match the one they found. I believe they're investigating the scene in the alley as we speak. Once you give your OK, someone will come by. You don't have to cooperate, but they'd probably be able to get a search warrant anyway."

"I don't mind if they come in now, but I don't want them to be here when my next patient arrives at 1:30."

"That's fine. I'll let them know. Do you want me to come over? I have an appointment, but I could cancel it."

"That's OK. Hopefully, this won't take long."

I hang up, and look around my office to see if anything looks suspicious. I don't know why I bother. I have nothing to hide. Still, the police always make me nervous. As I'm tidying up, José walks through the door with another officer.

"Hi Claire. This is Constable Birk." I nod at the young police officer standing beside José. "Cole says he spoke with you and it's fine for us to take a look around?"

"Yes," I respond. "But I'm going to need you to be out of here before 1:30 if that's alright. I have a client coming in then."

He looks at his watch. "That shouldn't be a problem."

The two officers walk past me and start looking around. I sit at my computer pretending to work while they do. I glance up every few seconds to see what they're doing, but they just seem to be checking out the area. Then they disappear into the treatment room.

After ten minutes or so, José approaches me. He has one of my white towels in his hand. "Do you mind if I take this? We just want to compare it to the one we found in the alley."

"Um. Sure. That's fine."

"Thanks for letting us look around Claire."

"No problem."

The two officers walk out the door. I feel like someone has wrapped their arms around me and is tightening their grip. I need to stay focused. It's still lunchtime and I have half a day of work left to do. I take a look in my treatment room to make sure things are still organized, and they are.

Sitting down at my desk, I take a deep breath and go over the events of the day. Steve knows that Brad and I were spending time together and may know more. But more disturbing than that, is Brad's phone being found in the alley behind my office. Could we have possibly come back here for some reason that night? My office is within walking distance from the hotel. But I can't think of any reason why we'd come back here. Also, that wouldn't explain why his phone was in the alley. I do have a door that exists out back, but I never use it. Why would his phone be in a different place than his ID? Nothing makes sense. It's also been almost a week since anyone has heard from him and I can't help but think the worst. The towel with blood on it isn't helping to ease my mind.

Placing my head in my hands I wonder how much longer I can deal with this, hiding my feelings and pretending everything is fine. I feel like my foundations are cracking. It was only a week ago when I was smiling easily throughout the day. But that snapshot of my life is gone. Someone has stolen it and replaced it with something empty, photoshopped and distorted.

The rest of the day is a struggle. It's a relief when my last patient finally leaves. The thought of driving home and making dinner is exhausting, so I text Jon to see if he wants to order in pizza. He does, so I quickly order it before leaving my office.

The pizza arrives five minutes after I get home. Jon and I sit down in the living room to eat while we watch the news. As I was driving home, I tried to mentally prepare myself for the possibility that there may be a news clip about Brad and the new development in his disappearance, but nothing could have prepared me for what actually showed up on my TV.

Jon and I are halfway through our pizza when it happens. I'm grabbing a slice from the box when I looked up at the TV to see Karen, my needy patient. She's standing at a podium beside a police officer and the caption underneath her reads: "Wife of Missing Man, Brad Carleton, Issues Plea."

Karen sniffs and wipes her eyes as she clutches a gold cross hanging from a chain around her neck. Then she starts talking, her voice trembling.

My name is Karen Huang and Brad Carleton is my husband, my best friend and the love of my life. The last few days have been very difficult for me and our families. This does not feel real.

She pauses to blow her nose and wipe her eyes.

34

My husband left at 5 o'clock on Saturday night. He kissed me goodbye and told me he loved me. I have not seen him since. Somebody out there knows something, and I just pray they do the right thing. Please come forward. Brad was my everything. If you've seen him or know anything about his disappearance, please call the police.

Tears are streaming down Karen's face as she walks away from the podium. A police officer steps up to the microphone.

Karen's husband, a 42-year-old man, was reported missing on June 15th when he didn't come home after a night out with friends. His ID was located in May & Lorne Brown Park, and his cell phone was found today in an alleyway behind the 1100 block of Mainland Street in Yaletown. Brad Carleton is described as 5' 11, 180 pounds, with short brown hair and blue eyes. When he was last seen, he was clean-shaven and was wearing blue jeans, a black hoodie and dark running shoes. Anyone with information is asked to contact the Vancouver Police Department.

I stare at the TV as if my eyes are waiting for my brain to catch up with what they just saw. I'm completely frozen. Then I start to process the information. Karen is Brad's wife. I find this hard to grasp. They have different last names, and neither mentioned that the other was also a patient of mine. Did Brad know his wife was coming in for treatments? Or maybe a better question is whether Karen knew Brad was seeing me. I think about all the times she brought up her husband and asked me about mine, and now it all makes sense. She must have known, or she at least suspected, that there was something between Brad and me. Either that or she asks inappropriately personal questions of everyone.

My thoughts are interrupted when Jon says, "I guess they still haven't found him. It isn't looking good."

I realize I'm still leaning over the pizza box with a slice of pizza in my hand. I sit back on the couch and see Jon studying me. "No. It doesn't," is all I manage to say before taking a bite of my pizza.

He continues to look at me. "Did you know him well?"

I feel my face flush. "Not really. I just feel bad for him and his family."

"I feel sorry for his wife," is Jon's response.

We continue to watch the news, but all I can think about is Karen. Didn't she tell me her husband disliked dogs? But Brad told me he loved dogs, and he even volunteered at an animal shelter. So which version of Brad is the truth? And if Karen is Brad's wife, then who the hell was the red head that Steve saw him having dinner with? Perhaps my answer to Jon's question was more honest than I thought. Maybe I really didn't know Brad that well.

I don't feel like I can spend the rest of the evening trying to act normal. I want to go to bed early, get some rest and be by myself but I don't want to seem suspicious. I also don't feel like talking to Jon. I'm edgy and he'll probably notice that something is wrong. I'm pretty sure he already noticed that I was acting strange, but hopefully he just thinks I'm upset that someone I know had gone missing.

After dinner, I tell Jon that I'm going to read a book in the bedroom. As I crawl in under my covers, I try to concentrate on what I'm reading, but it's hard to block everything else out of my mind. Eventually I give up and go to bed early after all. But as soon as I turn the light off, thoughts of Brad enter my mind. I want so badly not to think at all, to have my thoughts absorbed by the night. But instead, I feel like I've just downed a shot of espresso.

Hours pass and the usefulness of my thoughts evaporate. Now I'm thinking crazy things. Steve's comment about Brad having dinner with an attractive redhead plays over and over in my mind. And the same thought keeps popping into my head. *Could it have been Shelley?*

CHAPTER 7

As the first light of dawn creeps into the sky, I stand at the kitchen window mesmerized by the sun casting a warm, orange glow over my garden. I watch as the light touches each flower, causing them to glow as if on fire. Then I see it. A blue rose standing out like a beacon. Its petals are a deep, rich shade of blue, almost as if they have been dyed by the hand of a master. The stem is long and slender, and the leaves are a vibrant green. It seems to grow in the sunlight as if it were imbued with some kind of magic. I smile, excited that I'm able to witness such a beautiful creation of nature.

Then I wake up, and I'm filled with a sense of disappointment as I realize it was just a dream—the same one I had a couple of weeks ago. I know that blue roses don't actually exist in nature, so why do I keep having this dream? A symbol of the impossible made possible? Or maybe it's something more sinister. A symbol of deception, of something that seems beautiful and amazing but isn't real. I'm not sure. Perhaps it doesn't symbolize anything at all.

Rolling over, I look at my bedside clock. It's 5:30 a.m. As I turn back, the room starts spinning and I feel like I might be sick. My sleepless nights seem to be taking a toll. I lay still for a few minutes until the spinning stops, but I still feel nauseous. Pulling the covers aside, I slowly slip out of bed, trying not to wake Jon. Then I tiptoe to the washroom. After quietly shutting the door behind me, I lean over the sink. My stomach heaves but nothing comes out. I stay there for a while longer to be sure that I won't vomit. My face feels hot so I splash some cold water over it. Looking in the mirror, I see a pale reflection staring back at me. A stranger.

Why? seems to be the question that I keep asking myself these days. Why did I make the choices that I did? Why did Brad have to disappear? Why can't everything go back to the way it was when I was happy? Why can't I remember that night?

Knowing there is no chance that I will fall back asleep, I go to the kitchen and make myself a chamomile tea. As I sit at the kitchen table, I search Brad's name on my tablet to see if there's any news. I've been wondering about the towel that was found in the alley, but Cole told me it would probably be at least a week or two before the police get the DNA results.

All I find with my internet searches are a bunch of photos and videos of Karen making her plea for help. The images make me feel sick again. I still can't figure out whether she suspected that Brad was having an affair with me. The fact that she came in for treatments isn't that suspicious. Maybe she asked Brad who his massage therapist was and decided to go to the same person. But if that's the case, it's odd that Brad never mentioned it to me.

I've replayed everything I can remember from my conversations with Karen, but I can't think of any specific comment that would suggest she knew. There's only one conversation that stands out. It occurred about two months ago on one of her first visits.

I was asking how her back was, and she said it was particularly sore as she'd spent the previous day taking a tennis lesson. She said her husband played tennis and she was hoping to find something the two of them could do together, but she thought it would take a long time to catch up to his level. She described how he worked long hours and how she was home alone a lot of the time without much to do other than housework and errands. She told me that when her husband wasn't working, he'd often go to the gym or play tennis, which again left her home alone.

Karen then asked if I participated in any sports. When I told her I played tennis, she asked who I played with. Now that I know who she is, I wonder if she already knew that I played tennis with Brad. When I told her I had some friends who played, she started asking whether I did any outside activities with Jon. This was followed by a number of questions about how much time Jon and I spent together.

I remember finding the conversation awkward. It seemed like she was prying into my private life, and in particular my marriage. At the time, I thought maybe she was just wondering if most couples spent more time together than she spent with her husband. Still, something didn't feel natural about our conversations.

I shut down the website with Karen's image and log into my secret email. I still check it every day, not wanting to give up on the possibility that Brad is still alive. When I pull up my email, I do a double-take. Something is different. There's a read receipt on one of my emails. I had forgotten that I attached a notification request to it. I can feel my skin prickle with excitement. Did Brad read my messages? But there's no response.

Then my heart sinks as it dawns on me. It was probably just the police. I don't know how they would get into this email account with his fake name, but I'm sure they have ways. Still, I can't help holding out a bit of hope that it might have been Brad.

I contemplate writing another email just in case it was him. But if it's the police, which is the most likely scenario, then I don't know if I should. I was sending my emails from a fake email address, but the police know about our affair and must know it was me. I'm not even sure what I'd write if I did send another email. I can't think of anything that I'd want the police to see. After thinking about it for a while longer, I type:

Brad? Are you getting these? I received a read receipt on one of my emails. If you're reading this, can you please let me know if you're OK? I've been so worried about you.

38

I think of telling him I love him, but since I don't know who's looking at this email account, I decide not to. I attach another request for a read receipt and send it. At least I'll know if someone reads this email.

Shutting my tablet, I take the last sip of my tea. I'm glad it's finally Friday. I'm exhausted and I need a break. My brain has been stuck in overdrive.

As much as I've tried to stop it, my mind keeps replaying the image of Shelley and Brad meeting for dinner. I know it's irrational. I can't think of any reason why the two of them would be meeting and not telling me unless they were romantically involved. But I can't picture Brad doing that. Then again, that's probably what most people who are cheated on say to themselves before they catch their partner with someone else.

Brad did tell me that he had been unfaithful to his wife before meeting me. And the fact that he cheats on his wife, who he claims to love, means he's capable of doing the same to me. One thing I've learned in life is that if someone does something once, they'll do it again.

As for Shelley, she cheated on her husband along with other boyfriends in the past. She's very flirtatious and loves attention from men. I think back to the only time she met Brad. It was a couple of months ago. We were in a loud lounge and I left them talking for a bit while I used the washroom and got us some drinks. They were standing very close together when I returned and I wondered if Shelley had been flirting with him. But when I joined them, I had Brad's full attention and I never thought anything of it.

In any event, I've never questioned Shelley's loyalty. Not since that night that changed our friendship forever. The night neither of us talks about. The night we both want to forget. I push the thought out of my head. I'm feeling too fragile right now to deal with that memory. It's been locked away for a long time, and I don't intend to twist that deadbolt open.

I need to get out of my house and clear my mind, but it's too early to go to work. It's been a while since I've worked out, which is probably contributing to my stress level, so I decide to go for a run. Creeping back into the bedroom, I manage to grab my running clothes without waking Jon. As I'm leaving the bedroom, I see his phone sitting on the dresser. I've been curious to know who he's been whispering to. I pause wondering if I should look at it. I know I shouldn't violate his privacy, but I can't help myself. Glancing back at the bed, I see Jon is still breathing heavily. Heart pounding, I pick up his phone and power it on.

Damn! It's password protected. I try to think what his password could be. We have a few common ones that we use for shared accounts. I try one and it doesn't work. I look over at Jon again. He hasn't moved. With a shaky hand, I try one more. This one also fails. Jon stirs. I quickly turn his phone off and put it back on the dresser before creeping quietly out of the bedroom.

I can feel a million little needles dancing on my skin as I walk down the hallway. I shouldn't have tried to get into his phone. It was wrong, but I only wanted to know who he's been whispering to. I wasn't going to snoop through everything. Maybe I should just ask him. Next time I catch him speaking in a low voice on the phone I think I will.

The morning run helps to clear my head, and I'm feeling much calmer when I arrive at work. Unfortunately, my feeling of serenity doesn't last long. When I open the door to my office, something catches my attention—a plain white envelope is lying on the floor. Presumably, it was pushed through the mail slot, which is rarely used for such purposes. My eyes fixate on the unassuming package, its presence unsettling. As I reach down and pick it up, a shiver crawls up my spine. I gingerly pull out the note that lies inside and carefully unfold it. As I do, large red letters jump out at me.

I KNOW WHAT YOU DID. RUN RABBIT RUN!

CHAPTER 8

The words seem to leap off the page and I almost drop the note. Adrenaline rushes through my body. Fear wells within me as I walk over to the window and look outside. Finding the parking lot empty, I look back at the note. My thoughts spin like a frenzied carousel. Who put this through the mail slot? What do they think I did? Are they referring to my affair? Brad's disappearance? Or could it be something else? There's only one other thing I can think of. But that happened many years ago. No one knows about it. Shelley and I vowed never to tell anyone. I can't imagine someone could have found out about *that* after all these years.

If the note is about Brad, then who could have written it? It would have to be someone who knew about our affair. I can only think of two possibilities. Karen and Steve. Shelley also knew about our affair but it wouldn't make sense for her to write the note.

I consider calling the police, but I'm worried they'll think the note has to do with Brad's disappearance and I don't want to become a suspect. I put the piece of paper back in the envelope, holding it between two fingertips in case I change my mind about giving it to the police. They would probably want to test it for fingerprints or other clues. I cautiously put the envelope in the back of my desk drawer and shut it.

Goosebumps cover my arms as I look out the window again. There's no one there, but I have a strange feeling someone is watching me. I walk back to my desk and sit down putting my face in my hands. Could someone have coincidentally found out about the secret from my past at the same time Brad disappeared? The thought is disturbing. I need to tell Shelley about the note. She should know just in case. I pull out my phone and send her a text.

Hey. Are you free for lunch today? I need to talk to you.

She responds a couple of minutes later and we arrange to meet at Bella's, a nearby Italian restaurant. It's never that busy, so we will be able to have a private conversation there.

Distracted by the morning's events, I fail to notice the blinking message light on my work phone. As soon as I see it, I pick up the phone and log into my voicemail. When I hear the voice on the other end, my heart stops for the second time this morning. It's Karen.

Hi Claire. It's Karen Huang.

Her voice sounds quiet and shaky. She sniffs and then continues.

Sorry for the last-minute cancellation earlier this week. There's been a lot going on, as I'm sure you've heard. Could I schedule an appointment for next week? Preferably Monday or Tuesday if you have something available. Thanks.

I hang up. Is it just by chance that she calls me on the same day that someone leaves a creepy note? I'm sure I could fit her in on one of the days she's requested, but now that I know who she is, I don't think I want to. Then again, I can't really tell her I'm booked up forever. Maybe it would be good to see her. I might be able to figure out if she knows something about my affair with her husband. Also, she may have some information about Brad that isn't being shared on the news. Reluctantly, I decide to call her back. Thankfully she doesn't answer. I leave a message scheduling her in for Monday morning.

When I arrive at Bella's, Shelley is already there, seated at the back. I wave and make my way over to her table.

"How are you doing?" She asks tilting her head to the side as I sit down across from her.

"Not well."

"What happened? Is it Brad?"

"No. When I arrived at work this morning, I found a note on my floor."

"A note?"

"Yes. It was in a plain white envelope." I describe what it said.

Shelley's eyes widen. "That's scary. Do you think it's about Brad?"

"I don't know. If it is, then I'm not sure who'd have written it. You're the only person I told about our affair."

"Well, I definitely didn't write it," she says in a defensive voice.

"No. Of course you didn't. But then who did? It would have to be someone who knew about me and Brad. And what does the note mean? Does someone think I was involved in Brad's disappearance?"

"It sounds threatening. Did you call the police?"

"No. Brad's cell phone and a towel with blood on it were already found behind my building. I'm worried about becoming a suspect." I go on to tell her how Karen was my patient, but also Brad's wife, and how she's made another appointment.

"That's odd. Maybe she wrote the note."

"Yeah. Maybe." I tear a bread bun in half and put butter on it. "Do you think there's any way it could be about—" I pause and give her a look. I know she'll understand what I'm referring to. I watch as her face becomes one shade paler.

"But nobody knows about that." She looks at me with concern. "You didn't tell anyone did you?"

"No. Of course not. Did you?"

"No," she says glancing sideways and then back again. It looks like she's about to say something more but then stops.

"I just wanted to let you know in case," I say in a reassuring voice. She nods her head. "But I'm sure it's about Brad, which isn't exactly comforting. It means someone knew about our affair, or at least suspected."

"Do you think Jon knows?" she asks.

I hadn't considered that it could be him. He has been acting strange lately. But I can't see him slipping a note through my office door. What would be the point of that? I think he'd just confront me.

"No," I respond. "I'm pretty sure he doesn't know. Even if he did, I don't think he'd write a note like that."

"Yeah. I don't think Jon would do that either. It's probably Brad's wife."

Since we're talking about Karen, I decide it's a good time to discuss another subject that has been bothering me.

"There was another strange thing that happened. One of my patients recently saw Brad at JJ's having dinner with an attractive woman with long red hair."

I leave my statement hanging and study Shelley to see her reaction. Her face falls. She knows I'm asking if it was her.

"Oh. Really? That's strange." She pauses and I feel my stomach sink as I wait and prepare myself for her to lie. "It wasn't me," she says and laughs nervously.

I don't know if I believe her. I decide to try a different tack. "Do you think he could have been seeing another woman?"

Shelley shrugs her shoulders. "I'm not sure. I don't know him. He cheats on his wife, so I guess he could be. But from what you told me, it seemed like he was in love with you, so I can't imagine he'd be with a third woman." She pauses and sips her water. "Unless he's some sort of a pathological liar."

The thought bothers me. Could Brad have been lying to me and seeing another woman? That in itself is heartbreaking, and if he was cheating on me with my best friend? I just can't believe he'd do that. But I know Shelley, and I still think there's something she isn't saying.

"Yeah. You're right," I respond. "I don't think he'd be with a third woman. But then who is the redhead he was having dinner with?"

"Who knows? Maybe it was just a business dinner or an old friend or relative or something."

"Yeah. I guess it could have been anyone," I say unconvinced.

The rest of our lunch seems awkward and I make an excuse to leave early, saying that I have to set up for my next appointment.

As I park in front of my office, the feeling that someone is watching me returns. After shutting the car door behind me, I look around the parking lot. There are a lot of parked cars, but no one in sight. As I unlock the door to my office, I start to second-guess my decision to keep the note a secret. What if someone abducted Brad and now they're after me?

43

Locking my office door behind me, I carefully pull the envelope out of the drawer with my fingertips. Maybe I'll call Cole and ask him what I should do. I look at the time. I only have 20 minutes until my next patient arrives.

I dial Cole's number, but he's out of the office so I leave a message. It isn't until the end of the day that he gets back to me.

"Hi, Claire. Cole here. You called?"

"Hi, Cole. Something weird happened and I just wanted to get your opinion on what I should do."

"Sure. What happened?"

"When I arrived at work this morning, I found an envelope that had been pushed through my mail slot onto the floor." I describe the note to him. "I don't know if I should tell the police. If they think the note is related to Brad's disappearance then they might start investigating me."

"I understand your concern, but I think you should notify the police. It seems like someone is threatening you, and given that the person you had an affair with is missing, it may mean you are in danger too. Maybe the police can help to figure out who wrote it. Also, if the note is connected to Brad, then it may help the police in their investigation.

"Yes. I guess you're right," I respond reluctantly.

"You should be careful not to handle the note though. There could be fingerprints or other evidence that may help the police to identify the person who wrote it."

"I was careful. After I opened it, I held it by its corners."

"Good."

The line is silent as I contemplate giving the note to the police. I still feel uneasy about it. Cole seems to read my mind.

"Don't worry Claire. This isn't going to make you a suspect."

"OK," I say hesitantly. "I'll call the police."

After I hang up, I consider how to handle this. It's 4:30 p.m. and Jon is expecting me home at 5:00 p.m. If I call the police now, they'll probably want to come to pick up the note and ask me some questions. I'll have to invent a reason why I'll be home late. I don't think I can use Shelley as an excuse again. I'll have to say I had a last-minute emergency appointment, a walk-in.

I decide to call the police first to see if they even want to come by tonight. I manage to reach José, who unfortunately does want to send someone over right away. After I get off the phone, I text Jon to give him my excuse for being late. There's no response. He's probably getting suspicious if he wasn't already.

My foot is tapping on the floor as I sit in my office chair and wait for the police to arrive. I look over at the closet where my jacket hangs and see my tennis racket and gym bag on the top shelf. Brad was the only person I played tennis with and every time I see that racket it reminds me of him. There's no point keeping it at my office. I will take it home today. The thought makes me sad, so I try to think of other things.

A police officer arrives 15 minutes later. "Hello," he says in a formal tone. "I'm here to pick up a note that you received today?"

"Yes." I point to my desk. "There it is."

The officer puts on latex gloves and then picks the envelope up by its corners. He removes the note from inside it in the same manner, unfolding it and reading it. Then he looks at me with an odd expression, and I wonder if he suspects I wrote the note myself. He puts both the envelope and the note in a plastic bag and thanks me saying he will take it with him so the lab can examine it. I notice he doesn't make eye contact as he's speaking.

After he drives off, I grab my gym bag and tennis racket out of the closet. I will have to leave them in the trunk of my car until I have a chance to bring them into the house without Jon seeing. I don't want to be questioned about who I was playing tennis with.

As I walk across the parking lot, I glance up at the sky. Dark grey clouds are forming and it looks like it might rain. A cool wind starts to pick up, blowing leaves and debris in the air. I shiver as I reach my car and click the key fob to pop the trunk open.

As I throw my gym bag in the trunk, something catches my eye. There's a dark piece of clothing crumpled up in the back corner. Confused, I grab it and hold it up so I can see what it is. It's a black hoodie. Brad's! It looks like the one he was wearing on Saturday night. I have no idea how it got in my car.

Bile rises in my throat as I quickly place it back in the trunk and look around to see if anyone is watching. Finding no one in the parking lot, I pick it up again to take a closer look. The front of it is ripped and stained with something dark. Blood.

CHAPTER 9

Sitting in the driver's seat of my car, I can feel the sweat beading on my forehead. Brad's hoodie remains in my trunk, taunting me with its presence. I try once again to remember what happened on Saturday night. I've played it over and over in my mind, but my memory always ends after I leave the hotel. I need to figure out what's going on. If I didn't put that hoodie in my trunk, then who did and why? It looks like someone has gone to great lengths to set me up. But right now, my immediate concern is what I'm going to do with it.

My mind races with possibilities. If I tell the police, will it implicate me in Brad's disappearance? Surely the police will want to seize my car for inspection and may even want to search my house. What would Jon think? Even if I didn't become a suspect, and I'm sure I would, Jon would wonder about my connection to Brad.

I think about calling Cole, but he'd tell me to call the police and I just can't do that. And in all honesty, I'm starting to doubt myself. What if I did do something to Brad? My gut clenches at the thought. Knowing I'm not going to figure anything out tonight, I start to drive.

As I pass through the busy streets, I think back to the events of the last few weeks, trying to figure out who would want to harm me in such a devastating way. My mind runs through every conversation, every encounter, every detail, but nothing stands out as suspicious.

Lost in thought, I almost miss my turn, my headlights catching the street sign just in time. I take a deep breath and try to calm myself, but the fear still lingers at the back of my mind. As I pull into my driveway, I look around, my eyes searching for anything unusual. I get out and lock my car to make sure no one can access the trunk.

As I open the door to my house, my nerves are in overdrive. Jon greets me right away. "Busy day?"

"Yes." My voice sounds shaky. I clear my throat and try to smile. "I'm glad it's Friday." I walk past Jon into the kitchen and place my purse on the counter. Then I grab a bottle of wine from the wine rack and proceed to open it and pour myself a large glass. My life is falling apart and I need something to help me calm down. I take a few large sips before noticing that Jon has come into the kitchen and is watching me.

"Everything OK?"

I place the wine glass down on the counter. "Yes. Why?"

"You just seem kind of stressed."

"Oh. Yeah. Maybe I am a bit. It's just been a long day. Would you like a glass of wine?"

"Sure." He looks at me for a moment, and then says, "If you don't feel like cooking tonight, we could just order in."

Why is he being so nice to me? "Great idea," I say, trying to smile. "You can order whatever you feel like. I'm fine with anything." I pass Jon the wine bottle to pour himself a glass, and I take my glass of wine down the hallway to the bedroom so that I can change out of my work clothes.

I down the rest of my wine while changing, and wonder how I will make it through the rest of the evening without having a breakdown. I need to get that hoodie out of my trunk, but I don't know where to put it. I could throw it in a dumpster, but that may be hard to do without being seen, and I might change my mind about giving it to the police. Maybe it will help them find Brad. But if I did something to harm him, I need to get rid of it. I can't think clearly, and I don't know if it's the wine or the stress.

As I walk back into the kitchen, I can hear Jon on the phone finishing his take-out order. I will have to do a better job of acting normal.

"So, what was the emergency?" Jon asks after hanging up the phone.

"What?" The question takes me by surprise.

"Didn't you say there was an emergency and you had a last-minute appointment?"

"Oh. Yeah. It was one of my new patients. She had just strained her back and wanted a treatment before she left on vacation. Not really an emergency, but I guess she saw it that way."

Jon doesn't usually ask about my patients and I wonder why he is today.

"You fixed it for her?"

"Yes. I think so."

"Did you hear anything more about your patient who went missing?"

I can feel my heart thumping in my chest. *What's with all the questions?* "No. I think he's still missing."

"What a nightmare," Jon says.

I nod and Jon stares at me for a few seconds and then says, "I ordered Chinese food."

"Great," I say in a squeaky voice that sounds like a cartoon character. I immediately refill my wine glass and take another sip.

Jon walks into the living room and sits down in front of the TV. I linger in the kitchen for a few minutes while I try to calm my emotions. It's been a rough day. I tell myself that I will not think about Brad, the note or the hoodie for the rest of the evening.

Sitting down beside Jon on the couch, I sip my wine and try to concentrate on watching the news. Ten minutes pass before Jon gets up and says, "I'm going to go pick up the food now."

"Oh. Where did you order from? Don't they deliver?" I ask somewhat surprised.

"They do. I ordered from Wing Lee, but they said it would be 45 minutes to an hour for delivery, and I don't want to wait."

"OK," I respond feeling a bit confused. I've never known Wing Lee to take that long to deliver.

"Do you mind if I take your car? Mine is almost out of gas," Jon says.

My chest tightens, and for a moment I feel like I can't breathe. "Sure. That's fine," I reluctantly respond. I have to say yes, otherwise it would seem suspicious.

He grabs my keys from my purse, and I can hear the front door open and shut. Then I hear the sound of an engine starting. As I stand up and look out the window, I see Jon driving off in my car.

He never asks to use my car. Well, hardly ever. And he never picks up take-out. Why does he want to use my car? Is he going to look in the trunk? I feel like I'm going to have a heart attack. *Calm down, Claire. He's probably just hungry. You did get home later than usual.*

But I'm not convinced. After sitting there for a little while, I get up and take my phone out of my purse. Finding the contact I'm looking for, I call the number.

"Wing Lee. How can I help you?" The man's voice is barely audible over the background noise of the restaurant.

"Hi. I wanted to make an order for delivery to West Vancouver. How long will it be?"

"Ah. About 20, 25 minute," he responds with a heavy Asian accent.

"Thanks. I'll call back later," I say, and hang up.

Could the wait time have changed since Jon called? It's still unclear if he lied. I look out the window at his car in the driveway. Then I look at the time. He's only been gone for about ten minutes. I have five to ten minutes until he gets back. I can feel my pulse quickening as I jog down the hall to the bedroom and open the top drawer of Jon's dresser. His spare key is there. I grab it and head out the front door to where his car is parked in the driveway. Unlocking it, I hop in. The gas gauge is just below 1/4 full. More than enough gas to pick up the food.

I sit there for a moment trying to process what is going on. If he's lying about needing to use my car, then what is the reason? He either wants to search my car because he's suspicious about something, or—Could Jon be the person who put the hoodie in my trunk? No. That doesn't make any sense. I often leave my car unlocked, so anyone could have put it there. But if it was Jon, it means he knew about my affair, did something to Brad, and is setting me up. No. That's crazy. But he has been acting strange lately.

It occurs to me that I'm still sitting in Jon's car and need to get out before he gets home. But before I do, I take a quick look in his glove box. I'm not sure what I'm looking for, but since I'm already in his car, I might as well snoop around a bit. When I open it up, all I find are his insurance papers and some napkins.

Next, I try his console where I find a few receipts. I pick up the first one. It's a gas receipt from last week. I put it down and look at the second one. A liquor store receipt for beer. The last one is a parking receipt. As I'm putting the receipts back in the console, something occurs to me. The gas receipt was from Pay and Save, and I'm pretty sure there are none in our area. I pick it up again and take a closer look at the location. Georgia Street. Close to Yaletown. The date is last Saturday, the same day Brad disappeared. The receipt was printed at 5:22 p.m. I feel a shiver throughout my body. He had to have left the house shortly after I did.

Did he follow me? No. I met Brad at 5:30 p.m., and I parked at my office and walked for ten minutes. So Jon must have left the house about ten minutes after me. What was he doing downtown? He never mentioned that he was planning on going out. He was watching TV when I left. Something is definitely wrong.

I hear the sound of a car in the distance. Our residential road isn't that busy, and we are located at the end of a cul-de-sac, so it's most likely Jon. I quickly put the receipt back in the console and shut it. After exiting the car, I rush back inside the house shutting the door behind me. As I do, I hear my car pull into the driveway. Sprinting down the hallway, I put Jon's spare key back in the top drawer. I make it back to the kitchen just as the front door opens. My face is flushed and I'm breathing heavily. Grabbing my wine, I take a big gulp.

Jon walks into the kitchen and places the take-out on the counter. I find myself staring at him, examining him. What does he know, and what did he do in my car? Jon must feel my gaze on him because he turns and looks at me with a quizzical look.

"Is everything alright?"

I try to act normal. "Yes. Why?" Not wanting to make eye contact, I turn and open the cupboard to grab some plates.

"You were giving me a strange look."

"Oh. I didn't mean to. I was just watching you unpack the food to see if you bought any chow mein."

"Yep. Right here." He holds one of the plastic containers up. His hand seems to be shaking a bit, or is that my imagination?

"Good." I force a smile. "I had a craving for it."

Jon looks at me again. "Your face looks flushed. Are you feeling alright?"

"Yeah. I'm fine," I say. "It's probably just the wine."

We sit down for dinner and I can't stop thinking about my car. He took it for a reason. So he either searched through it or planted something in it. Or did he really just think his was low on gas?

"Claire?" His voice snaps me out of my thoughts.

"Yes?"

"I was asking if you wanted to watch a movie on TV tonight. Are you sure you're OK?"

"Yes. Sorry. I'm just exhausted. It's been a long week. I think the wine is hitting me too. I probably shouldn't drink on an empty stomach." I put some chow mein on my plate and say, "Sure. Let's watch a movie." Watching a show is probably the best option at this point. Then I don't have to talk to Jon. He's obviously noticed my suspicious behaviour.

Dinner is awkward with little conversation. Jon seems quiet, and at one point, while I am opening my fortune cookie, I look up to find him staring at me, the corners of his mouth twisted in disgust. He knows something. I'm sure of it.

CHAPTER 10

The next morning, I wake up at 6:00 a.m. It's Saturday and Jon usually sleeps in. Not wanting to wake him, I take my time sliding the covers off of me, so I can get out of bed without disturbing him. I move silently out of the bedroom and down the hall in my pajama bottoms and T-shirt.

When I make it to the entryway, I slip on my flip-flops and slowly undo the lock on the front door so it won't click too loudly. My heart is racing as I step outside and quietly close the door behind me. I go straight to the trunk of my car and click it open. Peering inside, I scan its contents with a growing sense of unease. My tennis racket and gym bag are still there where I left them, but the hoodie is folded in half beside them. Is that how I left it? I don't think so. I thought I shoved it back into the corner of my trunk where I found it. But I was so panicked at the time, I can't be sure.

"Morning Claire!"

I quickly jerk up knocking my head on the hood of the trunk. Turning, I look over to see our neighbour, Tim, in his shorts and T-shirt with sports socks pulled up over his shins. I grab my gym bag and racket out of the trunk and slam it shut.

"Oh. Hi," I respond in a breathless voice. "Going for a run?"

"Yep. I like to get my workout in early," he says as he lunges forward to stretch his calf.

Tim lives across the street from us. I've seen him jogging in the morning lots of times before and he always waves or says hello. He's also often outside his house gardening, and he likes to chat. I don't want Jon to hear me outside the house talking to Tim, so I cut the conversation short.

"Looks like a nice day for a jog. Enjoy!" I say, as quietly as I can, but loud enough so that he will hear. Waving, I turn around and start walking back toward my house with my gear. When I reach the door, I turn back to see Tim jogging off down the road.

Crap! That was bad luck. I look through the window hoping Jon didn't wake up and hear me outside talking to Tim. The lights are still off, so I slowly turn the handle to the front door and step inside with my tennis racket and gym bag. Pausing for a moment in the entryway, I listen. The house is silent. Jon must still be asleep. Great. I quickly go downstairs and place my stuff in the storage room.

I can't decide what to do with the hoodie, so I leave it in the trunk for now. If I bring it into my house there's a greater chance of Jon finding it, assuming he hasn't already. I feel guilty about not informing the police about it when I found it. But as much as I hate to admit it, I don't know what role I played in Brad's disappearance. What if I did something to him? Just thinking about it causes me to shiver. Then it occurs to me, if I injured or killed him, I would have had to have moved him somewhere. The only way I could do that is with my car, and there was no blood in it. *Or was there?* I peer out the living room window at it. Then I quietly open the door and go back outside.

After looking around to make sure there is no one in sight, I quickly make my way to the back of my car. With a deep breath, I pop open the trunk, bracing myself for the worst. This time I examine the material that lines the trunk space more closely. I'm relieved to find that there aren't any visible blood stains. Next, I open the door to the back seat and stick my head in. I examine the black leather seats and dark floor mats. Nothing there either that I can see. The tension starts to leave my body until another thought enters my mind. Maybe he died another way, like a blow to the head.

Then I catch myself. This is the first time I've thought of him as being dead. I've been trying to keep positive thoughts, but I suppose if I'm being honest with myself, there's always been a part of me that doesn't believe he's alive. I try to push that thought out of my head.

After quietly shutting the door to the car, I sneak back into the house without making a sound. The house is still silent, so Jon is still sleeping. The thought of him makes me tense. He's been acting strange lately and I want to know why.

I can't shake the feeling that he's hiding something from me and I'm determined to find out what it is. I need to get into his phone. But unfortunately, it's with him most of the time. My only opportunity to get into it is either when he's sleeping or when he's in the shower. The shower would be the safest. But my nerves are shot and I need to come up with some password ideas, so I decide to wait for another opportunity.

It comes on Sunday morning. I'm up early, feeling anxious and unable to sleep; my new norm. Jon eventually gets up and has a coffee. His mood is off. He barely speaks to me and is avoiding eye contact. After watching the morning news, he finally turns the shower on.

As soon as I'm sure he's in the shower stall, I grab his phone. Biting my lip, I nervously stare at the locked screen. I will need to be quick and have his phone back on the dresser by the time the shower turns off. I've come up with six potential passwords, as I only have six failed attempts before his phone will lock.

My heart pounds in my chest as I clutch his phone. The first password I attempt is our address. Fail. Next, I try the last four digits of his phone number and repeat the first two digits. Wrong. I try the same with his work phone number. Another fail. Next, I enter his birth date. Nope. I try his name spelled twice, but that doesn't work either. Frustration mounts as I realize I have only one last attempt. I enter our anniversary date and hold my breath while I watch the screen. Sadly, that doesn't work either. Feeling defeated, I put his phone back where I found it. I will have to try again another time.

An opportunity presents itself on Monday morning. By this time, I've researched the most common passwords. I could see Jon using one of them. He's not exactly the most sentimental person. After he enters the shower, I once again pick up his phone to see if I can unlock it. Sweat beads on my forehead as I try the most popular password: 111111. The screen blinks and goes back to the login page. The second most popular password is apparently the word, *password*. I almost hope Jon isn't dumb enough to use that one. It turns out he isn't. Next, I try 123456. To my surprise, the phone opens up and I'm presented with the home screen. I stare in disbelief. *Really Jon?* But I'm in! I can feel the adrenaline rushing through my body. There isn't much time.

I quickly navigate to his messages, scrolling through his texts and searching for any suspicious conversations. I can see a few from me and a couple from Jon's friends. But there is nothing of much interest.

Then I look at his call history. There are a bunch of numbers that I don't recognize, probably work-related. I scroll down to last Saturday. There was one phone call that afternoon. I need to write down the number. Frantically, I glance around the bedroom for a pencil or pen but don't see one. The shower is still on. Do I have time to make it to the kitchen? I think so. I rush to the kitchen with Jon's phone in my hand and quickly write the number down on a piece of paper.

While I'm there, I scroll to the morning when I heard him whispering on the phone. The same number appears. I think this is all I need. In any event, I now have his password and I can log in again if necessary. I shove the paper into the bottom of my purse and sprint back down the hall to the bedroom. My heart stops when I realize the shower is off.

I quickly try to power off the phone but my sweaty hand slips and hits the call button instead, dialing one of Jon's friends. Panic sets in as I end the call and desperately try to turn his phone off. The bathroom door opens, and as Jon walks out of the bathroom, I drop his phone back on the dresser. The phone's light is still on. Jon looks over at me standing frozen. I try to compose myself as if nothing is amiss. I need to direct his attention away from the phone.

"Did you hear that dog barking last night?" I ask as I walk toward the closet on the opposite side of our bedroom. His eyes follow me.

"Um. No. I didn't hear anything."

I can feel my heart pounding in my chest. He's looking at me with a furrowed brow. Does he know I'm up to something? The light on his phone goes out just as he glances over at it. He looks back at me with pursed lips.

"It was the middle of the night. It woke me up," I say, as I turn and grab a cardigan out of the closet.

"Huh. I wonder whose dog it was."

I may be wrong, but I think he's trying to suggest that there are no dogs in the area. I try to think if I've seen any of our neighbours with one, but I don't think I have.

"Not sure," I respond. "But it was quite loud. I'm surprised you didn't hear it," I add as I walk out of the bedroom with my cardigan. It's probably best not to continue this conversation. As I pass out the doorway, I glance over at him. His jaw is clenched as he grabs his phone from the dresser. He looks at it and then glances over at me. Something is definitely off with him.

CHAPTER 11

Traffic is light on the way to work and I arrive early. I park as close to my office as I can, and nervously scan the area before getting out. Seeing nothing unusual, I walk to the back of my car and take a deep breath before opening the trunk. The hoodie is sitting there like an uninvited guest at a party. Its familiar fabric and faded colour send shivers down my spine. I cast a furtive glance around the parking lot, making sure no one is watching before quickly stuffing it in my large handbag. Then I walk with purpose toward my office. Once inside, I lock the door behind me. As I look down at my handbag, I can't help but wonder what would happen if anyone found out what I was hiding.

I glance out the window once more, scanning the parking lot again before placing my handbag on my desk. No one is watching, so I remove the hoodie and place it on the top shelf of my linen closet and then push the door shut. It will stay out of sight there until I figure out what to do with it.

Now I need to get ready for my first appointment of the day. Karen. I can feel a tension headache coming on. I wonder if she knows about me and Brad. Either way, our conversation will be awkward.

I have about ten minutes until she arrives, so I decide to quickly check my secret email. As I log in, the screen awakens and I stare at it in shock. There's a read receipt from my last email. It was opened today at 8:04 a.m. But as the seconds tick by, my initial excitement quickly turns to confusion and doubt. Could it really be Brad reading my emails? I can't shake the feeling that it's someone else. Something doesn't feel right. I try to push the thought aside. Is it possible that Brad is reading my emails but for some reason is unable to respond? No. The more I think about it, the more certain I am that it isn't him. It's probably just the police, which is why there's no reply.

I stare a long time at the screen wondering whether I should write another email, but I decide against it. Instead, I make myself a cup of tea and busy myself setting up for Karen's arrival. It will be a relief to get her appointment over with.

She arrives right on time in her sweats and T-shirt. Her face is pale and her eyes are puffy. It looks like she barely slept. My heart sinks, and I can feel the weight of my guilt bearing down on me. A heavy suffocating feeling, like a rock lodged in my chest, refusing to budge.

"Hi Karen," I say in a soft voice. "How are you holding up?"

She looks down at the floor. "I'm doing OK. It's been really difficult, but my family has been very supportive."

"That's good," I say with a smile. "I'm glad you have family that can help you through this."

Karen looks up and her eyes lock on mine. I can't read her expression. Angry? Stoic? Accusing? I glance away. "Have there been any leads?" I hold my breath as I wait for her to answer.

"No. Just his ID cards that were found in the park and then his cell phone that was found outside your office." I can feel her eyes lock on me as I pretend to be examining some papers on my desk.

"Yes. That was odd that his phone was found out back. I can't imagine how it got there. This whole ordeal has been so surreal."

"Yes. It has been." Karen's voice sounds hard now. There's a long pause and I'm not sure what to say, so I remain silent.

"He was coming here for treatments, right?" As she asks the question, she watches me with a cold, unflinching stare. Is she guessing or does she know? I don't want to be evasive. I think she knows.

"Yes," I answer. I want to say more, but I'm afraid of saying too much.

"Was he here on Saturday? The day he went missing?"

I suck in a deep breath. This conversation is making me uncomfortable. Does she know about us? "No," I respond. "I'm not open on the weekends."

"Oh. I'm just trying to figure out how his cell phone ended up in the back alley."

"I'm not sure. Hopefully, the police will be able to figure that out." My mouth is dry now, and my voice sounds hoarse. I don't want to continue this conversation, so I abruptly change the subject. "Well, let's get you changed, and we'll get started on your treatment."

Karen wipes at the corner of her eye. "I'm just going to use your washroom, and then I'll get changed," she responds.

"Sure. It's out the door and down the hallway to your left," I say, pointing in the direction of the washroom that I share with the other businesses in the building.

As Karen walks out the door, I let out a deep breath. This is going worse than I thought. I hope she doesn't continue talking about Brad throughout her treatment.

Karen returns a few minutes later and I direct her into the treatment room to get undressed. As I wait, I organize my desk. When I walk into the room, she's lying face down on the massage table.

"I've been so tense lately with everything that's happening," she says with her head facing down in the face cradle. "I feel like my back is seizing up."

I prod her upper shoulder area where she usually has issues. "Yes. It's quite tight. We'll get it loosened up."

For the next ten minutes or so, Karen doesn't say anything. Then she says what I feared she might say.

"I have the feeling he was meeting someone."

"Sorry?" I ask, trying to keep my voice steady.

"Brad."

I can't breathe. *She knows.* "Oh," is all I manage to say in response.

She turns her head to look at me as if she's trying to gauge my reaction. I don't look at her. Instead, I concentrate on my treatment. I'm wondering whether I should say something more. If it wasn't me he was seeing, would I have responded differently? But before I have a chance to say anything, Karen continues.

"The police spoke to the friends he said he was with on Saturday and they all say they weren't with him, that they hadn't even made plans to see him that night."

It feels like a vice grip is closing in on my throat. "I'm sorry," I say. And I truly am.

Karen continues. "The more I thought about it, I realized that he had been working late or coming home tired and not wanting to spend time with me. He had become a lot more distracted and distant in the last few months. I thought he was just busy with work or things weren't really going well with his job." Her voice cracks and I think she's crying. I don't know what to say.

"Maybe it was just work-related," I offer.

"No. I don't think so," she replies. "Looking back, the intimacy had disappeared as well. And why would he lie about going out with friends unless he was meeting a woman?"

"I don't know," is all I can think to say. It comes out of my mouth too quickly and I wonder if I sound suspicious.

A long silence follows, and I hope this conversation is over. But she's not finished.

"I just don't understand why married people cheat." Her voice is louder now, almost angry. "If you're not happy in your marriage, why wouldn't you try to fix the issues, and if that's not possible then why wouldn't you get a divorce and find someone who you're more compatible with?" She lets that question hang for a few seconds. "Cheating is a coward's way of dealing with things. It's selfish. People who cheat want all the benefits from their marriage but also want to get whatever's missing from someone else."

I feel like I've been hit by a dump truck. "Yes. Cheating isn't the right way to deal with problems in your marriage," I say in a voice that doesn't sound like my own. She's right. I know what I did was wrong. I knew it all along. I should never have done it, and now I'm paying dearly for it.

"It's just strange. I still can't believe he would cheat on me. We had a great sex life. Better than most married couples, at least if what I read on the internet is true."

I feel a pain in my heart. Is that true, or does she suspect I was having an affair with her husband and she's just saying it to hurt me? Brad told me they only had sex a couple of times a year.

Karen continues in a shaky voice. "I know we could have spent more time together, but I thought he was happy." Turning to look up at me she adds, "Sorry to dump all this on you. It's just been a really difficult time for me, not knowing what happened."

"No. Of course," I reply. "It must be a horrible thing to go through. I hope they find him."

Karen doesn't bring Brad up again. In fact, she barely says anything throughout the rest of the treatment. When she leaves, all she says is, "Thanks, Claire." She doesn't ask to book another appointment. I suspect this appointment was just an information-gathering endeavor. But I can't figure out if she knows about my affair with Brad or not.

After Karen leaves, I sit down at my desk and rest for a couple of minutes. I really hope Brad is found alive and this nightmare ends soon. And if there wasn't already enough stress in this day, I'm about to add more before my next appointment arrives.

Reaching down to the bottom of my purse, I grab the piece of paper that contains the number I found on Jon's phone. I pull my phone out and turn off the setting that shows my caller ID. Then I punch in the number. As it rings, I hold my breath and wait for an answer.

"Malcolm Investigations. How can I help you?"

I quickly hang up. I wasn't expecting an investigation company. Why? This is who Jon was whispering to on his phone in the morning? Could he somehow be using this company for work? Or did he suspect my affair? I turn my computer on and type in *Malcolm Investigations Vancouver*. A website pops up so I click on it and read the description.

Malcolm Investigations is a full-service private investigation company with a team of experienced, professional private investigators. We have over 20 years of experience, along with the skills and resources to conduct any type of investigation. Our team consists of men and women from all backgrounds including private investigation, military and law enforcement. Whether it be infidelity surveillance, in-depth asset investigations, or simply locate investigations, we have the experience, resources and the best technology available to obtain the information you need.

Is Jon investigating me? It seems likely given that he was on the phone with this company on the Saturday that Brad went missing, and also left the house shortly after I did, ending up in the same area.

I suddenly feel like I'm going to be sick. Rushing down the hallway to the treatment room, I lean over the sink. I can feel bile in my throat but nothing comes out. As I stand up, I catch a glimpse of my reflection in the mirror. My face is pale, sweat glittering on my forehead and I have dark circles under my eyes. I have to look away. The person I see disgusts me. What have I become? A liar? Cheater? I glance back at my reflection. Murderer?

CHAPTER 12

For the rest of the day, my head is throbbing with pain. It feels like a hundred tiny hammers are pounding against my skull. Each strike sending waves of discomfort throughout my entire body. My mind feels clouded and fuzzy as if it has been wrapped in a thick blanket of fog. Does Karen know? Does Jon? Did one of them slip that envelope through my mail slot? Or was it someone else? I really can't see meek Karen writing threatening notes and sliding them through my door. I also can't see Jon doing that. But then again, he seems to know about my affair and it looks like he was following me, so who knows what he'd do.

There's one further possibility that keeps popping into my mind. Maybe it's someone from my past. Someone holding a grudge from that disastrous night with Shelley. Thinking about it makes me shiver. I wonder how my life might have been different if I'd just stayed home that evening.

It happened many years ago. We were in our early twenties and still in the party phase of our lives. It was Friday, July 13th, and we'd made plans to go to an all-white-themed party on a boat. I've never been a superstitious type of person, so I didn't think twice about going out that night. But now I prefer to stay at home on a Friday the 13th.

I remember the night clearly. Shelley arrived at my apartment at 6:30 p.m. I opened the door and my mouth dropped open. She was wearing a sleek, white, sleeveless, mini bodycon dress that accentuated her perfect shape and brought out her auburn hair and bright blue eyes.

"Wow. You look gorgeous Shelley!"

"Thanks. So do you." Shelley smiled coyly. She knew she looked amazing.

I was wearing a white A-line dress, with the bottom flaring out a bit. It was more classy than sexy. I didn't look as sexy as Shelley. But I felt pretty good in it.

Shelley entered my apartment and sat on my couch. I had set out some crackers and cheese for us to snack on.

"Do you want a cooler?" I asked.

"Sure. Thanks." She followed me to the fridge.

I handed her a cooler and grabbed one for myself. Then I put on my party music playlist. We had been looking forward to this night for weeks. The party was being held on a three-level charter yacht that could accommodate up to 385 people. It had a huge 3000 square foot deck outside, an indoor dance floor, a DJ and a bar. It was like a floating nightclub that cruised around the harbour. The party was from 8-12 p.m., and Shelley assured me that there would be a bunch of singles from our age group.

"Cheers!" Shelley held her cooler up and clinked it against mine.

"Cheers!" We both took a sip.

"So, are you ready to meet some hot men?" Shelley asked with a playful smile.

"Absolutely! But are the hot men ready for us?"

Shelley laughed and then reached into her purse and pulled out a small silver tube. "I brought something for us," she said, raising her eyebrows and smiling. After twisting off the top, she turned the tube upside down letting a joint fall out into her hand.

I wasn't into doing drugs. I'd tried it a few times, but generally it didn't do anything for me other than make me antisocial and tired. But I didn't want to bring down the mood and Shelley seemed excited about it, so I smiled and tried to seem enthusiastic.

"Great! Where did you get that?" I asked.

"Tygh. He says it's really good. Premium stuff."

Tygh was one of Shelley's friends. The stoner type, with long hair and baggy jeans that hung down below his underwear.

"Nice." I tried to sound animated.

Shelley put the tube back in her purse. "Do you think anyone else will be there that we know?"

"I don't know. Maybe," I answered. I had been wondering the same thing. I didn't really like going out with just Shelley because if she received any attention from a guy that she was interested in, I would become invisible to her. And it's always awkward wandering around a party by yourself. I had hoped that our other friends Kathy and Christie would be joining us, but Kathy got sick last minute and Christie had a family celebration she had to attend. So it was just the two of us.

Shelley and I finished two coolers each before catching a cab to the dock. When we arrived, we could see a large yacht with a bunch of people crowded around outside. I scanned the crowd to see if there was anyone I recognized. There wasn't, but I did see a lot of cute guys dressed up in their white pants with matching white tops. The coolers had hit me, and I was feeling a bit tipsy already.

"Check out those guys," Shelley said nodding her head to the side in the direction of a group of four attractive men. One woman was standing with them, but it was hard to tell which one of them she was with.

"They're hot," I said looking over at them again. As I did, I noticed one of them was looking over in our direction, probably checking Shelley out.

"Come on." Shelley pulled my arm. People had started to board the boat. "Let's hit the bar before there's a line-up."

We walked quickly toward the entrance of the boat and up the gangway. After entering, we made a beeline for the bar and bought ourselves a cooler. Then we made our way up to the top deck and watched as the crowd slowly boarded. The boat left the dock about 20 minutes later.

It was a warm night, but I could feel the breeze out on the deck when the boat began moving and I wished I'd brought a jacket. The drinks had warmed me up a bit, but it was still a little chilly. Shelley and I were leaning against the railing, looking out toward the shoreline as it passed by. The sun was starting to set, painting the sky with shades of orange, pink and purple.

"Enjoying the cruise?"

We both turned toward the voice. Standing in front of us was a tall, attractive man with dark hair, dark eyes and a chiseled face. His full lips complimented his prominent cheekbones. He was wearing snug-fitting white pants with a button-up short-sleeved shirt. He looked classy. It was the same guy we were checking out before boarding the yacht. Beside him was another man who was attractive in a more rugged sort of way. He had stylishly messy brown hair and green eyes. He looked more like a jock.

"I'm Ethan," said the dark-haired man.

"Jeff," said his friend in a confident voice.

Shelley and I introduced ourselves, and we all started chatting. It was clear that Shelley and Ethan were attracted to each other. Jeff wasn't really my type. He was a wannabe actor who was working as a waiter while he found small roles in various movies and TV shows.

A few minutes into our conversation, I realized it wasn't one. It was a monologue. He spoke about 90% of the time. All. About. Him. He seemed nice, but I wasn't feeling any chemistry and I don't think he was either. One of the ultimate turn-offs was him telling me he enjoyed hunting. Being an animal lover, I knew I could never be interested in him. Plus, and this is maybe a bit silly, his last name was Pusey. If somehow we hit it off and ended up getting married, I couldn't imagine myself with that last name. I think he knew it was an unattractive name because he mentioned that he went by the last name, *Best*, for his actor roles. That name suited him, given that he seemed to think he was—the best.

Ethan and Shelley, on the other hand, seemed to like each other. Shelley was laughing and touching Ethan's arm, and Ethan had a big smile on his face. He gazed into her eyes when he spoke. Shelley always had a way with men.

After about half an hour, Ethan announced that they were going to go grab a bite to eat and find the rest of their group. He said they'd come to find us later. Shelley seemed absolutely giddy as they walked off into the crowd.

"So? Do you like Jeff?" she asked excitedly. "He's cute!"

"I don't really think he's my type," I responded. Shelley's face fell. "But you seemed to hit it off with Ethan," I added.

This made her face beam. "Yes. He's sooooo hot. He's training to be a pilot!"

"That's cool," I replied. Of course he had to be not only hot but also successful.

"He's super smart too. And funny," she added

I was starting to feel a bit jealous. She always got the good ones. "Great," I commented with a lack of enthusiasm.

We chatted a bit more about Ethan while enjoying the view. It was getting cool out on the deck so I suggested we go in and get some more drinks.

"Brilliant idea!" said Shelley.

We went down to the main level of the boat, past the dance floor and toward the bar. As we were approaching the bar, we passed Ethan and Jeff talking in a small group. Ethan saw Shelly and smiled at her. There was an attractive woman with shoulder-length dark hair standing beside him. She was the same woman we saw standing with that group outside the boat. She turned to see who Ethan was smiling at. I noticed the scowl on her face as she turned back.

"Did you see that girl looking at us?" I asked.

"No. Who are you talking about?" Shelley seemed clueless.

"That girl standing beside Ethan. She looked jealous that he smiled at you."

Shelley glanced over at the group. The girl was talking to Ethan now. Shelley turned back toward me and shrugged her shoulders. "Oh well."

After we got our drinks, we grabbed some appetizers and wandered around exploring the boat. The music was blasting and people were already dancing and having fun. Shelley and I stepped out onto the dance floor for a couple of dances. Two men joined us and bought us a round of drinks afterward. They were nice, and I kind of liked the one I was talking to, but Shelley appeared uninterested and suggested we go back up to the top deck. She seemed to be searching around for Ethan. I secretly hoped she wouldn't find him because I was enjoying walking around and meeting people.

When we got to the top deck, I was relieved to see that Ethan was nowhere in sight.

"I know what we can do," Shelley said smiling.

Then she reached into her purse and pulled out the tube containing the joint. I was already feeling quite tipsy and didn't want to add marijuana to the mix, but I also didn't want to disappoint Shelley, who was now holding the joint up to a zippo lighter.

After taking a deep drag, she passed it to me. I sucked some smoke into my mouth but tried not to inhale it. After a couple of puffs, the two guys who we were dancing with downstairs came over and asked if they could join us. Shelley shared her joint with them, which was good because I didn't want any more. Once the three of them finished most of it, Shelley put it out on the railing and dropped it back in the tube.

Even though I barely inhaled any, I felt like my head was spinning. It appeared to affect Shelley too. After putting the joint out, she stumbled backward a bit like she was off balance, and her eyes were bloodshot.

Someone walked out the door from the stairway and the dull thud of the music suddenly became louder. The song that was playing was one that Shelley liked.

"Come on. Let's go dance!" she yelled and grabbed my arm, pulling me away from the two guys we were talking to.

We hurried back down to the dance floor, which was now wall-to-wall people. Pushing our way through the crowd we found a spot on the floor and started dancing. The music pounded relentlessly. I could feel the bass thumping through my body as sweaty, intoxicated people pushed up against me while gyrating to the music. Shelley was laughing and throwing her arms in the air, singing along to the song that was playing. Even in her intoxicated state, she was as graceful as a gazelle.

Halfway through the song, Ethan appeared.

"Can I join you ladies?"

"Of course!" yelled Shelley over the music.

I looked around but didn't see his friend Jeff or anyone else with him. When I looked back, Ethan was grinding against Shelley. A few seconds later, they kissed. I awkwardly continued to dance on my own while the two of them made out. Ethan glanced over and seemed to pick up on my uncomfortableness. He stepped back so that I wouldn't be dancing solo. It was nice of him to try to include me, but I still felt like a third wheel.

When the song finished and the next one started, Shelley and Ethan continued dancing. I decided it was time to go to the washroom. There was a lineup at the one next to the bar, but I remembered finding one on the bottom floor when we were exploring around the boat. It only had two stalls, but it was way at the back corner of the yacht, and when I saw it earlier it had been left largely undiscovered. I was feeling lightheaded and grabbed the railing as I made my way down the stairs. Happily, when I arrived at the washroom there was no line-up outside.

As I entered, I saw the dark-haired girl from earlier who had been standing near Ethan. She was applying some makeup in the mirror, and when I passed by to enter a stall, she looked over at me.

"Where's your slutty friend?" she asked in slightly slurred words.

I turned to face her and saw that her eyes were red and puffy. It looked like she'd been crying. "Sorry?" I responded. I wasn't sure if she was talking to me, but I figured she must be since no one else was in the washroom.

"Your redhead friend who's trying to steal my boyfriend," she spat.

"Oh. She's—" I didn't know what to say. "Is Ethan your boyfriend?"

"Yes. He is. And he's not interested in whores, so you can tell your friend to stay away from him."

I didn't want to get in a fight with this girl. She seemed a bit unstable. "I don't think he mentioned he had a girlfriend," I responded. Then I carried on and entered the stall. As I shut the door behind me, I could feel my heart pounding. The girl looked a bit crazed and I was afraid to be alone in the washroom with her.

"Well, he does!" she shouted through the door. "So tell your friend to find someone else to hit on."

I could hear the bathroom door open and close, so I assumed that she left, but I stayed in the stall for a while longer than I needed to, just in case. Before I opened the stall door, I peeked through the crack to see if I could see anyone in the washroom. Seeing no one, I finally came out and breathed a sigh of relief when I found the washroom empty. Then I rushed back upstairs and found Shelley at the bar buying another drink.

"Where did you go?" she asked.

"I just went to the washroom, and guess who was there?"

"Who?" Shelley's eyes seemed a bit unfocused.

"That girl that was standing by Ethan earlier. She called you a slut and said Ethan is her boyfriend. She said to tell you to stay away from him."

"What a bitch!" yelled Shelley over the music. "I was dancing with Ethan and she just walked up and grabbed him off the dance floor. Her name is Cassie. Ethan said she's an ex, who doesn't seem to be accepting that the relationship is over."

"She seemed to think he was her boyfriend and she was pretty pissed at you."

"Well, she can come talk to me in person instead of calling me names behind my back," snapped Shelley. Then she sipped her cooler, spilling some on her dress. She was definitely intoxicated, although I wasn't sure if it was the drinks or the joint.

I thought about what Ethan had told Shelley. "If she's an ex why would he let her pull him off the dance floor?" I asked.

"He probably didn't want to cause a scene," Shelley responded.

She might be right. Ethan did seem to be an empathetic type of person. "Come on. Let's go find some food," I suggested. We both needed to sober up a bit.

Shelley fished around in her purse and pulled out the tube containing the remainder of her joint. "Let's finish this," she slurred and headed back towards the stairs to the upper deck.

Not wanting to lose her, I followed her back up the stairs. I wondered if she was looking for Ethan again. But when we stepped outside, she dumped the joint into her hand.

I didn't want any, and I didn't think Shelley needed to have any either. "I think I'm good," I said, waving my hand sideways. "I've had a lot to drink and so have you. Maybe you should save that for later."

"Are you saying I'm drunk?"

"No. We've both had a lot. I just think we don't need that," I replied.

"Suit yourself." The tube slipped from her hand as she was pulling the lighter from her purse. I bent down and picked it up. Shelley didn't seem to notice that she had dropped it.

She lit up the remainder of the joint and took a long drag. There wasn't a lot left, so she finished it pretty quickly. When she was done, she threw the roach over the railing into the water. She was acting strange, much quieter than before, and her eyes were racing around everywhere.

The sun had gone down and it was dark outside, apart from the dull yellow lights on the boat. It had also gotten a lot cooler and neither of us had a jacket.

"Let's go back inside and get some water," I suggested.

Shelley's eyes darted behind my shoulder and then back again. "Do you mind getting me one? I'm feeling a bit dizzy and the fresh air is helping."

I turned to see what Shelley had looked at. As suspected, Ethan was standing in a group of people behind me, quite a bit further down the deck. I hadn't seen him when we first came outside. Cassie was with the group, but she had her back to us, so I don't think she knew we were there. I felt a bit uncomfortable leaving Shelley outside by herself, but we both needed water and I was cold.

"OK, I'll grab us some water," I said as I turned toward the door. "I'll be back in a few minutes."

When I reached the bottom of the stairs, the party was still booming with lots of drunk people on the dance floor. There was also a big lineup at the bar. I considered trying to signal the bartender from the side of the bar so that he could pour a couple of glasses of water, but I didn't want the people in the lineup to get upset with me, so I joined the back of the lineup. Lucky for me, two attractive guys were standing in front of me.

"Hey. How's it going?" I asked as I stepped in behind them. I was feeling bold after having had several drinks.

They both turned to look at me. The taller one on the left smiled. "Good. How's your night going?"

"Great! This is an amazing yacht," I replied, perhaps a bit too enthusiastically.

"It's always a great party," said the second one. "Did you come last year?"

"No. This is my first time."

They introduced themselves. The tall one was Richard and Greg was his friend.

"Who are you with?" asked Richard.

Did he want to know if I was here with a guy? Or was he wondering if I had a friend he might be interested in? I wasn't sure, but the way he looked at me made me think he was interested in me. "I'm just here with my friend Shelley. She's upstairs. I'm grabbing us some water."

"Water?" He replied with a bit of a frown. "Not drinking?"

"Oh. We are. We're just taking a break."

"Breaks aren't allowed." He laughed. "Can I buy you and your friend a real drink?"

It was nice of him to offer to buy us both a drink, but Shelley didn't need another one. "I think my friend has had too much already."

"OK. Water for her. What are you drinking?"

When we got to the front of the line, Richard bought me a cooler and I ordered two glasses of water. I couldn't pack all three, so he and Greg came upstairs with me. I was hoping they would. I wanted to keep talking to Richard, and I thought Shelley might like Greg.

But when I got upstairs, Shelley was gone. My eyes scanned the area where Ethan and his group had been standing but they weren't there either. I looked at Richard and Greg. "I left my friend here. I'm not sure where she went." Greg looked disappointed.

"Maybe she went to the washroom," offered Richard.

"Yeah. Probably," I replied. But I had a suspicion that she was with Ethan somewhere.

A cool breeze hit me, and I shivered. Richard handed me his jacket and I happily put it on while I sipped my drink. If Shelley had gone to the washroom, she should be back soon and I wanted to stay where I was so she could find me.

Richard and Greg chatted with me until we had all finished our drinks. It was 11:30 p.m., about half an hour since we came upstairs, and Shelley was still nowhere in sight. I was beginning to worry about her. She was clearly intoxicated when left to get us some water, and the boat would be docking soon.

"I think I should go look for my friend," I said.

"Do you want some help?" asked Richard.

"Sure. That would be great." I didn't feel like wandering around the boat by myself.

Greg looked at Richard with an annoyed look. "I need to use the washroom. I'll meet you downstairs."

"See you in a bit," replied Richard. Then we headed off in search of Shelley.

We started at the top deck, and as we left the shelter of the wall we were standing next to, I could feel the wind gust through my hair. I shivered and was glad that I had Richard's jacket. Shelley didn't have a jacket, and if she was still out on the top deck, she would be freezing.

It was dark as we began exploring. The lighting from the boat was dim and I had to look carefully at each group as we passed by to see if Shelley was there. We passed Jeff standing with a couple of people, but I didn't see Ethan or Shelley with him. After circling the top deck, I peeked in the washroom and looked under the occupied stalls for Shelley's shoes. None of them were hers, so Richard and I headed downstairs to check out the main level of the boat.

This area was much more crowded. It was difficult for us to make our way through all the people. The once bustling scene now felt suffocating, the noise and chatter now closing in around me as I searched. My eyes scanned the dance floor, trying to find Shelley's familiar face. But she wasn't there. Someone bumped my arm, and Shelley's water spilled everywhere.

Richard and I continued walking around the main floor, the crowd becoming a blur of faces, none of which belonged to Shelley. As our search went on, my nerves frayed. Shelley was nowhere to be seen. We ran into Greg near the bar, so I returned Richard's jacket and left him with his friend while I checked out the ladies' washroom on that level. Panic began to set in when I didn't find Shelley there, and I also realized that I hadn't seen Ethan or Cassie anywhere.

The boat was about to dock, and there was only one last area to search. Down on the bottom level. There were fewer people on that level, which had little atmosphere. But I figured Shelley and Ethan may have snuck off to be alone down there.

As I made my way down the stairs, most of the partygoers were gathering on the main level to disembark from the yacht. When I reached the bottom level, I glanced around but I didn't see Shelley. It wasn't until I approached the washroom, that I heard loud voices. I recognized Shelley's voice immediately.

As I opened the door, I found Shelley and Cassie alone in the washroom in the middle of a loud argument.

"He's not your boyfriend. He doesn't even like you!" Shelley was yelling with slightly slurred words.

Cassie wiped her eyes. Her mascara streamed down her face in small black rivers.

"You think you're so perfect, so much better than me. He'd never want someone like you. We've been together for five years. He loves me. We're just on a break."

"That's not what Ethan told me. You're delusional. Why don't you take a hint and stop following him around? He's not interested in you," yelled Shelley.

Cassie had stepped forward and was right in Shelley's face. "You're a man stealing whore!" They were both drunk and acting stupid. I needed to get Shelley out of here. But before I could do anything, Cassie's drink went flying into Shelley's face.

"You bitch!" yelled Shelley and pushed Cassie, who went sailing backward toward me. I put my hands out to prevent her from hitting me, but as she moved backward, she slipped on the spilled drink. I still remember it, playing out in slow motion. Her arms flailing, the loud crack as her head hit the edge of the counter. Then her body slumping to the floor.

Everything was silent for a few seconds as Cassie lay motionless. Shelley looked at me with wild eyes. I bent down and pulled Cassie's hair away from her face. Her eyes were shut and I couldn't tell if she was breathing. "Cassie?" I said with mounting panic. I shook her a bit, but there was no response.

"Let's go!" yelled Shelley. "We need to get out of here."

I didn't know what to do. The alcohol was clouding my thoughts. I felt Shelley grab my arm and pull me up. Then we both rushed out of the washroom and left Cassie lying on the floor. I tripped as we ran up the stairs, catching myself on a person going down in the opposite direction. Looking up, I saw it was Jeff.

"Sorry," I whispered, out of breath.

Jeff scowled at me and continued down the stairs.

When we reached the top of the stairs, we saw Ethan, who was probably waiting for Jeff. Shelley hurried past him. He tried to grab her arm but she pulled it away and we frantically moved through the crowd of people who were waiting to get off the boat, which had now docked. I remember seeing Richard and Greg, who were somewhere in the middle of the crowd. Richard waved and signalled me to come over, but I looked away, pretending not to see him.

"Shouldn't we tell someone where she is?" I whispered to Shelley as we made our way to the front of the crowd.

"No. We need to get out of here," she responded. "She'll be fine."

But she wasn't. She was later found dead.

CHAPTER 13

The next day it was all over the news that a woman in her early 20s had been found dead on the washroom floor of the party cruise boat. According to the report, one of the cleaning crew had found her about half an hour after all the guests had disembarked. Cassie's full name was released the day after the incident. Casandra Pusey. It turns out she was Jeff's sister.

The cause of death was initially unknown but was later determined to be due to a head injury that was caused when she hit her head on the counter. I always wondered if it was our fault for leaving her there. Would she have lived if we had gotten help instead of running away?

It's a horrible feeling, knowing that I may have contributed to Cassie's death. I tried talking to Shelley about it, but all she would say was that it wasn't our fault and that we shouldn't talk about it. She seemed strangely detached from the whole incident. I found out weeks later that she was dating Ethan. It only lasted a few months, but she saw Jeff from time to time. I never understood how she could be so removed from what happened. That night still haunts me to this day.

I look out the window and watch the raindrops trickle down the glass. Did Jeff figure out that we were coming from the washroom on the bottom floor of the yacht when he passed us on the stairs? Did Shelley tell Ethan or someone else what really happened to Cassie? No. That doesn't make sense. Years have passed. If it has something to do with Cassie, why would someone put a note through my door now? And why target me? Why not Shelley? There are a thousand questions prowling around in my head. But nothing will get resolved today.

My next patient is arriving in half an hour and I need to set up. As I'm walking toward the treatment room, I hear the *ding* of my front door opening. Turning back, I see José with a few police officers.

"Good morning, Claire." José presses his lips together to form a straight line.

My stomach clenches. *Did they find Brad?*

José passes me a document. "We have a warrant to search your office and car."

I stare at him blankly for a couple of seconds as I try to process what's going on. "Why?" I ask, as the police officers enter my office and start looking around.

"We received the test results back from the towel that was found in the alley. The blood on it matches Brad's and the towel matches the ones you have here."

I stand frozen, unable to speak. *How?*

"Could you please provide me with your car keys?"

I take them from my purse and hand them to José, who gives them to one of the officers standing beside him. The officer walks out the door toward my car.

"We'd also like to ask you some more questions. Could you come down to the station? You can contact Mr. Hayes if you'd like to have him present."

"Are you arresting me?" I ask, my voice sounding shrill.

"No. At this time we would just like to ask you some more questions."

I look out my window and watch as a police officer starts to examine my car. I can feel the frantic beat of my heart reverberating throughout my body.

"I'm going to call Mr. Hayes," I tell José. "I will also need to call all of my patients who were scheduled for massage therapy today and cancel their appointments."

"Yes. That's fine. Go ahead and make those phone calls," José says.

"I need to access my appointments on my computer," I tell him.

José nods and follows me to my desk. He watches as I log on and print out a copy of my appointment list for today through Wednesday. I glance over at the linen closet and wonder if there is any chance I could grab Brad's hoodie, but it would be impossible. There are too many police officers milling about, and José is watching me like a hawk.

Grabbing my printout, I walk outside to find somewhere quiet to make my phone calls. The air is heavy with tension and unease. As I sit down on the curb at the far end of the parking lot, my thoughts are racing. What will happen when the police find Brad's hoodie in my office? How will I explain that?

A sour taste creeps into my mouth as waves of dizziness wash over me. Leaning over, I throw up in the shrubbery beside the curb. It takes a few minutes before my head stops spinning. I find a stick of gum in my purse and pop it in my mouth to remove the taste of vomit.

My hand shakes as I call my patients and cancel all of my appointments for the next three days using the excuse that my office was broken into. The only appointment I keep is a Tuesday appointment for Steve. There's something important I need to ask him if I don't wind up in jail.

When I finish contacting all my patients, my next call is to Cole. Luckily, he is in his office. He answers in a calm voice.

"Cole here."

"Cole, it's Claire. The police are at my office. They're searching it and my car."

"Do they have a warrant?"

"Yes. They said the blood they found on the towel in the alley matches Brad's, and the towel they found matches the ones in my office."

"Do you have any idea how one of your towels could have ended up in the alley with Brad's blood on it?"

"No," I say in a frenzied tone. "I have no idea. I've told you everything I know." I pause. "Except one thing."

I hear Cole taking a deep breath on the other end of the line. "What's that?"

I look around to make sure no one can hear me. Then I say, "I found Brad's hoodie in my trunk. It was ripped and it had blood on it."

"What? When did you find that?" he asks.

I don't know what to say. I don't want him to think I'm hiding anything so I decide to tell him a half-truth. "I just found it this morning."

"So, the hoodie is still in your trunk?" he asks.

"Well, no. Not exactly."

"What do you mean, 'Not exactly'?"

"I moved it into my office and put it on the top shelf of my linen closet. I was going to leave it there until I figured out what to do with it." I can almost see him clenching his jaw. "Someone planted it. Someone's setting me up," I say, my voice rising.

There's a long pause. "Well, you didn't do yourself any favours by moving it, Claire."

"Will I be arrested?"

"I don't know. I don't think they will arrest you today unless there's anything else you aren't telling me."

"No. There's nothing else. Actually, there's one thing that might be relevant."

I hear him exhale loudly. "What's that?"

"Brad's wife, Karen, is one of my patients."

"And you didn't think to tell me this?" he asks.

"I didn't realize until I saw her on the news. She has a different last name. She was just in my office this morning."

"I assume your office is now closed for the day?"

"Yes. The police want to ask me some more questions at the station. They said I could call you first."

"I will rearrange my schedule. Can you come to my office now?" he asks.

I tell him that I don't have a car, but I can catch a cab. He instructs me to tell the police that I'm meeting him and I'll be in to answer questions this afternoon. I do what he says, and I arrive at his office 30 minutes later. He asks me some more questions about Karen, the hoodie and the towel and gives me some advice on what I should say to the police. Then we go to the police station where we meet again with José and Dianna.

Dianna is the one asking questions and she is as cold as she was during our first visit.

"Can you explain why the hoodie that Brad was wearing on the night of his disappearance was found ripped with blood on it, hidden in your linen closet?" I can feel the frost in her voice and it sends chills throughout my body.

"This morning I was putting some things in my trunk and saw it there. I don't know how it got there. Someone must have put it in my trunk," I say, trying to sound confident.

"Mmmmmhmmmmm." Dianna looks at me like you would look at a child saying, "It wasn't me."

"Did you contact the police when you found Brad's hoodie in your trunk?"

She knows I didn't. "No," I say. "I wasn't sure what to do, so I brought it into to my office. I was worried that if I called you guys, I would become a suspect."

"Right," she says and I can tell she doesn't believe me. "Who has access to your trunk?"

I think about this for a moment, and then I answer. "I don't usually lock my car, so I suppose anyone could have had access."

"Did you open your trunk at any point between the time that Brad disappeared and this morning when you discovered the hoodie?"

"No," I lie.

"Did anyone else use your car during that period of time?"

I pause. I don't know whether I should say Jon used my car. What if they want to question him?

"No," I answer, not looking directly at Dianna.

"No?" She asks staring directly at me. "Your husband didn't use your car?"

"No." I lie. "He has his own car."

She asks some further questions about where I park my car at home and where I parked throughout the time Brad has been missing. Then she tells me they will be keeping my car for a couple of days to examine it. I wonder how I will explain this to Jon.

Before continuing with her questioning, Dianna looks at me for a few seconds and says, "Claire, you can see how this looks from our perspective, can't you? You were having an affair with Brad. You were the last person to see him before he disappeared. There is a lot of time that is unaccounted for between the time you left the hotel and when you got home. Brad's cell phone and one of your towels with his blood on it were found in the alley behind your office. Now the hoodie he was wearing on the night he went missing has been found hidden in your office."

I feel nauseous. I do see how this looks. "I didn't *hide* the hoodie," I explain. "I just put it in my closet until I could figure out what to do." I try to swallow but my throat is dry. I look at her and she stares back at me with stern eyes. "I'm being set up," is all I can say.

"Do you know who would want to set you up?" she asks.

"I don't know. Maybe Brad's wife. Maybe she found out about our affair."

"Do you have any reason to believe she found out?"

"Not really," I respond. "But she's been coming in for treatments and talking a lot about her marriage. She was also asking me questions about mine."

Dianna looks at me with a puzzled expression. I add, "I didn't know she was Brad's wife until I saw her on the news."

Dianna seems interested in this information. She asks more about Karen's appointments and my conversations with her. I tell her what I can recall.

"What about your husband? Do you think he knew about your affair?"

I was expecting this question, but I still feel my stomach tighten. "No. I don't think he knows."

"How can you be sure? Is it possible he knows?"

"I don't think he does," I reply. "He hasn't said anything. I don't think he'd hurt Brad or set me up if he did know."

"No? But he does have access to your car, correct?"

"Yes. But I don't usually lock it, so anyone could have accessed it."

"Could he have gotten a hold of the keys to your office?" she asks.

I have to think about this. "My office key is on my keychain, which I keep in my purse. I also have a spare key that I leave at home in the top drawer of my dresser, but I don't think Jon knows about it."

I don't like where this conversation is leading.

"Did you tell Jon about the note that you found on the floor of your office?"

I shake my head no.

"The hoodie?"

"No."

"I assume he knows Brad was your patient, and he is aware that a towel with blood and his cell phone were found behind your office? This was on the news and is public information."

"Yes. He knows that," I say, looking down at the table.

Dianna nods. "Claire, we need to interview Jon." She looks at me and I can't read her expression. "We don't need to tell him about your affair, but we need to know where he was on the night Brad disappeared."

I take a deep breath and nod. Somehow, I knew this would happen. I'm relieved that they aren't going to mention my relationship with Brad. At least not yet. But I wonder if their questioning will make Jon suspicious. I also wonder what they will discover Jon was doing that night.

The rest of the interview is a blur. At the end, Dianna informs me that they've received access to my cell phone records. I watch her examining me to gauge my reaction. I'm not too concerned. I never communicated with Brad on my cell phone, and I can't think of anything else on there that I should be worried about, so I just nod my head.

When the interview is over, Cole walks me out and offers to drive me back to my office.

"How do you think that went?" I ask when we step outside.

"I think it went fine. We'll have to see if the police find anything else in their search today. It appears that someone is trying to set you up, and we will need to figure out who that is."

"Did they find out anything about the note that was slipped through my mail slot?" I ask as we walk toward Cole's car.

"No. Unfortunately, there were no fingerprints or anything else that would indicate who wrote it, and there are no security cameras in the vicinity." He looks at me with a sympathetic gaze and adds, "They did say that the paper that was used for the note was the same brand as the printing paper in your office, but I wouldn't be too concerned about that. It's a common brand."

I walk the rest of the way to Cole's car in silence. Things aren't looking good for me.

CHAPTER 14

The police are still at my office when Cole drops me back off, so I walk down the street to a nearby cafe and buy a sandwich. As I sit at the counter with my lunch, I contemplate what I'm going to tell Jon. I will have to tell him that my office was searched and my car was taken. I think I also need to tell him about the hoodie, given that he will likely be questioned about my car.

I'm worried that the police might contact Jon before I get home, so I decide that it would be best for me to call him now and explain what's happening. I'm sitting in the back of the coffee shop and there are only two other customers. They are engaged in their own conversation so they won't hear mine.

Jon answers on the third ring.

"Hi." He sounds a bit breathless like he's walking outside. He's probably grabbing lunch.

"Hi," I respond, followed by a long pause. I hadn't really thought this through before I called and I'm not sure what to say, so I just launch into it. "The police are here at my office."

"The police?" He sounds worried.

"Yes. They're searching my office and my car."

"Why?" He asks, in an anxious tone. "Does this have to do with your patient who went missing?"

"Yes. Apparently, the towel that they found in the alley was they same make as the ones I have in my office."

"Do they think you had something to do with this guy's disappearance?" His voice raises an octave. "Why are they searching your car?"

I take a deep breath. "This morning when I opened my trunk, I saw a hoodie in there. It had blood on it. They think it's his." I don't mention that I moved it into my office.

"How did his hoodie get in your trunk?" His voice is getting louder and is beginning to sound accusatory.

"I don't know. I think someone is trying to set me up," I say, and in the back of my mind I can't help but wonder if that someone is Jon.

There's silence on the other end of the line, and I consider telling him about the note, but he will wonder what someone thinks I did, and why I didn't tell him about it earlier, so I decide not to.

Eventually he says, "Why would someone try to set you up?"

"I don't know," I reply. "I'm as confused as you are." Then I add, "The police took my car for a couple of days."

I can hear Jon breathing, but he says nothing. After a few seconds he asks, "Do you need a ride home?"

"No. Thanks. I'll rent a car. I'll need one until mine is returned."

"OK."

There's a long pause before I force the next words out of my mouth. "I think they said they might want to speak to you as well."

"What? Why?" He sounds almost frantic.

"I don't know. Maybe to see if you saw anyone around my car, or if you know anything."

"Great." I can tell he's mad. "Look. I'm just grabbing lunch. I've got to go."

"OK. I should be home at the usual time," I say, and then realize Jon has already hung up.

That didn't go well. It was an awkward conversation, but I guess I knew it would be. I take a bite of my sandwich and watch the couple sitting at the front of the coffee shop talking and smiling. I wish that could be me having lunch without a care in the world. It's a tough pill to swallow, but I brought this on myself, and now I will have to deal with it.

I remember my father once telling me, "There are wolves and rabbits in this world, Claire, and if you don't know which one you are, you are not a wolf." I decided at that moment that I would never be a rabbit. Whoever put that note through my mail slot misjudged me. I will not run. In fact, I think it's about time that I start hunting down whoever did this to me.

Lifting my phone off the table, I start to search for private investigation companies in Vancouver. I come across the company I found on Jon's phone and consider calling it. If they tell me they are in a conflict of interest then I'd know Jon is investigating me. But they probably wouldn't say that. They'd likely tell me they're too busy to take this on right now. Then they might tell Jon I contacted them. I can't take the risk of him knowing I've called a P.I., especially since he's one of the people I will be asking them to investigate.

After scrolling through several more companies, I find one that looks good— Extreme Spy. It states that they investigate everything from long-lost family members and infidelity to employee background checks and fraud. They say that they use every method in the book to help their customers and they go beyond a typical investigation.

I call them from a pay phone outside the coffee shop. I don't want their number showing up on my cell phone if anyone is tracing my calls.

"Extreme Spy. How can I help you?"

"Oh. Hi. I wanted to retain an investigator."

"Sure. We can help you with that," says the lady on the other end of the line.

"But first I need to know if my information will remain confidential," I say.

"Absolutely. You have no need to worry. We are bound by a Code of Ethics and Professional Conduct that says we cannot disclose any confidential information that we receive from clients. Also, all of our files are securely maintained. We can only disclose a client's information if compelled by a process of law."

Feeling confident that my information will remain private, I make an appointment to come in this afternoon to meet with one of their investigators.

The next thing on my agenda is renting a car. When I finish my sandwich, I catch a cab to the closest car rental place that I can find and rent a small economy car. As I'm paying for my rental, José calls to inform me that they have finished their search of my office if I want to come back and lock up.

Hurrying outside to the rental car lot, I find my car, a small silver sedan. I pause for a moment, taking in the sight of it. It isn't exactly what I imagined, but it will do. Hopefully, I will only need it for a few days. After climbing inside, I adjust the mirrors and seat positioning and start driving back to my office.

When I pull into the parking lot, there is only one police officer left and he is sitting in his car directly outside my building. I could swear he scowls at me as I pass by. I guess they found the hoodie. I take a deep breath as I open the door to my office and let myself in. As I do, I can hear the police officer drive off.

I glance around. My office is in disarray, but it's not as bad as I had anticipated. I thought it would be a lot more disorganized after the search. I look toward the linen closet and approach it with a sense of dread. As I open the closet door, I see that the hoodie is gone. I knew it would be, but I'm still left with the sickening feeling that I've been caught.

By the time I get everything back in order, it's time to leave for my appointment with Extreme Spy. As I start to drive, I feel a sense of excitement and apprehension build within me. I've never hired a private investigator before, but I feel like this is the best chance of getting the answers I need.

When I'm halfway to my destination, I glance in my rearview mirror and see a black SUV a few cars back. I've noticed it driving behind me for most of the trip. As I drive, my eyes dart back and forth between the road ahead and the rearview mirror. I try to concentrate on where I'm going, but the SUV is pulling at my attention like a magnet. I turn off of the main road and check to see if the SUV is still there. I see it round the corner behind me and my breath quickens. Am I being followed?

I need to stop at the bank, so I pull over to the side of the road a few blocks down and park at a parking meter. I watch as the SUV passes by, but I can't see in through the tinted windows. It continues on down the street. I sit in my car for a few minutes to make sure that it doesn't return. Satisfied that it's gone, I get out of the car and withdraw some money from the bank.

When I arrive back at my car, I look around for the dark vehicle, but it's nowhere in sight. Maybe I'm being oversuspicious. Nevertheless, I decide to take a roundabout route to get to my appointment.

I arrive at my destination right on time. It's a small unassuming building nestled among the bustling city streets. After I park in an underground parking lot, I wait a few minutes before exiting my car to make sure I'm not being followed. Then taking a deep breath, I step out and make my way inside.

Extreme Spy is located in a small office, and I get the impression that most clients don't come here in person. A man at the front desk asks for my retainer fee, which I was expecting. I give him the cash I just withdrew from an ATM. This way there will be no bank records indicating that I hired a P.I.

The man asks me to take a seat and says Jenna will be with me shortly. There are only two seats in the waiting area, so I sit in the closest one. After a few minutes, a lady with shoulder-length brown hair walks out. She looks to be in her mid-30s.

"Claire?" she asks in a friendly voice.

"Yes." I stand up and shake her hand.

"I'm Jenna Sherwood. Please follow me into my office."

Her office is neat and tidy, with a large oak desk taking center stage. Jenna seats herself behind her desk and smiles warmly, gesturing for me to take a seat across from her.

"Hi, Claire. What brings you in?" She leans forward slightly as she studies me.

I inhale deeply and try to compose myself. I figure I might as well cut to the chase. "Have you seen the story on the news about the man who has gone missing in Vancouver? Brad Carleton?" My voice wavers slightly as I speak.

Jenna's eyes widen. "Yes. I have."

I knew she would have, given that the story has been all over the news. I go on to explain that I was having an affair with him. Jenna nods, seemingly unsurprised by my revelation. She's probably heard it all in this line of business.

I continue with my story as Jenna sits back in her chair steepling her fingers together. I tell her that Brad disappeared on the night that we were secretly meeting, and I explain everything that has happened since, including his cell phone being found outside my office along with a towel that had blood on it. At certain points Jenna stops me to ask questions.

Then I tell her about the letter that was slipped through my door and the hoodie in my trunk, explaining that I think someone is trying to set me up. She listens attentively and takes notes from time to time as I relay everything I can remember. When I'm finished, I feel like a weight has been lifted.

Jenna asks, "Do you have any idea who would want to frame you?"

Shaking my head, I say, "I honestly don't know. I can't think of anyone who would have a reason to."

Jenna seems to know there is a "but" coming, and waits for it.

"But my husband Jon has been acting strange lately. He was whispering on his phone one morning, so I looked at his call history." I decide to edit out the part where I broke into his phone. "I found the number of a private investigation firm."

Jenna asks for the firm's name and I provide it to her.

"Interesting," she says, making a note. "They investigate infidelity, but that's not exclusively what they do."

"Right," I respond, as I'd already looked them up.

"Is there anyone else that may be holding a grudge against you?"

I think for a moment. "Possibly Brad's wife," I answer, "if she knew about our affair."

Jenna nods in agreement. "Do you have any reason to think she knew?"

"Yes. Kind of." I tell her about how Karen had been making appointments with me and about my strange conversations with her.

"That does sound a bit suspect," Jenna says and makes some more notes. "Anyone else?" she asks.

"It's a long shot," I reply, "but something happened a number of years ago, and it's possible someone is blaming me for it."

Jenna raises her eyebrows.

I consider telling her the true story, but I'm worried about her considering it a crime that she has an obligation to report. So instead of telling her what actually happened, I tell her that Shelley and I were on the yacht when Cassie died and that Cassie had been accusing Shelley of stealing her boyfriend, Ethan. I say that Cassie's brother was on the boat cruise as well and we passed him at the end of the night going up the stairs.

After I finish telling Jenna everything I can think of, she stands up and shakes my hand.

"It was nice to meet you, Claire. It sounds like you have been through a lot lately. I'm sure this must be a very stressful time for you."

"Yes," I say. "It hasn't been easy."

"I will start doing some research right away to see what I can dig up."

"Thanks," I say with a smile. "I really appreciate it."

"No problem. I will be in touch shortly."

As I drive out of the underground parking lot, I feel like I'm finally gaining some control over my situation. But then I see it, and a chill spreads throughout my body. A black SUV is parked on the opposite side of the road. It's impossible to tell if it's the same one I saw earlier. I try to look through the driver's side window as I turn the corner into traffic. I'm pretty sure there's someone in the driver's seat, but I only get a quick glance.

On the drive home, I check my rearview mirror repeatedly, but I don't see the SUV again. It must be my exhausted mind imagining things. My nerves have calmed by the time I reach my street, but a new anxiety is causing a different stress. I'm dreading the conversation that I know is coming with Jon. He knows I haven't been completely honest and he didn't sound happy when I spoke with him earlier today.

As I approach my driveway, I see a police car parked in it and my heart rate instantly quickens. *Am I being arrested?* But then it occurs to me that they are probably just talking to Jon.

Taking a deep breath, I get out of my rental car and walk through the front door. When I reach the top of the stairs, I see Jon sitting in our living room with José and Dianna. He looks over at me, eyes filled to the brim with hurt and anger. He gives me a fake smile. "Hi, Claire."

My stomach turns as I walk into the living room and look at the three of them. "Hello," is all I manage to get out of my mouth.

Silence fills the room. Then Dianna stands up. "We were just leaving." She looks over at Jon and smiles. "Thanks for speaking with us."

"Of course," Jon says as he stands up and walks José and Dianna to the door. I notice that José avoids eye contact with me as he passes by.

When the door shuts, Jon turns around and glares at me.

"What did they want?" I ask as he passes by me into the kitchen.

"They were just asking what I was doing on the night Brad disappeared, and whether I'd used your car or had been to your office." Jon takes a beer out of the fridge. "They were asking some questions about you and our relationship as well," he says with his back to me.

"What did you tell them?"

"Oh. Nothing really. Just the truth." His tone seems almost sarcastic.

I wait to see if he's going to say anything more, but he doesn't. He sits back down in the living room with his beer and turns the TV on. He seems upset, but I'm happy not to engage in a conversation about this, so I say, "I guess they're trying to figure out who's setting me up. I told them it wasn't you, but I suppose they needed to ask you some questions anyway."

"Yeah," is all he says, as he chugs back a third of his beer. I feel like asking him if he needs a funnel for the rest of it, but I decide not to. Instead, I ask, "Did you tell them you were home on Saturday night?" Then I hold my breath while I wait for his response. There is none, so I ask, "Did you say you used my car?"

"Yes. I told them I used it to pick up the takeout on the weekend. Why?"

Crap. Now they know I lied. "I don't know," I respond. "Just wondering."

"Why would I lie about using your car?" His voice seems agitated, and I don't answer.

"And why didn't you tell me about everything that was going on sooner?" He's now facing me, and he looks like he's about to jump up out of his seat.

"I was planning to," I say, "but I had a lot going on today with my office being searched and my car taken, plus the police were asking me a bunch of questions."

"Right. I'm sure you did. I guess with all that was going on, you didn't have a chance to call me until the afternoon." He abruptly turns and leans back against the couch, facing the TV.

"Actually, I didn't," I say, knowing it isn't true. I don't want to argue with him and I don't want to talk about the investigation any longer, so I walk down the hall to the bedroom to change out of my work clothes. He doesn't bring it up again and neither do I. In fact, we barely speak for the rest of the evening. It's amazing how accustomed we have become to sweeping things under the rug.

CHAPTER 15

The next morning, I go to my office at the usual time. On the drive there, I periodically look in my rearview mirror and I'm relieved to find that no one is following me. I also don't find any SUVs in my parking lot when I arrive at work.

Today I only have one appointment—the one I kept with Steve. He arrives right on time.

"Good morning, Claire," he says in a chipper voice. "How are you?" I see him studying my face as he waits for my answer.

"I'm doing well, thanks," I say with a fake smile. "How are you?"

"Great!" he says enthusiastically. He seems in a particularly good mood.

I get him settled on the massage table and start working on him. Steve is chatting throughout the treatment like he usually does. Partway through, he brings up Brad, just like I knew he would.

"Have you heard anything more about Brad?" he asks, turning his head toward me.

"No. As far as I know, he's still missing."

"Yeah. I thought so," he replies. "I didn't hear anything on the news."

"No. I haven't either," I respond.

"I feel bad for his family." He pauses, then he says, "I saw his wife on TV, and she looked really upset. Of course, anyone would be in that situation."

"Yes. It must be awful to have a loved one go missing," I reply.

He doesn't say anything further on the subject, which is a relief.

Near the end of his massage, he asks if I'm still playing tennis. I get the feeling he's hinting that we should play together, so I tell him I injured my shoulder and I won't be playing for a while. He seems disappointed, and there's a break in the conversation. This seems as good an opening as any to bring up the subject I've been waiting to discuss.

"So, how's your dating life going?" I ask.

"Still single," he responds. "It's difficult to meet women in Vancouver. I don't hang out at bars, and I'm not interested in dating sites. It's hard to find someone who I'm physically attracted to, but is also smart and has similar interests."

I nod in agreement. "Yes. I know what you mean. It's like looking for a zebra in a herd of horses."

"I'll tell you something for free," Steve says with a grin. "There aren't many women like you out there." He glances over at me to see my reaction.

I laugh and ignore his flirting. "I know what you mean about dating sites," I say. "I've never been a fan of them either. I always found it was best to meet someone through work or friends."

"Yes," he says sighing. "You're probably right."

I pause for a moment before speaking. "I have a friend who's recently single. I'm not sure if she's ready to date, but I could introduce the two of you."

"Thanks," he replies. "I don't really want to go on a blind date, though. But maybe if you were there too." He's dropping hints like confetti. He seems to be coming on strong with his flirting today. I wonder what's gotten into him.

I ignore his comment. "She's actually quite attractive," I say. "Here. Let me show you a picture."

I stop my treatment and wipe my hands. Then I pick up my phone and pull up a picture of Shelley and hand it to Steve. He takes it and stares at the photo for a while. I hold my breath. *Does he recognize her?*

As he passes my phone back to me, he says, "She is attractive. Nice hair."

I take my phone back and smile. *That's it? Nice hair?* He didn't recognize her. I feel the stress leave my body as I place my phone back on the counter.

Then Steve says, "You know it's strange, but I'm pretty sure I've seen her before."

"Oh?" I reply as my heart sinks. "I don't think she's ever been in here at the same time as you." I can feel my body tense as I await his response.

"No. I don't think it was here. I think she may have been the woman I saw at JJ's with Brad." My stomach clenches. So, it was her. Although I suspected it might be, I hoped Steve would prove me wrong. Why was she meeting up with Brad? I'm at a loss for words.

"Are you sure?" I ask, my voice cracking. "She never mentioned that she knew him."

"Yes. I'm quite sure it was her. I have a pretty good memory for faces, especially attractive ones."

"Hmmmm. Well, when she's ready to start dating again, I'll set up a meeting between the two of you."

"You mean the three of us." He turns to me with a mischievous smile. "Sure. That would be great Claire."

Pretending not to notice his flirtation, I say, "Of course I would make sure it wasn't awkward for either of you."

"Great. I should have my new boat soon. Maybe the three of us could take it out one day and you could introduce me."

He must see the expression on my face because he adds, "You could bring Jon too if you want."

"Thanks," I respond, trying to sound enthusiastic. "Sounds fun."

Then it occurs to me. How does he know Jon's name? I don't remember ever mentioning him to Steve, but I guess it's possible that I said his name at some point.

I try to imagine Jon, Shelley, Steve and I all going out on a boat together and I almost laugh. It would never happen anyway, as I have no intention of introducing Steve and Shelley. I have the information that I set out to get. Unfortunately, my suspicions were correct. It appears that my best friend is a liar.

Steve leaves my office 30 minutes later and all I can think about is why Shelley lied to me. She specifically told me that she was not the woman who Steve saw with Brad. And why didn't Brad tell me that he had met up with Shelley? The only logical explanation is that they were hiding something from me, and I can only think of one thing that could be. A relationship.

I must be missing something. Shelley has been my best friend for almost 20 years and although she has her flaws, I can't see her going behind my back and having a relationship with Brad. I also can't picture Brad doing this to me. But I suppose if I'm honest, it wasn't all rainbows and butterflies with him. We had our issues, most of which were caused by the nature of our relationship.

It was difficult to spend time together or to communicate when we weren't physically together. Whenever Brad was spending time with his wife I would hardly hear from him, which meant no communication over the weekends, none in the evenings and only a few short emails when he was on vacation. We also rarely spoke on the phone, fearing that other people might overhear our conversation.

The email communication between our meetings was unfulfilling. When we first started our relationship, Brad would always send emails saying how much he missed me or couldn't wait to see me. But as time went on, he would often just send a quick note about how his day was going or about our plans for our next meeting.

It was our in-person meetings that formed the basis of our relationship. But the problem with that was that we could only see each other for a couple of hours at a time, a few days a week. Both of us had busy work schedules that we needed to work around, so our meetings were somewhat rushed. Also, when we met, we were both on edge because we needed to avoid running into anyone we knew.

And then there were the phone calls. His wife phoned him every lunch hour for some reason. He would often have to leave and go somewhere quiet to answer the phone or call her back. I initially thought she was suspicious and checking up on him, but he told me they always talked on the phone at lunch and sometimes throughout the day. Once she called him three times in the hour and a half that I was with him. It was very odd.

Trust was also a big issue. Brad is attractive, successful, smart and charismatic. He told me about previous infidelities that occurred throughout his marriage. Yet, he always maintained that he loved his wife, had a good relationship with her and had no intention of ever leaving her. It made me think, if he'd cheat on his wife who he had a longer and deeper relationship with, wouldn't he also cheat on me?

I often wondered what life would have been like if Brad and I had left our spouses and moved in together. Would we trust each other? Would the excitement fade? Would there be things that I didn't like about him? Things that annoyed me? It seems like in most relationships, you meet someone and everything is great. You are attracted to the other person's appearance, personality, intelligence, sense of humour or other traits. You initially accept your differences. You may even be more attracted to your partner because of how different you are.

But after a while, you begin to notice little things that you think your partner could improve upon, and there are things that you start to find unattractive. They don't like to cook. They watch too much TV. They cancel plans last minute. Would this have happened with Brad over time?

It's hard to say because our relationship was never conventional. It was more of an addiction. I continued to see him, even when I knew our connection was destructive. I was on a high when we were together and went through withdrawal when we were apart, always craving another fix of Brad's love and attention. Yet, like an addiction, I couldn't bring myself to end the relationship. Looking back, I can't say it was worth what I'm going through now. I feel like I've woken up from a dream and into a nightmare.

Walking over to the window, I look out into the parking lot. My stomach tightens when I see a black SUV parked at the far end. It's difficult to tell whether it's the same one I saw yesterday. I will keep an eye on it and see if it follows me when I leave later today.

As I start to turn away from the window, a movement outside catches my attention. A dragonfly. Its playful, shiny blue body with delicate legs shimmers in the sunlight as it hovers mid-air. Its iridescent wings, thin as silk, move so fast that it appears almost motionless. I look at it, and it stares back at me with big bulbous eyes. Then it backs up and darts off into the sky in a graceful and effortless movement. Such a beautiful creature. I read once that dragonflies symbolize transformation and self-realization. Perhaps that's true.

As I turn away from the window, my mind wanders back to my conversation with Steve, and I'm wondering if I should confront Shelley. Would she lie and say Steve was mistaken? That she wasn't at JJ's with Brad? Or would she tell me the truth?

I guess there's only one way to find out. Grabbing my phone out of my purse, I send her a text.

Are you free to meet for lunch today or tomorrow?

A few minutes later I hear a *ding*. It's Shelley's response.

Sure. I'm free for lunch tomorrow. I hope everything's OK.

She follows this with a heart emoji. For some reason, the emoji makes me scowl. It seems fake given what I now know. I text her back.

Great. Do you want to meet at Bella's at noon?

I get the thumbs-up emoji in response. I will have some choice questions for Shelley tomorrow. I'll have to give some thought as to how to approach it.

A wave of nausea passes through me as I place my phone back in my purse. Then a thought escapes from the corner of my mind. The corner that I keep locked with unpleasant truths. I've been trying to ignore it for a while, but I think I have to face the fact that I have yet another problem to deal with.

My period is almost a month late. I started taking birth control pills when I began my affair with Brad. Buried in the bottom of my makeup bag at home, there were occasions when I had forgotten to take one, but I don't think it would be that easy to get pregnant at my age. I'm pretty sure it's just the stress and anxiety that I've been dealing with that has caused me to miss my period. But the alternative would be disastrous. If I'm pregnant, Jon would know the child isn't his. He's sterile.

Thinking about it causes my anxiety to grow like a crack in a windshield. I need to deal with this now. I can't handle the stress of not knowing in addition to everything else that is happening. There's a large retail drugstore a few blocks away. I can buy a pregnancy test there. Putting on my jacket, I get ready to leave. But I stop just before opening the front door. Someone might be watching me. So instead, I lock-up and leave out the back door into the alley.

As I reach the end of the alley, I look both ways. Finding no one in sight, I quickly turn the corner onto the main street and come face to face with Brad. I almost drop my purse. It's a Missing Person's poster stapled to a telephone pole. Karen must have put it there.

It takes me a moment to pull myself together. Then I walk as quickly as I can to the store, looking back several times to make sure no one is following me. On the walk there, I decide that I should also buy a cheap prepaid phone while I'm there so I can make sure my calls aren't being traced.

When I arrive, there are various people milling about. As I walk past the rows of toiletries and cosmetics, I try to avoid eye contact with anyone. Reaching the electronics section, I find what I'm looking for—a small display of pre-paid phones tucked away in the back corner. I scan the selection and grab the cheapest one I can find, placing it in my basket.

Next, I find the aisle with the pregnancy tests. I can feel sweat form on my forehead as I stand in front of a shelf lined with various boxes. My eyes frantically scan the packages trying to find the right one. I need to hurry before someone sees me. I reach out to grab a box but hesitate and pull back as a group of giggling teenagers round the corner into the aisle. They pass by as I pretend to check my phone messages.

Taking a deep breath, I try to compose myself. I know I have to do this. Reaching up with lightning speed, I grab the first box I can get my hand on and place it in my basket, hidden behind the phone. Then I make a beeline for the checkout counter.

When I reach the front of the line, I look around once again before placing the items on the counter, trying to avoid the gaze of the cashier. I feel a sense of relief when she scans the pregnancy test and places it in a white plastic bag. I pay in cash and quickly leave the store. Mission accomplished.

I'm out of breath when I arrive at the back door to my office and let myself in. It feels like I've just run a marathon, and it takes a few moments before I'm able to breathe normally again. As I empty the contents of the shopping bag onto my desk, I see the pregnancy test sitting there like a coiled snake, ready to strike. It's silly because I know it doesn't have the power to change my reality, but I'm afraid of it nonetheless. Am I being irrational? It's not the first time I've missed my period.

As I stare at the small box sitting on my desk, my mind goes to a place I don't want it to go. What would I do if the test were positive? I get a warm feeling thinking of Brad being the father of my child. He told me that he always wanted children and the only reason he didn't have any was because his wife didn't want them. But the feeling leaves me as quickly as it came. The reality is that Jon would leave me if I were pregnant and I don't even know if Brad is alive. I'd likely be raising the child on my own. I may even be raising it in prison if I don't figure out what's going on soon.

My hand unconsciously rubs my stomach, and I quickly pull it away. *I'm not pregnant*, I tell myself. But if I am, I don't think I could handle the stress of dealing with it today. I grab the pregnancy test and shove it in my desk drawer. So much for being brave.

I try to distract myself by setting up my prepaid phone, which is more complicated than I had anticipated. It takes about 20 minutes. When I'm finished, I create a new email address. Then I call Jenna to give her my new contact details. I also tell her about my conversation with Steve. To my surprise, she's already done some research on my case and says she will report shortly.

Next, I call Cole to see if he has any information about what Jon told the police or when I might get my car back. When I receive his voicemail, I leave a message giving him my new phone number and asking him to get back to me on those things.

I'm finally gaining some control over my situation, and it feels good. I'm tired of sitting back and letting life happen. It's time to take the reins.

After making myself a cup of tea, I do my daily login to my secret email account that I used to communicate with Brad. There are no new emails, which isn't surprising. I also search the internet for any news on Brad. I'm always tense when I do these searches, afraid that one day I will find a story about our affair.

As I scroll down past old news stories, something catches my eye and my stomach tightens into a ball. It's an article saying the police have found a person of interest in Brad's missing person's case, but no further details are provided. *Are they referring to me? Or is there someone else?* I look at my phone willing it to ring. Cole will probably know what's going on.

My phone remains silent, so I continue to browse the internet. As I do, I come across another article that takes me by surprise. Apparently, Karen has arranged a search party for Brad that is to take place throughout Stanley Park tomorrow. I don't know why she wouldn't have mentioned this to me when she came in for her treatment. And why Stanley Park? It's about a 10-minute drive from where Brad's ID was found. But it's a big park and I guess it's the most likely area where someone would dump a body.

Feeling on edge, I walk over to the window and look out. The sky is a muted grey, casting a dull light. The black SUV is still parked in the same spot, its tinted windows blocking my view of the interior. The uneasy feeling in my gut grows stronger. The sound of my new phone ringing startles me and I jump. Then, realizing it must be Cole, I rush over to my desk to pick it up.

CHAPTER 16

"Hi Claire. It's Cole. I got your message. I was just speaking to José, and there have been some developments." His voice sounds somber, which is not a good sign.

"Oh. What did you find out?" I ask hesitantly.

"Unfortunately, it's not good news."

Brad's dead. They found his body. "What is it?" I ask, voice shaking.

"The police sprayed luminol throughout your car, and apparently there was evidence of a fair amount of blood in the back seat, which had been cleaned up with some sort of cleaning detergent. There were also trace amounts in the trunk, but that may have been from Brad's hoodie."

I don't know what to say. I'm completely frozen. My fingers lock around my phone as Cole continues.

"They also found evidence of blood in the washroom at your building. They've sent samples from your car and office for testing to see if it matches Brad's."

I feel like I've been hit by a semi. I can't believe this is happening. Someone is setting me up. I don't know of any other explanation. A dark thought surfaces. *Could I have done something to Brad?* Is it possible that I drank so much that I don't remember? Or could I be suffering from some form of amnesia caused by the traumatic event of killing Brad?

"That *is* bad news," is all I can think to say. Then I add, "I have no idea how blood could have gotten in the back seat of my car. No one ever uses it."

"Well, it looks like someone is trying to frame you," says Cole. "We've discussed this before, and you are going to have to think hard and make a list of anyone who may be holding a grudge against you."

"I really can't think of anyone," I respond. "I don't know who would do this to me."

Cole pauses as if he's deciding whether to say something. Then he asks, "Do you think it's possible that your husband found out about your affair? Is it possible that he's setting you up?"

I feel sick. I can't say that the thought hasn't crossed my mind. But I really can't see Jon murdering Brad and then trying to make it look like it was me. I haven't told Cole that Jon hired a P.I. and that he may have followed me that night. I just can't see Jon as a murderer and I don't want Cole thinking of him that way either.

"I don't think that Jon knows about my affair and I can't see him framing me," I respond. "I'll give it some more thought, but I don't know anyone who hates me this much. Maybe Brad's wife found out about the affair."

"Yes. That's possible," says Cole.

"Have the police checked her house for blood?" I ask hopefully.

"I understand that she allowed them to search her house, but they have no reason to suspect her of doing anything at this point. She hasn't indicated that she was aware of your affair, and according to her, their marriage was going well."

I'm not sure she really believes that. She was complaining to me about how much time he spent away. And if anything he said is true, they didn't have much of a sex life. But who knows what the truth is. People lie all the time. I read once that the average person is lied to about 10 to 200 times a day.

"There's something else," Cole says.

I suck in a deep breath. "What?"

"The police were interviewing some of the neighbours on your street to see if any of them saw anyone around your car. One gentleman who lives across the street from you said he saw you on Saturday morning getting something from your trunk."

Crap. I'd forgotten about Tim. Of course he had to mention that he saw me going through my trunk. I knew I shouldn't have lied about when I found the hoodie.

"Is this true?" Cole asks when I don't respond right away. I know I can't continue the lie. Obviously, I've been caught. "Yes. I forgot about that." My voice sounds weak.

"And you didn't see Brad's hoodie in your trunk at that time?"

I think at this point I need to tell the truth. I shouldn't have lied in the first place. "Yes. I knew it was there. I saw it on Friday when I put my gym bag in my trunk." I hesitate for a moment, unsure of what to say. Then I continue. "I panicked. I didn't know what to do. I thought of calling you, but I was afraid you would make me turn it in to the police, and I didn't want to become a suspect in Brad's disappearance. I'm sorry."

There is silence on the other end of the line. Then Cole speaks in a calm voice. "Look, Claire. If you want me to represent you, you are going to have to start trusting me. I can't be your lawyer if you continue to lie to me."

"I understand. I'm sorry." I realize he's right. I do need to trust him. He's the only person that I can trust at this point.

"Is there anything else you aren't telling me?" he asks.

"I hired a private detective yesterday," I respond.

"That's good news. I was going to suggest that we do that. Who did you hire?"

I give him Jenna's information. He tells me he's heard of Extreme Spy and thinks they're a good company.

After we're finished discussing Jenna's investigation, I say, "There's something else I should tell you."

"Yes?" he asks, and I can sense the annoyance in his voice.

"You were asking if it there is anyone else who could possibly be holding a grudge against me. I'm not sure if this is relevant, but something happened a long time ago." I take a deep breath and then proceed to tell him about Cassie. The real story.

"I wish you had told me about that earlier," he says. "It's possible that someone from the boat cruise is harbouring negative feelings toward you, but it seems unlikely given the amount of time that has passed."

"Yeah. That's what I thought," I respond. "That's why I hadn't mentioned it earlier. But I did tell Jenna about it, so she may look into Jeff and Ethan to be sure."

"Makes sense," Cole replies. "We shouldn't leave any stone unturned."

I consider whether I should tell him about Jon potentially following me on the night of Brad's disappearance and that Steve thinks he saw Brad out with Shelley. I don't want to implicate my best friend and my husband in this if they had nothing to do with it, but I don't want to keep anything from Cole. I ultimately decide to tell him. However, I make it clear that I don't want this information being shared with the police.

"I'm glad you decided to trust me, Claire. We need to be a team on this." He pauses for a moment. "I know you don't want to believe that Jon had anything to do with Brad's disappearance, but you should know that he lied to the police about being home on the night Brad disappeared and if he knew about your affair, he had a motive to hurt Brad and set you up. He also had access to your car and possibly your office."

I know Cole is right. But I still don't think Jon has anything to do with this. "Let's just see what Jenna turns up. I don't want the police to question Jon any further if that can be avoided. I've already caused enough problems."

"Claire, I don't think you realize the seriousness of the situation. If those blood samples taken from your car come back with Brad's DNA, there is a good chance you will be arrested."

It feels like someone is slowly tightening a noose around my neck.

"Right now, you are the only person of interest."

I feel a lump form in my throat. So I was the person of interest who was referred to in the news article. I guess it was wishful thinking that it might be someone else.

"But what would they arrest me for?" I ask. "There's no body. We don't even know if Brad is dead."

"True. But he's disappeared without his ID or phone and hasn't been seen or heard from since. His cell phone and a towel with his blood on it were found outside your office. You were having an affair with him, and you were the last person to see him. Apparently, the back seat of your car lit up like a Christmas tree when the police sprayed luminol on it. If they can prove that the blood in your car is his, then they will probably have enough circumstantial evidence to lay charges."

Cole pauses as if trying to decide whether to continue. Then in a calm, slow voice he says, "If the blood is his, it's a logical conclusion that he is deceased and that he was in the back of your car bleeding."

I'm gripping my phone so tightly that my knuckles have turned white. I don't know what to say.

Cole sighs heavily. "I hate to say it Claire, but even if the bloodwork is inconclusive, which might be the case as luminol is known to destroy DNA, there is still a good chance that you will be arrested."

Anxiety wells up inside me like a geyser ready to explode. I thank Cole for the call, my voice barely a whisper, and then I tell him I have to go. After I hang up, I run down the hallway to the washroom and throw up in the toilet. As I rinse my mouth with water, I look up at my reflection in the mirror. My hair is wet and sticking to my face. My make-up is smudged and there are dark circles around my eyes. I can't stand the sight of myself.

Crumpling back down onto the floor, I hold my knees against my chest and cry. My situation is getting worse with each passing day. I feel like a goldfish trapped in a plastic bag. Is this my punishment for having an affair? Is it karma? I could tell myself that everything happens for a reason, but I hate it when people say that. Things don't happen for a reason. Things happen randomly. People just give things a reason.

I know that the blood in my back seat will be Brad's. Who else's could it be? And with that realization, I also know that Brad is dead. And although I refuse to believe it, I have to consider the possibility that I killed him and disposed of his body. So far all of the evidence is pointing in that direction. But if I did something as crazy as that, wouldn't I remember it? Is it even possible to forget that you killed someone?

I get up off the bathroom floor and walk back to my office where I log on to my computer to search crime-related amnesia. I'm surprised to find a study stating that 20-30% of those accused of violent crimes claim to have no recollection of the event.

Apparently, there are two different explanations for this type of memory loss in violent offenders. The first is that during the commission of the crime, an offender may suffer from a brain dysfunction that prevents the memory of the criminal event from being stored in that person's memory. This is called organic amnesia.

The second occurs when the offender is in an extreme emotional state, such as rage, when committing a violent offence. The details of the crime are stored in that person's memory while undergoing strong emotions. When the offender later returns to a calmer state, that person is unable to remember the event because of a mismatch in emotional states from the time it was stored to the time of its attempted retrieval. This is called dissociative amnesia.

I search some more and see that alcohol may also have a negative affect on your memory. Not surprisingly, excessive drinking can cause one to forget the commission of a violent crime. I suppose this is the same thing as blacking out when you've had too much to drink.

So, it's possible that I could have killed Brad in a state of drunkenness or in a state of high emotions, and I could have tried to cover it up. I just can't think of anything that could possibly make me do that.

Looking at my watch, I see it's already lunchtime. It's been a busy day and I'm exhausted. I feel like all the energy has been sucked out of my body. Yet I can't sit around doing nothing. I need to work on proving my innocence. It occurs to me that Jon is at work, and I have a prime opportunity to search through his things to see if I can find anything that would suggest he is involved in any of this. I feel a bit guilty even considering this, but Cole has me thinking about it and I need to do this for my own peace of mind.

Stepping out the front door of my office, I glance over at the black SUV before getting in my car and driving off. I check my rearview mirror to see if the SUV also leaves. It's not until I am a block away, that I'm pretty sure I see it pulling out of the parking lot. A thousand tiny needles dance across my skin. Gripping the steering wheel a bit tighter, I speed up, weaving through traffic. The light up ahead has just turned yellow, so I push the gas pedal and careen through the intersection just as it turns red. Looking back, I can see the SUV stopped a couple of cars back at the light. I breathe a sigh of relief as I race the rest of the way home.

I only start to relax when I near my house. That is until I see Jon's car in our driveway. It's only 2:00 p.m. What is he doing home at this time?

CHAPTER 17

I pull into our driveway beside Jon's car, still confused as to why he would be home. When I get out of my car, I see Tim standing outside his house watering the plants. He smiles and waves. *Jerk*. Doesn't he have a job? I feel like giving him the finger, but I know he probably didn't realize all the problems he caused for me by telling the police he saw me with my trunk open the other day. So instead, I give him a fake smile and a short wave before entering the house. When I do, it's completely silent, which is unusual. I expected to find Jon in front of the T.V., but no one is there. Something doesn't seem right.

My stomach is in knots as I quietly walk down the hall toward our bedroom, where I find Jon walking out of the ensuite bathroom, wiping his wet hands on his jeans. When he sees me, his eyebrows shoot up and his mouth forms into a perfect "O". I can tell from his expression that he wasn't expecting to see me.

"What's going on?" I ask.

"Nothing," he says, not meeting my eyes.

"What are you doing at home? Shouldn't you be at work?" I ask.

His jaw hardens. "Shouldn't you?"

Fair question. "I took the afternoon off," I respond. "But why are you home?"

"I quit my job," he calmly says as he shuts a partly open dresser drawer.

My mouth opens, but nothing comes out. It takes me a moment to process what he said. "You didn't tell me that you lost your job. When did that happen?"

"I didn't *lose* my job," he snaps. "It's not like, 'Oops. I can't find my job anywhere. Where did it go?'" He pauses to glare at me. "I quit!"

"When did you *quit*?" I ask, emphasizing the last word.

"A couple of weeks ago."

I allow his words to percolate for a moment before responding. "So all this time you were lying to me and pretending to go to work? What were you doing? Just sitting around the house?" I'm furious now. "Last week you told me you couldn't help with the dishes because you were too exhausted from working!"

"Did I say that? I guess I lied." His face is smoldering with resentment.

What's wrong with him? I don't even know how to respond to that. I was expecting an apology, but I don't think one will be forthcoming. I glare at him.

"Have I offended you?" he asks, his eyes narrowed. "Why are you acting so damn sanctimonious? You lie all the time. In fact, I think you have reached an Olympian level at lying, haven't you?"

I look at him with confusion, not knowing what to say.

"You don't think I know?"

My heart starts pounding in my chest. "Know what?" I ask, even though I'm pretty sure I know what's coming.

"That you were fucking Brad Carleton."

It hits me like a slap in the face. He knows. Or does he? Is he guessing? Should I admit it? Before I have a chance to decide, he says, "I know about the tennis games, the lunches, the hotels."

He knows.

I take a moment to process this and then I say the only thing I can. "I'm sorry." I don't know what else to say so I add, "It was a mistake."

A vein on his forehead protrudes. "You're sorry? Sorry for what? Sorry that I found out? Or are you sorry for cheating on me? Sorry for the constant lies? Sorry that I wasn't good enough for you? Sorry that you made me feel like crap every day?"

Guilt washes over me like a tsunami. I feel like I need to explain, justify. "I know I hurt you, and I know I was wrong. But neither of us has been very happy lately. Things have changed between us. Ever since we tried to have a child. It just seems like you're distant, like you're angry all the time."

"No. I'm not even angry anymore Claire. I'm just done. I'm done with your games. I'm done with your lies. I don't care about your secrets and your excuses. I'm done."

"Jon—"

He cuts me off. "I know you are going through your own hell, and you have a lot on your plate right now. But you brought this on yourself. If you weren't happy, you should have discussed it with me. We could have tried to work it out. But instead, you chose to betray me, to sneak around and lie, to sleep with another man. And now you're a suspect in his murder investigation. How ironic. The thing that you thought would make you happy has now ruined your life. You've lost me. You've lost him, and I hope to God you've lost your self-respect."

He takes a deep breath before continuing. "You'll probably lose your freedom as well. But if you somehow get out of this, I wonder how many patients you'll have left after your name is all over the news as a suspect in a murder investigation." He pauses and looks at me, almost with sympathy. "You've lost everything, Claire." He tilts his head. "And for what? Sex? Excitement? Your egotistical need to feel attractive or wanted? I hope it was worth it."

And with that, Jon storms past me and out the bedroom door. A few seconds later, I can hear the front door open and slam shut. Then I hear his car start up and screech out of the driveway.

I'm still standing frozen in the bedroom. I can hardly breathe as I sit down on the edge of our bed. Tears spill down my face. Jon's right. I've lost everything. I *destroyed* everything. I don't even have a close friend to confide in. Brad is gone and my trust in Shelley is fading.

I pull my cell phone out of my purse and start to dial my parents' number. But then I stop. What would I tell them? That I cheated on Jon and I'm a suspect in my lover's disappearance? They would be so disappointed in me. I stick my phone back in my purse. It's amazing how your life can change so quickly. Two weeks ago, I was laughing and feeling in love. And today—today I'm a different person. I'm lost. I sit on the edge of my bed thinking about what a mess I've made of my life.

I understand why Jon is so upset with me. I would feel the same way in his shoes. But the state of our relationship isn't all my fault. Marriages don't fail. People do. It's never just one person's fault. Although I was wrong to have cheated, Jon played a role in our failed marriage as well. He can't just pull the emergency cord on the responsibility train and exit off.

After a few minutes, I get up, wipe the tears from my face and blow my nose. It's early afternoon, but I feel like a need a drink to numb the pain. Making my way to the kitchen, I pour myself a large glass of wine. Then I sit down in the living room and finish it. As I do, I can feel my nerves start to calm. It's time to stop dwelling on my bad choices. I can't change the past, but maybe I can change my future.

As I'm sitting there, I remember the reason I came home early. The thought of searching through Jon's things now feels wrong. But after seeing his rage and knowing that he was aware of my affair, I have to accept that there is a possibility, however small, that he is the person setting me up.

I start by going through Jon's drawers, taking all of his clothes out of each one to be sure that nothing is hidden in them. There isn't. Next, I search through the ensuite bathroom, which is the only one he uses. As I'm going through the bathroom drawers, I find a bottle of pills. Xanax. I'm familiar with the name. It's used to treat anxiety. I feel a heaviness in my chest. I had no idea he was taking these. I look at the prescription date. They were prescribed a month ago, but I suppose he could have been taking them for longer. I feel sad that Jon didn't confide in me about this, and I wonder how much I contributed to his need to take them.

Putting the pill bottle back in the drawer, I continue my search. After finding nothing else of interest in the bathroom, I look through our closet. I need to get a chair to reach the top shelf, where I find what looks to be a half-smoked marijuana joint. Another thing I didn't know about Jon. When I first met him, he'd occasionally smoke a joint with his friends but since we've been together, he hasn't mentioned that he was continuing to smoke. I don't know why he felt the need to hide it from me. I'm starting to wonder what else he hasn't disclosed.

While looking through the drawer on Jon's bedside table, I find his tablet. I pull it out and open it. The screen asks for a password. Would he use the same one he uses for his phone? I try it, and the screen opens up. It worked! I can feel myself tense as I click on his browser and check the history.

There are lots of searches about jobs, the news and the weather. As I scroll down, a section of searches catches my eye and I freeze. They all relate to Brad Carleton. They include searches for his address, his phone number and several social media searches. I check the date, and my stomach turns. They were done weeks ago, before Brad went missing.

Jon must have found out about our affair and was looking for information about Brad. But why? Could he have followed me that night that Brad disappeared? Did he follow Brad after I caught a cab home? Was he even here when I arrived home? I wish I could remember.

I hear a car approaching outside and I quickly slam the tablet shut and return it to Jon's drawer. I jump up and run to the living room and look out the window to see if it's Jon. But it's just one of the neighbours parking outside.

Returning to the bedroom, I finish looking through Jon's tablet, but I don't find anything else of interest. It's late afternoon by the time I finish my search of the house and my bottle of wine. I wasn't able to find anything further that would suggest that Jon has any involvement in Brad's disappearance. But the internet searches have me rattled.

I try texting Jon a couple of times to see if he is planning on coming home, but he doesn't respond. Feeling exhausted and depressed, I lay down on the couch and shut my eyes. I wake up hours later to an empty house and realize that Jon isn't coming home.

When I eventually turn in for the night, I regret having had a nap. I can't sleep. My mind keeps circling back to Jon and how he knew about my affair. I was very careful to make sure that there was no evidence of it on my phone or any other devices I kept at home. I didn't think I was acting suspiciously, at least not enough for him to suspect anything.

If he knew that I was playing tennis with Brad, he may have been following me. Or maybe he hired someone else to do that. That might be why he had a private investigator's number on his phone. But it's also possible that someone he knows saw me with Brad and told him. I wish I'd asked Jon how he knew, but it didn't seem like an appropriate question to raise at the time, and I'm not sure he would have told me anyway.

Although I don't fall asleep until about 2:00 a.m., I wake up early and can't fall back asleep. Thinking a jog might help release some stress, I drag myself out of bed and put my workout clothes on. My eyes are heavy and my body feels tired as I bend down to tie my running shoes. But I force myself out the door anyway. Once I start jogging, I begin to feel a bit better. The endorphins always help. But after I return home and shower, I can feel the anxiety start to well up again.

The thought of sitting around the house all morning waiting to see if Jon will return doesn't appeal to me. I contemplate whether I should attend the search party for Brad at Stanley Park. I have a few hours to kill before meeting Shelley for lunch, and it seems like the right thing to do. It will probably be a bit awkward, but I feel I owe it to Brad. I don't think being there will arouse anyone's suspicions as he was one of my patients. Well, it might arouse Karen's suspicions but I think that ship has already sailed.

According to the newspaper article, the search is scheduled to begin at 9:00 a.m. at the parking lot near Lost Lagoon. Stanley Park is huge, larger than New York's Central Park, and surrounded by the waters of the Burrard Inlet and English Bay. It is mostly made up of dense forest with some trails, but there are also beaches, lakes, and playgrounds. I'm assuming the search will be through the forested area.

It looks like it will be a hot day, so I put on some yoga pants and a tank top and grab my baseball cap and sunglasses. As I'm walking out to my car, I start to have doubts about attending the search. Maybe it's best to lay low. But the alternative is to sit around my empty house all day stressing about Jon, so I get in my car and start driving.

When I reach the end of my block, I see Jon's car pass by me in the opposite direction. I look over at him, but he's staring straight ahead with his sunglasses on. He probably saw me but is ignoring me. I consider turning back but decide against it. He doesn't want to talk to me right now. I wonder if he's just picking up his things or if he'll be home when I get back. I tend to think it's the former, but I guess I'll find out later.

I arrive at Lost Lagoon at 8:45 a.m. As I'm driving into the parking area, I can't help wondering if this will somehow refresh my memory. Was I here the night Brad disappeared? I immediately push the thought out of my head as being insane. I did not drive here a week and a half ago in the middle of the night with the dead body of a man I love in my car, even if I was drunk. In any event, the drive here hasn't stirred up any memories.

I find a spot at the end of the parking lot where the search party is supposed to meet. Half of the parking lot has been cordoned off with orange pylons and there is already a bunch of people in that area, crowded around a few mobile whiteboards with large posters of Brad taped to them. I also see a couple of police officers talking to a small group of people off to the side. I'm relieved to see that it's not José or Dianna.

As I walk to the other side of the parking lot, I see Karen standing beside one of Brad's posters handing out pamphlets and water bottles. More people are arriving in small groups, women in their early forties wearing their capris pants, some couples, and a fairly large group of men that look to be about Brad's age, perhaps a group of his friends or co-workers. The thought makes me feel a bit awkward. I don't know if Brad told any of his friends about us. Would anyone recognize me?

I start walking toward the poster of Brad. Seeing his face makes me sad. I miss him. Karen catches sight of me and I can't read her expression. She isn't smiling at me in recognition, but she also doesn't look upset. It almost appears as if she were expecting me.

"Hi Claire, I'm so glad you could make it out," she says with a fake smile, not sounding glad at all.

"Yes. Of course," I respond. "I wanted to help in any way I could."

Karen looks like she is about to say something, but then catches herself. Instead, she says, "That's very kind of you. You must have had to take a day off work."

"Yes," I reply, not adding that I had taken it off before learning of the search she'd organized.

"Claire?" The deep voice comes from behind me and I jump. Turning around, I see Steve standing there in his sunglasses and baseball cap. *What's he doing here?*

"Hey. Are you joining the search?" he asks, his voice a bit rushed.

"Yes. I have the morning off, so I thought I'd help out for a few hours."

"Me too," he says enthusiastically. "We can search together."

"Great," I say, trying to sound like I'm happy with the prospect. I'm not. I feel drained and I'm not in the mood for trying to hold a conversation with Steve, whose energy seems to be through the roof today.

"So, how's everything going?" he asks. "Is your business closed? I heard on the news that the police were searching a place in Yaletown."

I hadn't looked at the news today. I couldn't bring myself to check it this morning. I guess it would have been hard to miss all the police vehicles and commotion that was going on outside my office the other day.

"Yes," I respond. "I closed my office for a few days. The police did search it."

"Is that because they found Brad's cell phone in the alley behind your place?" He's speaking fast and sounds wired, almost manic. He must have loaded up on coffee today.

"Yes. That's what I understand."

"Do they think he was murdered in your office?" he asks.

I glance over at Karen, who is thankfully busy talking to another group of volunteers. If Steve is asking this, it will probably be a question that most people have. I wonder if Jon's right that I'll start losing clients.

"No," I respond. "I think they were just checking for evidence."

"Oh. That's kind of unsettling." Steve frowns. "Are you worried about your safety?"

"No. I don't think there is any threat to my safety," I lie.

"You should put a security camera up outside your door," he suggests.

How does he know I don't have one? It's not something most people would notice. But maybe he looked when he came in for a treatment after Brad disappeared.

"I'm planning on doing that," I respond. "I ordered one the other day and it should be arriving soon." And I did. I intend to catch the person who broke into my car and put a note through my door.

Karen finishes talking to a small group of volunteers and they head off to the other side of the parking lot toward the police officers. She turns back toward us. Steve looks at her and says, "I'm really sorry about your husband. I can't imagine what you're going through."

Karen nods. "It's been a nightmare. But thanks for coming out to help with the search." She tilts her head and asks, "Did you know Brad?"

"No," Steve responds. "I just saw on the news that he was missing and that you had organized a search today."

"Oh. Well, thanks again. Are you a friend of Claire's?" Something about the way she says "friend," makes me wonder if she's implying something.

"Yes. I'm Steve," he says, extending his hand out and shaking hers. "I'm a patient of Claire's, but I'd say we are also friends." He looks at me and smiles.

I try to smile back, but I'm feeling very awkward and Karen is looking at me strangely. How did she know Steve wasn't my husband? I wonder if she thinks I'm in some sort of romantic relationship with him. I decide to change the topic.

"So, what can we do to help with the search?" I ask.

"The officers are assigning groups of five to different trails. If you head over there," she points to two police officers, "they will put you in a group and tell you what trail you will be assigned to. They will also give you some tips on what to look for."

Karen reaches down to the table in front of her and passes us both a pamphlet. "Here's a picture of Brad and a description of what he was last wearing. There is also a map of the trails on the back."

I look down at the pamphlet and see a recent picture of Brad with a big smile on his face. It looks like he's on a hike. Did Karen take the picture? I feel a sudden pang of jealousy and quickly flip pamphlet over to the trail map side.

When I look back up, I see Karen looking at me. "You'll probably be assigned to the Lovers Walk Trail," she says pointing to it on the pamphlet. "I think it's next on the list."

I nod and start walking away. As I do, I wonder if her comment had some sort of hidden meaning. Was she suggesting something about my relationship with Steve, or perhaps Brad?

Steve and I stand in front of the two police officers and wait while they finish sending a group of five people off. When it's our turn, we're told we will be conducting a search of Beaver Lake Trail (not Lovers Walk) with three other volunteers.

The ladies we are assigned to search with, look to be in their late 30s. All three are wearing short jean shorts and crop tops, their hair styled and make-up on. They are busy spraying bug spray on themselves, but when they finish, they introduce themselves to me and Steve. The one named Debbie gives Steve a once over and I get the impression she finds him attractive.

"So how do you two know each other," she asks waving her finger between me and Steve. As she does, she pushes out her large breasts that have been shoved into her crop top that is one size too small. At least her breasts are real, which is more than I can say for her interest in me.

"I'm his massage therapist," I respond. "We just ran into each other in the parking lot." I'm hoping this will open the door for her to pursue Steve if she's interested.

She seems pleased with my response and immediately looks at Steve. "My brother's name is Steve," she says smiling at him.

"Yes. I guess it's a pretty common name," he replies, seemingly unaware that Debbie is flirting with him.

"It's not that common. I think I've only met two other Steves in my life," she says. "But they are both amazing people. Maybe there's something to the name." She smiles again.

"Maybe," Steve says returning her smile. I think for a moment he may be interested in Debbie, but then he turns to me.

"We should make our way over to the trail. I think we need to go this way," he says as he points to the right.

We all head off in that direction with our pamphlets to find the start of Beaver Lake Trail. On the walk there, Debbie tries a couple more times to start up a conversation with Steve, but he's fairly unresponsive so she and her two friends walk a few steps behind us and chat amongst themselves.

When we find the trail, we start searching. We are spread out on both sides of it as instructed. The sun casts dark shadows through the dense forest. My eyes scan the ground for any sign of disturbance as I make my way through the brush. As we walk, the group grows increasingly quiet, except for Steve, who seems more interested in holding a conversation with me than searching for Brad. It's almost as if he thinks we're on a date. He doesn't appear to be searching very hard as he spends most of his time looking over in my direction. I regret coming out to participate in this event. I don't think Brad will be found here.

After a couple of hours, we finish combing the area around our assigned trail and we start to make our way back. I'm feeling hot and sweaty. When we arrive at the parking lot, there is a flurry of activity. Two different TV crews are here to capture a story for local stations, and a reporter is interviewing Karen. I walk a bit closer to the crowd gathered around her to hear what she's saying.

"I just felt like I had to do something," she says to the reporter, tears filling her eyes. "I feel so helpless sitting around waiting and hoping for him to walk through the door."

I begin to worry the reporters will recognize me as being the owner of the massage therapy business that was just searched, so I put my head down and start to make my way back to my car. Steve, who has remained by my side, walks beside me.

"What are you up to now?" he asks with a hopeful look on his face.

"I'm meeting a friend for lunch soon," I say, checking my watch. "I should probably get going."

Steve's face falls. I think he thought the two of us would have lunch.

"Oh. OK.," he says not meeting my eyes. "It was nice running into you today. I guess I'll see you next week for my massage."

"Yes. See you next week," I say, waving goodbye. I watch as Steve turns and starts walking over toward the other side of the parking lot.

As I'm driving out of Stanley Park, I look in my rearview mirror. I'm not positive, but I think I see a black SUV exiting the parking lot. Is that Steve? I search my memory, but I don't think I've ever seen his vehicle before. Stepping on the gas, I quickly merge into traffic.

CHAPTER 18

When I reach the parking lot outside my building, I sit in my car for a few minutes to see if there is any sign of the SUV. As I wait, I check my text messages. Jon still hasn't responded to the text I sent yesterday. There's only one text and it's from Shelley.

I'm looking forward to seeing you for lunch today!

I'm not, but I respond anyway saying, *Me too!*

I have 20 minutes to kill until I have to meet her. Feeling satisfied that no one has followed me, I get out of my car and let myself into my office. There's no real reason for me to be here as I have no appointments today, but it's close to the restaurant where I'm meeting Shelley and I also want to pick up my pre-paid phone, which I left in my desk drawer.

When I open the drawer to retrieve my phone, my eyes fixate on a small box tucked away in the corner. Time slows as recognition floods my senses. The pregnancy test. With everything else that's been going on, I had forgotten about it, or perhaps it was subconscious avoidance. The sight of it causes anxiety, and I almost shut the drawer again.

I know I need to take it. Not knowing whether I'm pregnant is contributing to my stress levels, which are already off the charts. *Should I do this now? Get it over with?* My mind comes up with a bunch of reasons not to, but I end up convincing myself to do it. Snatching it out of the drawer, I open the box and read the instructions.

Then I take it to the washroom, my apprehension growing with each stride. I'm relieved to find the restroom empty. Opening the door to the first stall, I take the stick out of the box. My hand shakes slightly as I pee on it. *It will be negative,* I tell myself. When I'm finished, I carry it back to my office and place the test on the counter of my treatment room.

I need to occupy myself with something while I'm waiting, so I decide to listen to the voicemail messages that have been left on my work phone. There are a number of appointments that I need to schedule, but I'm not going to do that today.

I look at my watch. Have two minutes passed? Probably, but I'm not sure, so I pick up my new phone and check the email account that I gave to Jenna. I know I'm procrastinating, but this will only take a few seconds. When I log in, I'm surprised to find that Jenna has already sent me a short report. Interested to see what she found, I sit down at my desk and start reading.

The first heading is *Jeff Pusey*. I start to read.

Mr. Pusey's parents died in a head-on collision two years before the boat party, where his sister died. He has no other siblings and he never married.

Poor Jeff. He lost his whole family under tragic circumstances. Cassie's death must have hit him hard. I continue reading.

About three months after Cassie's death, Jeff was involved in an incident outside of a downtown nightclub where he assaulted another patron causing serious injuries. He moved to Los Angeles shortly after that and has played bit parts in various movies and T.V. shows.

Two months ago, Mr. Pusey was accused of sexually assaulting a woman in one of the changing rooms on a movie set. He denied the allegations, which were never proven. Shortly after this incident, he moved back to Vancouver and is now working in the downtown area at an acting agency located on Davie and Granville Street.

This last part sends a chill throughout my body. Jeff is working about ten blocks from my office. I had no idea that he worked so close by.

Jenna has attached a recent picture of Jeff, pulled from one of his social media accounts. He looks very different from what I remember. He's lost a lot of hair, and is now over-weight. His gaze appears distant and detached. There's a certain arrogance that emanates from his posture as if he believes that the world exists solely to serve as a stage for his grand performance. Although Jeff looks familiar, I don't think I would have ever recognized him if I passed him on the street. He's aged beyond his years.

Jenna also managed to track down Ethan (whose last name turns out to be Patterson) through Jeff's social media connections. The report states that Ethan is living a short distance outside of Vancouver, is divorced with two young children and works as a pilot. Unlike Jeff, Ethan doesn't seem to have been in trouble with the law. I look at his profile picture, which Jenna has attached, and he looks a lot like he did when Shelley and I met him, apart from a few new wrinkles.

My eyes widen when I look at a second photo that Jenna has inserted of Ethan. It's a picture of him standing with a group of men at a golf tournament, and one of the men standing next to him is Brad. The picture was taken five years earlier. According to Jenna, Brad is not listed as one of Ethan's connections, but nonetheless, they must have known each other. I'm not really sure what to make of this.

My mind turns back to the pregnancy test. Two minutes have definitely passed since I took it. In fact, it's probably been more than five minutes. Time to face the truth. I suck in a deep breath as I walk toward the treatment room.

As I walk through the doorway, I see the pregnancy test sitting there like a lone sentinel silently waiting to deliver its news. The instructions say that one line is negative and two is positive. I force myself to look down at it. For a moment I don't see anything, my brain struggling to make sense of the faint lines and symbols. Then I see it. A single dark pink line. *Negative*. I exhale, feeling a sense of relief as I pick the test up. But my mood switches quickly as I notice a second faint line. I look closer to make sure I'm not imagining it, but it's definitely there. Then, as if in slow motion, the truth dawns on me and I feel a wave of panic wash over me. *I'm pregnant.*

I quickly scan the instructions again to see if there is any other explanation for this faint line, but there's nothing. Maybe it's a mistake. The line isn't dark like it's supposed to be. Refusing to accept the result, I decide that I will need to take another test to be sure. I should have bought two in the first place. Disappointed that I don't have a clear answer, I throw the test in the trash can.

This day is not shaping up to be a good one, and now I have to meet Shelley. I feel like canceling, but it would be too last minute. It's already 12:45 p.m., and she's probably left to meet me. Shoving my new phone into my purse, I lock up my office and rush out the door.

When I arrive at the restaurant and look around, there's no sign of Shelley so I take a seat at the back to wait for her. She arrives a few minutes later. As she slinks toward my table in her tight-fitting sleeveless black dress and high heel shoes, I think how attractive she is. Would Brad have been interested in her?

"Hi," she says, slightly out of breath as she sits down across from me. "How are you?" She looks at me with concern, and I question if it's real.

"I'm doing OK," I respond. I consider telling her that Jon found out about my affair and left, but decide not to. I don't feel like talking about it right now. I have other topics of conversation on my agenda. So instead, I ask how she's doing. She talks about how busy she is at work these days before turning the conversation back to me.

"So, is there any news about Brad?" she asks, her expression unreadable.

Yes. His hoodie and blood were found in my car. "No," I respond, "I haven't heard anything. He's still missing."

The corners of her mouth turn down and she nods.

Here's my opening. "But there was something strange." I can feel the adrenaline starting to flow as I speak.

Shelley lifts her eyebrows. "Oh?"

"The patient who I was telling you about that saw Brad out for dinner with another woman—"

I pause and I can see Shelley shifting in her chair.

"Yes?" She takes the napkin from the table and starts to unfold it.

"Well, he mentioned he was thinking of going to the Calgary Stampede this year and I was telling him what a great time we had when we went a couple of years ago. I was showing him a few photos and he recognized you."

I can see the nervousness on her face. She picks up her glass of water and takes a sip.

"I don't understand," she says, but I think she does. "Do I know him?"

100

"No. I don't think so." I'm watching her carefully now to see what her reaction will be when I continue. "He says you're the woman he saw having dinner with Brad."

The colour drains from her face. "What?"

"It was you, Shelley. He was positive," I declare, not taking my eyes off of her.

She looks down at her lap, then back at me. I can tell she's trying to decide whether or not to deny it. Apparently, she decides to tell the truth.

"I did meet with him, but it's not what you think. I knew him before you ever met him. I should have told you, but by the time I figured out that the guy you were seeing was the same one I knew—," she pauses, "I thought about telling you, but you were so into him. I couldn't."

"How do you know him?" I ask, bracing myself for the answer I know I don't want to hear.

"He's the guy I was—," she looks down at the table and then back up at me, "with when Peter left me. The one Peter found out about."

I can't believe what I'm hearing. Shelley was one of the women Brad had an affair with? Why didn't he tell me about this? Why didn't she?

"I had only hooked up with him a few times," she says in a quiet, almost childlike voice. "It wasn't really anything, just sex. It's why I was so upset that I lost my marriage over it." Her words cut deep. Shelley and Brad slept together and neither of them told me. Sometimes friends turn out to be the worst enemies.

The waitress arrives and takes our orders. I've lost my appetite, but order anyway.

"Why didn't you tell me?" I ask when the waitress leaves our table. I'm sure Shelley can see the hurt on my face.

"I didn't know until you introduced us a month ago. It was really awkward, and when you went to the washroom, Brad made me promise not to say anything. Then the next day, he texted me and wanted to meet. That's why I was with him at JJ's."

"You couldn't have just met him for a coffee?" I ask, my voice raising. "Or talked on the phone?"

Her face flushes a bit. "It was his suggestion to meet at JJ's." She can see that I'm not softening and continues. "He convinced me not to say anything to you about our past relationship. He said he was in love with you and if I told you, you might end your relationship with him."

He's right. I would have. Not because he had hooked up with my best friend, although that is definitely a turn-off, but because he was deceptive about it. But something isn't ringing true. Why meet at JJ's in the evening for dinner?

"Why did your relationship with Brad end?" I ask, hoping the answer might shed some light on what was going on between them.

"Peter found out about us and I was trying to save my marriage. I couldn't risk continuing to see Brad. But as it turns out, Peter wanted nothing further to do with me, and neither did Brad." Her chin starts to quiver. "When Brad found out that someone had told Peter about us, he became worried that the same person would tell his wife. He said he thought it best if we cut all contact. I never saw or heard from him again until that night when you introduced us."

"When I told you about him, you didn't clue in that it was the same Brad that you had an affair with?"

"No. You said the man you were seeing owned a flooring business. When I met Brad, he said he worked in construction. I did think it was strange that we both had an affair with someone named Brad, but it's a common name and it didn't occur to me that it was the same person."

I search my memory, but I'm pretty sure Shelley never told me the name of the person she had been cheating on Peter with when their marriage ended. I would have remembered if she had told me his name was Brad. I didn't find out that she had been having an affair until Peter left her. She often kept her indiscretions to herself. Still, why did they meet for dinner?

"The night you met Brad at JJ's," I pause, maintaining eye contact, "did you and Brad hook up?"

It is only for a split second, but I see her eyes dart over to the door and back before she begins speaking, and I am sure she is going to lie. It's the worst feeling as I wait and prepare myself for it.

"No. Of course not," she says looking at me a bit too intently.

Right. Of course neither you nor Brad would do that. I'm not convinced, but I have enough on my plate, and I can't deal with this too. I guess in the end it doesn't really matter. Brad is gone, and even if he were here, our relationship would be over. There are a lot of contradictions piling up. He told me it had been years since he'd last cheated on his wife, but it appears it had only been months. He also told me he loved dogs and he volunteered at an animal shelter, but Karen told me her husband didn't like dogs. And why would he tell Shelley he worked in construction? Is that the same as owning a flooring business? I'm starting to wonder who the real Brad Carleton is.

There's another thing that's bothering me. "Did you know that Brad knew Ethan?" I ask.

Her face freezes for a couple of seconds before she answers. "Yes. I—That's how I met Brad."

"Through Ethan?" I'm confused. I didn't think she had kept in touch with Ethan. Somehow, I'm not surprised.

Shelley bites the corner of her lip. "I ran into him awhile ago. It was before Peter left me. He's divorced, but we just hung out as friends. He invited me to a wine-tasting event. It was a work function, but he thought it would be a good opportunity for me to network."

She pauses and then adds, "He was with a new girlfriend."

Somehow I'm getting the feeling she isn't telling me the full story.

"Anyway," she continues, "Brad was there by himself and Ethan introduced us."

I don't think I can stand to hear any more about the Shelley and Brad romance, so I decide to change the subject.

"Jon found out," I say.

Shelley appears confused with the abrupt change of subject and looks at me with a puzzled look on her face.

"About me and Brad." I clarify.

"What? How?" she asks, her eyes open wide in surprise.

"I don't know. But he did, and he left."

"What do you mean he left?"

"When I got home yesterday, he told me he knew about my affair. Then he stormed out of the house and didn't come back. But I think I saw him driving home this morning as I was leaving, so maybe he did return. Or maybe he was just packing his things."

"I'm so sorry Claire." She reaches across the table and rubs my hand. I instinctually pull it away. Shelley's face drops, but she quickly recovers.

"He just told you he knew and then left?" she asks.

"Well, we were arguing about something else before that. He quit his job weeks ago and didn't tell me. He's been pretending to go to work."

Shelley raises her eyebrows. "Oh. That's odd."

"The police were also at our house the other day questioning him. I don't think he was very happy about that."

"Why were they questioning Jon? Do they think he had something to do with Brad's disappearance?"

"I don't know. I guess they think it could be a possibility."

Our food arrives and I jab my fork into a piece of lettuce.

"It kind of makes sense. I mean, if Jon found out about my affair, he could have been angry at Brad. I don't think he had anything to do with it, but I could see why the police would question him."

"So did the police tell him about your affair?"

That hadn't occurred to me. They better not have. I will call Cole later and ask.

"No. I don't think so," I respond. "I have a contract with them that says they won't unless I become a suspect." As I say this, I feel a chill spread throughout my body. *Did I become a suspect?*

Shelley interrupts my thoughts with another disturbing possibility. "Do you think the person who told Peter about my affair with Brad also told Jon about yours?" I hadn't thought of this. Then Shelley says what I'm thinking.

"Could it be Brad's wife?"

"She would be my best guess, if that's what happened," I say. "But I don't know if someone told him. He might have figured it out on his own. I think he hired a private investigator."

"Why do you think that?" she asks.

"I saw the number on his phone."

"You looked through his phone?" She seems surprised by this.

"Yes. He was acting strange. I caught him whispering on his phone a couple of times, so I wanted to see who he was talking to."

She nods. "Do you think there is any other way he could have found out about you and Brad?"

"I'm not sure. I thought I was being careful."

"I don't know," Shelley says, shaking her head. "I have a bad feeling about this. I think someone told him."

CHAPTER 19

My lunch with Shelley has left me with more questions than answers. I don't feel like I'm any closer to figuring out who is setting me up. I seem to have reached a dead end in my investigation. However, there is one last thing I wanted to look into today—whether Steve owns a dark-coloured SUV.

I had written down his address before leaving my office to meet Shelley. Now I pull it out of my purse and type it into my rental car's navigation system. The map shows his house located a of couple blocks away from the park where Brad and I used to play tennis.

As I'm driving toward his address, I start to question whether this is a good idea. He might recognize my rental car, given that he just saw it this morning. But on the other hand, it's pretty generic looking. Also, what are the chances that he'd just happen to be looking out his window when I drive by? I tie my hair back in a ponytail and put on the baseball cap and sunglasses that I'd brought with me, just in case.

The closer I get to Steve's address the more anxious I feel. What if he sees me? It would be hard to explain why I'm driving down his street. But I carry on, deciding my fears are irrational. There's little chance of him spotting me, and even if he saw my rental car, he won't necessarily know it's me.

I slow down when I reach the entrance to his street. According to the map, his house is the fifth one in on the left side. I see a couple of houses with garages, and it occurs to me that if he has one with a door, I won't learn anything.

Turning onto his street, I drive slowly toward his house. It turns out he has a driveway without a garage and there is a boat parked in it, but it's otherwise empty. I feel the tension leave my body. He isn't home. This was a wasted trip.

But as I continue past his house, something catches my eye. A black SUV parked on the opposite side of the street. I look at it as I pass by, but I can't be sure it's the same one that was following me. It looks similar though. Not wanting to look suspicious, I continue driving.

Were the lights on in Steve's house when I drove past? I can't remember. I was too busy looking at his driveway. I don't want to risk driving by again. It was a bad idea to do this in the first place. Even if Steve does own a dark SUV, it wouldn't prove that he was the one following me. It would probably be better to ask Jenna to look into it.

It's been a long day, and I've been dreading the trip home. I don't know if I'll find Jon in the house or whether he will have packed his things and left. Part of me hopes he won't be there. The stress of the day has gotten to me, and I don't feel like dealing with him right now. I just want to rest.

As I approach our house, I notice a bunch of police cars parked outside. My stomach flips. What's going on now? I quickly park and rush inside. Did something happen to Jon?

There are several officers in my house. The one standing closest to the door sees me and asks, "Are you Claire Johnson?"

"Yes."

"We're searching your house. We have a warrant. It's posted on the door." He tilts his head toward it. "We're just wrapping up. We won't be much longer."

With all the commotion, I must have missed the notice on my front door. I'm relieved that nothing has happened to Jon, but now a new stress is surfacing.

"Is my husband here?" I ask.

"No ma'am."

"Why are you searching my house?"

"You'll have to read the warrant ma'am."

Well, isn't he helpful? I look around, and I'm pretty sure I see José in my kitchen. I don't know what to do. Should I stay in the house and wait for them to finish or should I leave? It's awkward standing by the doorway watching them go through my things, so I decide to leave and call Cole.

As I exit my house, I snatch the search warrant off the front door. While I'm walking to my car, I'm pretty sure I see Tim across the road ducking behind his curtain. I'd be willing to bet that all the neighbours will be gossiping about this.

Getting in my car, I drive a few blocks down the road to a nearby park and find a spot in the parking lot. I call Cole from my car. He answers on the first ring.

"Cole. It's Claire. The police are searching my house. They have a warrant."

"I'm sorry to hear that, but I'm not surprised," he responds. "As we discussed before, there's a good chance that you will be arrested and charged if the police confirm that the blood in your car is Mr. Carleton's."

It's not what I wanted to hear, but he did warn me.

"Do you know if they found anything in your house?" he asks.

"No. I just got home and they said they are wrapping things up."

"OK. Well, we should find out soon enough."

"I don't see what they could find in my house," I say. "It would be pretty difficult for someone to plant something there unless they broke in."

"True," Cole agrees. "I'm sure they won't find anything." His voice doesn't sound particularly convincing.

After I end our call, something occurs to me and I start to panic. The police may find my ripped jeans. They've been washed, but there is still a small blood stain on them. But as I think about it, I realize that even if they did find those, they couldn't possibly know I was wearing them on the night I was out with Brad. I exhale heavily and start to relax again.

As I sit in my car with nothing to do but wait, I decide to check the emails on my new phone. I'm happy to find that there's another report from Jenna. I need something to distract me.

The first heading of her report is *Brad Carleton and Karen Huang*. I can feel my heart rate speed up as I continue to read.

Mr. Carleton lived in Montreal, Quebec until 2012, at which time he moved to Vancouver, where he worked for a flooring company for approximately five years. In 2014 he married Karen Huang.

Sounds like everything he told me was true so far. I read on.

In 2017 Mr. Carleton started up his own business, Yorkville Hardwood Flooring Center, a Vancouver-based wholesaler and retailer of flooring and hardware supplies. This business filed for bankruptcy on May 27, 2022, listing approximately $520,000 in liabilities and $177,000 in assets. The company attributed its insolvency to a reduced customer base during the COVID-19 pandemic, resulting in an inability to pay vendors. It also noted the uncertainty of being able to extend its lease past the expiry on June 2022 given that the building was up for sale. Mr. Carleton was working as a floor covering installer at JI Flooring at the time of his disappearance.

I stare at the words for a while longer in disbelief. *He lied to me about his job.* Feeling sick, I force myself to continue reading.

Ms. Huang worked as a nurse at the Vancouver Hospital until 2014, after which she remained unemployed. Mr. Carleton and Ms. Huang are presently renting a condominium in Ocean Towers on Howe Street, Vancouver, where they resided before Mr. Carleton disappeared.

Another lie. Brad told me he owned his condo. Looks like Brad told a lot of lies. It seems his relationship with reality was tenuous at best. But why? Was he trying to impress me?

When I return home an hour later, the police are gone. I enter cautiously through the front door. The scene is surreal. My once orderly abode has been turned upside down. Drawers have been pulled out, papers have been scattered on the floor, and my belongings are in disarray. I feel violated.

I make my way to the bedroom, dreading what I might find. My eyes fall upon a pile of clothes on the floor and my heart skips a beat. Bending down, I start sifting through them, looking for my ripped jeans. Time slows to a crawl as I toss aside one piece of clothing after another. I swallow hard as I reach the bottom of the pile and realize the jeans aren't there.

Then I remember Jon's tablet and walk over to the other side of our bed. I check the contents of Jon's bedside drawer that have now been dumped on the floor. The tablet isn't there. Could he have taken it before the police arrived? The internet searches that Jon made won't look good for him. Unless he lies and says they were mine. The thought causes goosebumps to form on my arms.

The evidence is mounting against me, and I still can't figure out what's going on. Someone is playing me, but I can't seem to connect the dots. I must be missing something. But what? I feel like I've been walking aimlessly through a forest of stupidity. Feeling deflated, I sit down on the edge of my bed and rest my head on my hands.

I wonder where Jon is. I assume he's staying with a friend. I have no way of checking if he's at a hotel through his bank statements given that we have separate bank accounts. I try calling him, but there's no answer, so I send him another text.

Jon? Can you please respond to my text message?

I wait a few seconds for a reply, but there is none. As I put my phone back on the dresser, I hear a *ding*. It's my text message notification. I quickly grab my phone. It's a message from Jon.

What do you want?

My heart drops. What do I want? I want a night of untroubled sleep. I want to change the past. I want to stop looking over my shoulder. I want my old life back. But instead, I write:

Can we please talk?

I stare at my phone anxiously waiting for an answer. As the minutes pass, I begin to give up, but then I receive his reply.

I'm not ready to talk yet. I need a few more days to think about things.

Well, at least he responded. I text back.

That's fine. I understand

I hesitate before writing the next part.

I love you.

I haven't told him that for a while, but I should have. I do still love him. I stare at the phone waiting for his response, but there is none. I guess I deserve that. At least he's agreed to talk to me. I tell myself that I can wait a few more days if that's what he needs. But as it turns out, I never get the chance to talk to him because I'm arrested two days later.

CHAPTER 20

The first thing I remember is showering and getting ready to leave for work. The next thing I remember is hearing a knock on my door and thinking Jon had come home and had forgotten his keys. The last thing I remember is opening the door and finding two police officers standing on my doorstep. They tell me they have a warrant for my arrest in connection with the murder of Brad Carleton. Then they read me my rights and place me in the back of their police car.

Now I'm at the police station, getting my photograph taken and I'm still trying to figure out why I'm here. After being positioned in front of a white wall, a female officer says, "Look straight ahead." Her voice carries a tone of boredom. I straighten my posture, lift my chin and stare at the camera. *Click.* The camera's flash erupts, illuminating the small room where I'm standing. I feel a mixture of fear and distress, but as the flash fades, my resolve hardens. I will not go down for Brad's murder. I didn't do it.

"Turn to your left." *Click.* "Now to your right." *Click.* I make sure to keep my composure throughout.

"Please follow me to the processing room. We need to take your fingerprints."

I follow her down the hall into another room where a male officer greets me and explains the procedure for taking my fingerprints in a calm and professional manner. I watch nervously as he activates the scanner. A soft hum fills the room as it comes to life.

"Place the fingers of your right hand on the glass," he says in a manner that makes me think he's uttered those same words thousands of times.

I follow his instructions placing my fingers on the glass plate of the machine, feeling its cool surface against my skin. The scanner lights up with a soft blue light and beeps a few seconds later indicating that it has successfully captured the digital images. I can see the officer reviewing them on the screen. Then he repeats the procedure with my left hand and finally my thumbs. I remain silent, eyes on the scanner. I can't help but feel a sense of indignation knowing my fingerprints are now being catalogued as if I am a criminal.

When the fingerprinting process is at an end, I'm escorted into a room where all my possessions are itemized and recorded on a form. These are put into a sealed bag and I'm told they will be returned to me when I'm released. Next, I'm frisked and told to take off all my clothes except my underwear, an upper layer and a lower layer of clothing, plus my socks.

I slowly undress as the cold, stale air of the booking room stings my skin. My dignity is stripped away with each piece of clothing that I remove. When I'm finished undressing, I grab the prison uniform from the table in front of me. It's a dull shade of grey, devoid of any semblance of individuality.

Once I'm clothed, I am given an opportunity to call a lawyer. I dial Cole's number with a shaky hand. *Please answer,* I whisper to myself. He doesn't. Holding back tears, I leave a voicemail message describing what's happened. It occurs to me that I should let Jon know where I am, but I don't want to make that phone call myself, so I ask Cole if he can do it. The whole situation is humiliating.

Next, I'm led to a holding cell that is only about six feet by eight feet. It's cold and colourless with smooth walls. The steel door shuts behind me with a *clang* and I sit down on the hard bed covered by a thin mattress. Looking around the small cell, I see it contains only a steel sink and a toilet. I start to feel claustrophobic, like a bird trapped in a cage. To make matters worse, the cell smells of body odour and vomit.

My mind races with a thousand questions as I try to understand the events that led to this unfathomable moment. What did the police find? Why am I here? What's going to happen next? My heart aches with frustration as I think of the unfairness of the situation. The weight of injustice crushes my spirit.

Cole will be coming soon, I tell myself. Someone has to help me. But what if they don't let me out? My heart starts to thump in my chest and I feel like I can't breathe. Closing my eyes, I take a few slow deep breaths and try to relax. Eventually, I can feel my heart rate slow down.

Despite the bleakness of my surroundings, a flicker of determination ignites within me. I'm innocent. I will prove it. I have to stay strong.

After sitting in my cell for what feels like days, but is probably only a couple of hours, I hear the door clang open. The sound startles me and I look up to see a guard standing in front of me.

"Claire Johnson? You can come with me."

I stand up and the room spins. When I gain my balance, I walk toward the guard who takes me down the hallway to a meeting room where Cole is waiting.

"Claire." Cole stands up when he sees me. "Are you OK?"

The door shuts behind me and I turn to make sure we're alone. Finding no one behind me, I say, "I've been arrested for murder." My mouth is dry and my voice doesn't sound like my own.

"Yes. I've heard." Cole says softly. He sits back down and I seat myself across from him.

"Jon also found out about my affair with Brad," I blurt out without thinking.

Cole's mouth opens a bit like he's surprised. "I'm sorry. How did he find out?"

"I don't know. I wondered if the police told him."

"No. I'm pretty sure they didn't. I would have been notified. You have a contract." Cole touches my hand so that I will look at him. "Claire, the police would like to ask you a few more questions. You don't have to speak with them if you don't want to."

"I didn't do anything," I say, my voice cracking. And I'm not sure if I'm telling the truth, because the truth is that I don't remember anything.

110

"Yes. I know," Cole says, but he's not looking directly at me and I wonder if he actually believes that.

When Cole's eyes meet mine, I say, "I don't have anything to hide. If I refuse to speak with them, I'll look guilty."

"Not necessarily," Cole responds. "It's your right to remain silent."

"But if I'm not guilty of anything, then there's no reason not to speak with them," I argue. Before Cole has a chance to respond I ask, "You'll be with me, right?"

"Yes. Of course," he replies in a calm voice. "And if at any time you don't want to continue with their questioning you don't have to."

"OK. Let's talk to them."

Cole nods.

"Cole?"

"Yes."

"Can I leave after they speak with me?" My body tenses as I wait for his answer.

"If they lay charges, they will remand you into prison custody until we can get a bail hearing."

I feel like I've just been punched in the gut. "How long will that take?"

"It could take some time, but let's not worry about that just yet."

I *am* worried about it, but I nod my head. "And if I'm not granted bail?" I ask.

"Then you'll have to stay in jail until your trial."

I can feel the tears forming in my eyes and I blink a few times to stop them. "What are my chances of getting bail?"

Cole's furrowed brow and downturned lips answer my question before he speaks. "Typically, the chances of being released on a murder charge aren't great. It would really come down to whether you are a flight risk."

I look at him and say nothing, as I try to fight the tears that I know are coming.

"But we may be able to get around that if they place you under house arrest. That would involve you being confined to your house with an ankle bracelet."

The reality of the situation hits me like a landslide. I can't imagine spending even one night in that small cell, let alone months or years. I also can't picture being stuck at home and never leaving the house, although it's definitely a better option than a jail cell.

I swipe a tear from my eye, and Cole and I continue to discuss things for a short while longer before we are taken to another small room for my interview. José and Dianna are seated at a table in the center of the room waiting for us. We sit down, and after some formalities, Dianna looks at me with her usual ice-cold stare and begins her questioning.

"Claire, we have the results back from the lab, and the blood that we found in your car matches that of Mr. Carleton."

I sit perfectly still, rooted to my seat as a cold chill runs through my body. I say nothing because I literally can't speak.

"Do you know why his blood would be in your car?" she asks.

I shake my head.

"Did anyone else have access to your car that night?"

"I don't know. I might have left it unlocked." I think we've been over this before.

"Does anyone else have the key?" she asks.

"No."

"And Mr. Carleton's blood-stained hoodie that we found hidden in your office. The one you say you found in your trunk days earlier, but told no one about. You still don't have any idea how that got in your car?"

"No. But if my car was unlocked, anyone could have put it there."

Dianna's face is expressionless. "We spoke to the taxi driver who drove you home on the night Mr. Carleton disappeared. He says he picked you up in front of your office, not at the hotel. Do you know why you would be at your office so late at night?"

My gut clenches. "No. I don't remember that."

"Were you taking any medications that might have affected your memory that evening?"

"No. But I drank quite a bit. That probably affected my memory."

"Right." Her lips curve downward in a frown taut with skepticism. "The taxi driver also says that when he picked you up, you weren't with Mr. Carleton."

"OK. Brad must have decided to walk home," I respond.

"But it appears that Mr. Carleton was at your office that night, given that we found his cell phone in the alley along with his blood on one of your towels. We also found traces of his blood in the washroom located in your office building."

I look at her and say nothing.

"Can you explain this?"

"No."

"Did Mr. Carleton have a key to the building?"

"No."

Dianna pauses to make some notes and then continues.

"At your house, we found some jeans that were ripped and there was a blood stain at the knee. José, could you show her the jeans?"

I don't need to see them because I already know what she's talking about. I shuffle in my chair while José reaches into a box on the floor beside him and pulls out my jeans.

"Do you recognize these?"

"Yes. Those are my jeans."

"Were you wearing them the night Mr. Carleton disappeared?"

I hesitate. *Should I lie?* I'm not sure what to say, so I respond, "I'm not sure. I can't remember."

"No? What if I told you that we have you on the hotel security camera wearing a pair of jeans that look just like these?" I can see Cole looking at me. I never told him about the jeans.

"Yes," I finally say. "I think I was wearing those."

112

"Do you know how your jeans got ripped?"

I shake my head. I feel like I'm going to cry. This isn't going well.

"Did you cut your knee that night?"

"Yes. I think I must have fallen."

"Do you remember falling?"

"No."

"And the bruise that was on your arm when we first questioned you. Do you remember where that came from?"

"No." My voice cracks and I have to clear my throat.

Dianna shuffles some papers and then says, "We seized a tablet from your house."

I'm pretty sure I know what's coming.

"José, could you show Claire the tablet?"

José puts what looks to be Jon's tablet on the table.

"Do you recognize this tablet?"

"I can't be sure," I respond, "but it looks like Jon's."

"Did you ever use Jon's tablet?"

"No."

Dianna stares at me for a moment. "You didn't search for Mr. Carleton's home address on it?"

"No," I say somewhat defensively.

"Or his place of employment?"

"No," I respond again, "I didn't search anything because I didn't use Jon's tablet."

"So, you're saying Jon made these searches? Dozens of searches regarding Mr. Carleton within the days prior to his disappearance?"

I take a moment to think before answering. I don't want to implicate Jon, but the searches are obviously his if they aren't mine. "Yes," I answer. "I guess so."

"So, he knew about your affair?"

"Yes," I respond again.

Dianna nods and doesn't seem surprised, which makes me think that someone must have already spoken to Jon. Maybe they already questioned him about what they found on his tablet.

"Claire, did you kill Mr. Carleton and transport his body somewhere in your car?" Dianna asks.

"No!" I say loudly and immediately regret it. I didn't want her to see me lose control.

I can see the corners of her mouth turn up ever so slightly. Then she asks, "How can you be sure?"

I can't. "I just know I didn't," I say, jaw clenched.

"But you can't remember, can you?" It was more of a statement than a question so I don't bother to answer. It's clear she doesn't believe me.

A couple of minutes later, I'm escorted back to my cell where I sit for a few hours before being charged with second-degree murder.

CHAPTER 21

The cool, hard grip of handcuffs close around my wrists, causing me to shiver as I'm prepped for transport. Heavy shackles hang from my ankles, restricting my movement. I wonder how many other innocent people have been shackled like this. Did they, too, feel the sharp pang of disbelief as their freedom slipped away?

I guess I saw it coming. I was hoping Brad would be found alive, or that the person who actually killed him would be caught. But as the evidence started mounting against me, I knew that it was only a matter of time before I was arrested.

"Ms. Johnson, please follow me," says a male officer in a curt tone. "We're going to be transporting you to an all-female correctional facility." He turns and starts walking, and I follow as instructed. A second officer walks behind me.

I'm led outside to a van. To get there I have to do a stooping, shuffling walk and almost trip. When I try to step up into the van, I lose balance and the officer behind me places a hand on my back and pushes me inside. The door slams shut behind me.

The inside of the van contains a bench surrounded by steel walls. There's a small window but it's covered. The shadowy interior resonates with my somber mood.

I take a seat and stare straight ahead. I don't know how long the ride is but it seems like forever. The combination of heat and sliding around on the metal seat gives me motion sickness, and I feel like I'm going to vomit.

When I arrive about 45 minutes later, I stumble out of the van into the blinding light. I squint and when my eyes adjust, I see a large pale concrete building in front of me. I'm led inside, where I'm placed into a holding cell where I'm to wait until I'm processed. I sit with my eyes closed until the nausea subsides.

About half an hour later, my lunch is handed to me in a paper bag that contains four slices of bread, a slice of ham, mustard, peanut butter, jam, a muffin and an orange juice. I feel too sick to eat anything so I take the orange juice and leave the rest.

Over the next several hours, various staff come by to speak with me through the door, including a nurse and a psychologist. I suppose they want to make sure I have no medical or psychological issues. The latter is questionable, but the psychologist seems satisfied.

Eventually, I'm taken out of my cell and into a private room where I have to undergo a strip search by a female police officer, a process that involves me taking off all of my clothes and bending over—a humiliating procedure, to say the least. Also ridiculous in my opinion, given that I was arrested unexpectedly at my home.

I'm told to put on some prison clothes that consist of the maximum security dark green T-shirt, sweatshirt, sweat pants, underwear and cotton bra. I feel like I'm stuck in a bad dream and I can't wake myself up. If someone told me a few weeks ago that today I'd be checking into an all-female prison after being charged with second-degree murder I would have told them they were crazy.

After I change, I'm taken to a one-person cell, which is similar to the one I was in at the police station—cold and sterile. But at least it looks newer. It has a small plastic table, plastic storage bins, a stainless-steel toilet and mirror. There is also a stainless steel-encased TV with a remote control. Normally I'd be happy to see it, but I'm afraid that if I turn it on, I will see my arrest all over the news. Will my affair with Brad be broadcast as well? I don't think I could handle seeing that right now.

The lower level of the bunk bed has one sheet and two thin blankets, but no pillow. Instead, the mattress is sloped up a bit at one end. I sit down and stare straight ahead at the wall because there's nothing else to do. I spoke to Cole briefly after I was charged. He said he would try to get me a bail hearing as soon as possible, but it will probably take a few weeks. So, it looks like I will have a lot of time to reflect on my mistakes, and there were certainly a lot of them.

As I sit here alone in this small space with nothing to distract my thoughts, many questions start to swim around in my head. Is it possible that I killed Brad? Could we have gotten into an argument when I was drunk? Maybe I found out about him and Shelley. Could I have hit him? I'm sure I would never have hurt him on purpose, but could I have lost my temper and accidentally killed him?

And if I didn't do it, is it possible that Jon did? He had a motive. He knew about my affair. It's possible he was following me that night. He had access to my car and my office building, and I can't confirm that he was home when I arrived back after my night out with Brad.

I need to get out of my head. Closing my eyes, I try to empty my mind and drift off to sleep. But sleep is next to impossible with the guards coming by my cell every 30 minutes, their comings and goings punctuated with a loud banging of the heavy steel doors. I'm also cold. The blankets are too thin. And the lights never completely turn off in my cell. I have to throw a sweatshirt over my eyes to block it out. Eventually, I drift off to sleep, but only through sheer exhaustion.

By the time morning arrives, I've only managed to get a couple hours of sleep. The day goes by slowly. There's an inmate count first thing in the morning, right before breakfast. I also have an hour of recreation, but I'm otherwise left alone in my cell to ruminate over how I ended up here in the first place.

At least I am treated kindly by my fellow inmates, most of whom are struggling with addiction or trauma. But I feel like a misfit in this desolate place. I look up at the tiny window located near the ceiling, a small portal to the outside world. Through its narrow, clear surface, I catch a glimpse of the sky, painted with hues of orange and pink. A reminder of the beauty that still exists beyond my confines.

It will soon be evening, and I will have to try to sleep on the uncomfortable narrow bed once again. I ask for an extra blanket, and thankfully one is provided. I manage to get a bit more sleep than the first night, but still only a few hours.

When I wake up, my mind is occupied with thoughts of how long I'm going to be stuck in this prison. I feel a desperate need to get out of here. I try my hardest to remember the end of my evening with Brad. If I could only recall what happened, I might be able to prove that I didn't kill him. But as hard as I try, I can't remember a thing.

Sitting here in my cell, I don't think I've ever felt so alone. I haven't heard from Jon or Cole. Shelley has been trying to arrange a visit, but I'm not up to seeing her. I couldn't stand to be escorted out to the visitor's room in my prison uniform to see her sitting there in her designer clothes, face filled with pity. So instead, I sit on my bed and numbly stare at the wall while the day goes by in a blur.

I'm not sure what time it is on my third day in prison when a guard approaches and unlocks my cell.

"Ms. Johnson, please come with me."

"What's going on?" I ask.

"You're being released. The Crown has dropped the charges."

"What? Why?" I can hardly believe what I'm hearing. My mood immediately lifts.

"I don't know. I've just been asked to release you."

After changing out of my prison clothes back into my own, I'm given my personal belongings and I'm told that I'm free to leave.

As I walk towards the exit in a daze, I see Cole standing there. He smiles when he sees me and we walk outside together.

"Cole, what happened? How did you get me out?" I ask.

"I didn't. It was Jon."

Jon? He must see the look of confusion on my face.

"Apparently he placed a tracking device on your car the night Brad went missing. It shows a history of where you drove. It turns out that your car was parked at your office until you picked it up the next afternoon. There is nothing unusual in your driving patterns in the following days either. It proves that you didn't drive Brad anywhere in your car that night. Someone is setting you up."

It takes me a moment to comprehend everything that Cole has told me. When it hits me, I exhale all of my pent-up breath. My mind is juggling all my past, present and future thoughts. Then a cool breeze blows past me, taking all of my anxiety with it. Instinctively, I close my eyes and a feeling of calmness washes over me. I'm free. I'm no longer a suspect. Jon, of all people, came through for me. I hug Cole. He offers to drive me home, and I gladly accept.

When I arrive back at my house, I see a bunch of reporters camped outside on my driveway like a bunch of vultures waiting to pounce on their prey. As Cole pulls up beside Jon's car, the throng of reporters and camera operators part to make room. I take a deep breath before flinging myself out of the car. They set on me like a pack of wolves coming in for the kill. Flashing lights and microphones are shoved in my direction. It's surreal to see my home, once a sanctuary, now swarmed by the press who are hungry for a story.

I push my way past the reporters who are jostling for position, pelting questions at me and thrusting their microphones in my face. *Were you arrested for Brad Carleton's murder? Were you having an affair with him? Do you know where Brad is, Claire?*

My driveway feels like a battleground with the media as my opponents. The relentless clicking of cameras and barrage of questions makes my stomach churn with anxiety as I imagine the headlines, speculation and judgment that will be plastered all over the news.

Cole walks with me, pushing past the reporters as we make our way to the door. "Claire has been cleared of all charges," he yells. "Please leave her alone."

When I reach my front door, I thank Cole and quickly enter my house, shutting the door behind me and locking it. The sense of violation and invasion of privacy is overwhelming. I clench my fists. I will not let them bring me down. With renewed determination, I straighten my shoulders and brave it over to the windows and shut the blinds. Once I do, the chaos outside subsides like a fire doused with water.

As I walk down the hall to the bedroom, I find Jon sitting on our bed.

"Hi," I say, not really knowing how to start a conversation.

"Hi," he responds, glancing in my direction.

There's an uncomfortable silence, so I say, "Thanks for getting me out of prison."

"You're welcome." His tone is stiff and he has a blank expression on his face.

The conversation is getting awkward. I'm not sure if I should be addressing the fact that he had a tracking device on my car, which I find a bit disturbing, or whether I should just be thankful that he stepped up and provided the information to the police. I opt for the latter.

"I know you're upset with me, and you have every right to be. You could have said nothing and left me to rot in jail. I wouldn't really blame you if you did." I pause to see his reaction, but he continues to look at me with an expressionless face. "I am very thankful that you did this for me, especially given the circumstances," I add.

Jon takes a moment to respond. "I never once contemplated leaving you in jail. As soon as your lawyer called me, I went straight to the police station with the tracking device. I probably could have helped you earlier if you had been honest with me about what was going on."

He's right. If I'd told him the police were questioning me from the beginning and about all the evidence they were gathering against me, Jon could have provided the police with the tracking device before I was arrested—Before I underwent the most humiliating experience of my life.

"Yes. I should have been honest," I say. Then I add, "About a lot of things."

Jon clenches his fists. "You know what Claire? I wasn't happy in our marriage either, yet I would never have done what you did. But after all that's that's happened, I've come to realize something," he looks directly into my eyes, "I'm a good man. And I thank you for that because now I know that I deserve much better than this."

Tears blur my vision. "You're right Jon, you do deserve better than this. I'm sorry." And that, I know, is the truth.

Thankfully, the media didn't find out about my affair with Brad. Reporters speculated, but it was never confirmed. Stories were published saying that I was arrested, but also that the charges had been dropped. So, people may suspect that I'm a cheater, but at least I won't be known as a murderer.

I don't leave the house for the next couple of days and neither does Jon. Neither of us wants to deal with the circus of reporters outside. We don't talk much but when we do, we are civil. We have dinner together and even watch some TV, but Jon sleeps on a fold-out sofa in our rec room downstairs.

On the third day after my release, Jon leaves the house for a job interview. By this time, the reporters have left and things have gone somewhat back to normal.

I've been anxiously waiting for Jon to leave as there's something I need to do in private. As soon as he's gone, I put on a pair of sunglasses and a baseball cap and drive my car to a drugstore located about 20 minutes away. I quickly find the aisle with pregnancy tests and grab a different brand from the one I originally bought. Then I use the self-checkout.

I don't have much time before Jon gets home so I rush back to our house and immediately bring the test into the bathroom and read the instructions carefully. They are pretty much the same as the first kit that I bought—pee on the stick and check it two minutes later.

I unwrap the package and do as instructed. After placing the stick on the counter, I wash my hands and stand there beside it waiting. Since arriving home from prison, I've been thinking a lot about the first pregnancy test. I searched the internet, something I hadn't had a chance to do until then, and apparently a second faint line can appear if you leave the test sitting for too long. It's called an evaporation line. I won't make the same mistake this time.

Two minutes feel like two hours. I glance down at the test a few times while I'm waiting to see if a second line is forming, which would indicate that I am pregnant. But I only see one clear line. After two minutes have passed, I pick it up and look closely. There is only one line. I feel the knots of stress unravel like the air escaping from a balloon. I quickly grab the box and test stick and put them in a plastic bag, which I then place into another bag of garbage outside in our garbage container.

Although a part of me wanted to be pregnant, I realize that a larger part of me didn't. Brad is no longer here and could never be a father to my child. There's also no guarantee that I won't be arrested again, depending on what new evidence arises. And as much as Jon wanted a child, I'm quite certain he wouldn't want to raise Brad's. That is, if we are even able to salvage our relationship.

I have some hope that we can. Over the last couple days Jon has seemed less upset with me. Maybe he feels I've suffered enough for what I did. I've lost clients, spent time in jail for a murder I didn't commit, and I've been publicly humiliated with speculation that I was having an affair with a man who is likely dead. Lately, when Jon looks at me, it's not with the same anger or resentment that he had before. I actually think I see a hint of empathy in his eyes.

But the next day something happens that makes me question everything. I've just finished eating a Caesar salad for lunch and Jon is on his tablet in the living room. I go to my bathroom to brush my teeth, but my toothpaste is missing. Assuming Jon has borrowed it, I go to his bathroom to look for it. I find it sitting on the bathroom counter. As I grab it, I glanced down at the drawer where I found Jon's Xanax pills. I'd been thinking about them while I was in jail, and something has been bothering me. When I found the pill bottle, it appeared to be full even though the prescription was from over a month earlier.

I open the drawer and find the Xanax pill bottle stuffed away at the back. When I take it out and hold it up to look at it, I find that it's still full. It seems odd to go to the doctor, get a prescription, pick it up and then not use it. Curious, I pour the pills out onto the counter. The bottle says it contains 100 pills, but when I count them there are only two missing.

I try to think of a logical explanation. Maybe he tried them and didn't like them. But I've never known Jon to take medication. I don't even think I've seen him take an aspirin more than a handful of times. My mind concocts a number of explanations, but there is one particular possibility that I can't get out of my head.

I need to look something up on the internet. Retrieving my phone from the dresser, I conduct a search. My heart stops when I find what I'm looking for. This medication, when combined with alcohol, will cause memory loss. Is it possible that Jon used two of these pills to drug me on the night Brad disappeared so that I wouldn't remember anything? According to my search, a person's memory can be erased for a large part of the evening, even before taking the drugs.

But how could he have done it? I would have had to have eaten or drank something when I got home that night. The only thing I consistently do after a night out drinking is to pour myself a glass of water from the filtered water container in the fridge. And it was empty when I got up the next morning. I remember this because I never leave it empty. But it's possible that I had too much to drink and absent mindedly put it back in the fridge empty. However, it's also possible that Jon crushed up two pills and put them in the container with only one glass of water left. It would explain my memory loss.

He knew about my affair, and he was out on the night Brad disappeared in the same area where we were. It's possible that he followed Brad at the end of the evening after we parted ways, and then set me up. But why would he help clear my name? If he was setting me up, it wouldn't make sense for him to then get me off. Sweeping the pills back into the bottle, I decide that I'm being overly suspicious.

"Claire?"

I jump, almost having a heart attack. Then I turn to see Jon standing at the bathroom door. I quickly pull my hand back from the drawer where I've just replaced the pills. He must see the guilty look on my face because his expression drops and he asks, "What are you doing?"

I can feel my heart pounding. "I was just looking for my toothpaste," I say and grab it off the counter, while at the same time leaning against the drawer so it shuts.

His face relaxes. I don't think he saw the open drawer.

"Oh. Right. I used it this morning. Mine was empty."

I consider asking him about the medication but decide not to. We've been getting along well, and I don't want to embarrass him by asking, and I'm certainly not going to accuse him of drugging me. I think I'm being paranoid anyway. I guess that's what happens to you when someone tries to frame you for murder.

CHAPTER 22

It's been a week since I've been released from prison and I'm trying to get back to my normal routine. I've scheduled a few work appointments for today, hoping to slowly ease my way back into it. I'm concerned that there may be reporters hanging around my office when I arrive, but they seem to have lost interest in me for the most part. I think they got the message that I won't be answering any questions.

Steve tried to book an appointment to see me today, but I'm not ready to see him yet. In fact, I haven't seen anyone other than Jon because I don't feel like talking about my arrest and incarceration. And Steve is the last person I want to see on my first day back at work. I'm sure he wouldn't hesitate to ask a bunch of inappropriate questions. Sometimes his social etiquette is lacking.

There's another reason why I'm hesitant to see him. Before I was arrested, I asked Jenna to investigate Steve and in particular, whether he owns a dark SUV. I received an email from her when I was released from prison confirming that he does. It probably doesn't mean anything, thought, given that I haven't noticed any SUVs since arrived home from prison. I've come to the conclusion that it must have been the police following me. It makes sense given that I was their prime suspect for Brad's murder.

When I arrive at my office, I'm happy to see that there are no reporters hanging around. But when I get out of my car, I feel uneasy. Someone tried to set me up, and that person is still out there. I have some peace of mind, though, from the safety measures that I took to prevent any further incidents. I installed a security camera outside my office door and I've also bought some pepper spray, which I keep in my purse. I hope whoever was trying to frame me has now moved on. I don't think I could deal with any more surprises.

Unfortunately, I receive one almost immediately upon entering my office. Karen has left a voicemail message.

Hi Claire, It's Karen Huang. I understand from your out-of-office message that you will be open today. Could we please arrange to meet? I'm free this afternoon. I don't need any treatment. I'd just like to discuss some things with you if that's OK. Could you please call me back as soon as you get this? Thanks.

The tone of her message isn't particularly friendly and I have a feeling I know what she wants to discuss. I consider declining the meeting, but I know she knows where to find me, and I'd rather have a planned meeting than a surprise one. In any event, I feel I owe her that much after everything that's happened.

But since I'm not sure if she has revenge on her mind, I decide to plan our meeting for tomorrow in a public place. I choose the park where Brad and I used to play tennis. There are some picnic tables there where we can sit down and talk and we won't be overheard.

After setting up a meeting with Karen and treating two patients, I sit down at my desk to have a cup of tea and a sandwich that I brought from home. I'm not ready to venture out of my office just yet. I've been laying low these days, trying to avoid any reporters that might be lurking about.

But just as I take a bite of my sandwich, the next surprise walks through my door. The person I'm staring at is someone I never would have expected, and I have to blink a few times to make sure I'm not imagining it. I'm not. It's Jeff Pusey. He's wearing worn jeans and a wrinkled shirt. It also looks like he hasn't shaved in a while. I never would have recognized him if Jenna hadn't sent me his picture.

When I see him, I immediately leap up from my chair, grab my purse and start rifling through it for the pepper spray. I'm unable to get my fingers on it before he reaches my desk, so I settle for my cell phone. I might at least be able to call 911 if he threatens me.

"I saw you on the news," he says with slightly slurred words. *Has he been drinking?* "You were arrested in relation to that missing person, Brad." He takes a step toward me.

I'm standing frozen, clutching my cell phone, not knowing what his intentions are. "Jeff," I say in a voice that I hope sounds friendly. "I hardly recognized you. It's been a long time."

"Yes. I believe the last time I saw you was the night my sister died."

OK. This is definitely not a friendly visit.

"Right," I respond, backing up a bit to create some distance between us. "That was tragic. I'm really sorry for your loss." *Did that sound cliché?*

"Are you?" he asks. "Sorry?" He takes another step toward me. "One of the last things I remember about that night was you running up the stairs with your friend Shelley. She was all over Ethan, and it was upsetting Cassie. I always wondered if you and Shelley had something to do with her *accident*." As he says the last word, he puts the first two fingers of each hand up and bends them, mimicking quotation marks. He's clearly been drinking.

I look at him, not knowing what to say.

"It sure seemed like you and Shelley were in a hurry to get out of there," he continues. "Shelley had plans to go to a club with Ethan after the cruise, but the two of you just disappeared."

"I don't think we were in a hurry," I respond. "It was just late and Shelley was drunk so I took her home in a cab."

"Right," he says with a glare. He pauses as if he's remembering something. Then he says, "Ethan told me that there was an argument between you and Cassie in that same washroom earlier in the evening."

122

What? How would Ethan know about that? Did Cassie lie about it? Or did Shelley say something to Ethan? In any event, someone got the story wrong because there wasn't any argument. Cassie confronted me.

"It wasn't really an argument," I say calmly. "I saw Cassie in the washroom and she was upset with Shelley, but that was about it."

"Were you in the washroom with her when she fell?" He pauses and then says, "Or when she was *pushed*?"

"No." I lie.

Jeff shakes his head. "Why should I believe you? You're obviously a liar. How long were you lying to your husband? You were cheating on him with Brad, weren't you? Having an *affair*?" He spits out the last word like he's just put some expired food in his mouth. "What happened to Brad, Claire?"

OK. This is getting way out of hand. Does he really think I pushed Cassie and murdered Brad? He's clearly unhinged. I'm still clutching my phone but I don't want to dial 9-1-1. Jeff hasn't threatened me (yet), and I've had enough police encounters for one year. I glance down at my purse and wonder if I'd have enough time to grab the pepper spray if he becomes violent. Probably not. It's buried somewhere at the bottom.

"I think you should leave," I say calmly, trying not to provoke him. His lips are tight with anger, but then they form into a half smile before returning to their tight line. "I guess you know now how it feels to lose someone you love in tragic circumstances." His eyes narrow. "You may have been let out of prison, but I bet a lot of people wonder about you and Brad—whether you were having an affair with him. Whether you murdered him." He smirks. "How does it feel to be down in that rabbit hole Claire? The ride down is easy. But the climb back out won't be."

Jeff snorts and then turns and starts walking towards the door. As he opens it, he turns back and says, "Karma's a bitch."

I'm standing frozen with my cell phone in my hand. My heart is hammering in my chest. *Rabbit.* Was that reference coincidental, or was it Jeff who slipped the threatening note through my mail slot? RUN RABBIT RUN. It seems to fit. And what does he mean, when he says, *Karma's a bitch?*

I immediately call Cole and tell him what happened. He asks if Jeff threatened me. He didn't, although I think it could be implied. However, given that there was no threat, there's not much that can be done at this point. Maybe Jeff saw that I was arrested for murder on the news and he somehow associated me with Cassie's death. Nonetheless, the whole incident has shaken me up. The rest of the day is a struggle and I question whether I returned to work too early.

When I finally arrive home, I'm greeted with my third surprise of the day, but this one is a good one. Jon is standing in the kitchen sprinkling steak spice on some steaks which are sitting alongside some vegetable skewers.

"I thought I'd make dinner since I was home today and you were working."

There is a bottle of red wine open on the counter, and Jon pours a glass and hands it to me. I'm speechless. I can't remember the last time he made a nice dinner like this. Has he ever? I can't help but feel suspicious, but then I immediately feel guilty for doubting him.

"Thanks," I say. "It looks delicious."

Grabbing my wine, I walk down the hallway to the bedroom to get changed out of my work clothes. As I do, I have an uneasy feeling in my gut. *Why is he being so nice?*

I've spoken to Cole since my release from prison, and I can tell he still has his reservations about Jon. The pills did cause a small seed of doubt to start sprouting in my mind. OK, maybe it's more of a budding plant, but I've chosen to trust Jon. If he wanted to set me up, he wouldn't have helped to clear my name.

By the time I walk back into the kitchen, my wine glass is empty. Jon is busy cooking, so I pour myself another glass. He glances over as I do, and I expect his usual scowl but instead, he smiles and continues preparing the meal.

When it's ready, Jon and I sit down at the table. I still feel on edge.

"Looks delicious," I say, as I cut into my steak. I'm surprised to find that it's cooked perfectly. I didn't know Jon could cook.

"Thanks," he says in a cheerful voice.

"So, how was your day?" I ask forcing a smile.

"Good. Thanks for asking," he replies, returning my smile.

I can't help but wonder what he's up to. Is he trying to lull me into a false sense of security or am I just being silly?

"How was your first day back at work?" he asks and then sticks a piece of steak into his mouth.

"It was pretty uneventful," I lie.

Jon nods. "I'm sure it was nice to get out of the house and get back to your normal routine."

"Yes," I respond. "Things are finally starting to return to normal again."

Feeling like it might be a good time to ask the question that's been itching my brain, I say, "There's something I've been meaning to ask you."

"What's that?" he asks as every muscle in his face seems to tighten.

I pause for a moment, not knowing how to approach this. "When I went into your bathroom the other day to look for my toothpaste, I saw a bottle of pills in your drawer."

Jon's face pales and he stops chewing. A few seconds pass before he says, "When I found out about your affair I was suffering from some depression and anxiety, so I went to see my doctor. She prescribes some medication. I tried it once, but it didn't agree with me." He takes a large sip of his wine.

Is it my imagination or did that sound rehearsed? The clink of silverware against plates fills the silence as we each take a few bites of our food.

Breaking the silence, I ask, "Did you hear back about your job interview?"

"Not yet, but I have a good feeling about it," he says reaching across the table and taking my hand.

I feel a chill run down my spine as he grabs my hand. I try to pull it away, but he holds on.

"I've been thinking a lot about our future, and I think it's time to make some changes," he says.

I gulp. "What kind of changes," I ask, heart thumping in my ear. *Does he want a divorce? Did he make this nice dinner to soften the blow?*

"I want to start working on our relationship," he replies, his grip on my hand tightening.

A wave of relief washes over me. I wasn't expecting this. I'm almost not sure I heard him correctly. After taking a moment to collect myself, I say, "I think that's a good idea."

"Good," he says, releasing my hand. "I'm glad we're on the same page."

I stab a mushroom with my fork and put it in my mouth. I can't believe he wants to work on our relationship after everything that's happened.

We continue eating and Jon carries the conversation, making small talk throughout dinner. When we've finished, he takes both of our plates and rinses them in the sink before putting them in the dishwasher. He's going all out tonight.

As the night wears on, Jon continues to be kind and attentive. There's no arguing or criticizing, just friendly conversation. He even suggests we go for a walk after dinner, something we haven't done in ages.

By the end of the evening, I'm feeling good about our relationship. I don't know what motivated Jon to be a model husband tonight, but I can't complain. It felt good. It reminded me of how things were at the beginning of our relationship. I'd given up thinking that my life would ever be normal again, but Jon making an effort after everything that's happened has given me new hope. I feel the best that I've felt since the night Brad went missing.

CHAPTER 23

Today is the day I meet with Karen. I wake up early after a restless sleep. My mind is spinning, going over every possible scenario that might occur. I'm convinced she's going to ask me about my relationship with Brad, and I'm not sure how to approach it. Part of me wants to be honest, but another part thinks that maybe it's best if she's left with good memories of her husband.

Then again, maybe she already knows the truth. Jon knows and the police know. I wonder if the police have now said something to Karen. If I'm no longer a suspect, maybe she's become one. Plus, she must have watched the news where reporters speculated that Brad and I were having an affair. Ultimately, I decide that after all the lying I've done, it's time to be honest. Maybe it will help her move on.

At 10:25 a.m., I'm sitting in my car in the parking lot outside the park. It's five minutes before I am supposed to meet Karen. I can see her in the distance, sitting at a picnic table under the shade of a towering oak tree with her back to me. Her slender frame is bend forward, head resting on her hands. She must have arrived early. Part of me wants to turn around and go home. But I know I can't. I have to do this.

A cool breeze hits me as I open the car door and get out. When I shut the door behind me, I see Karen turn and look back toward the parking lot. She sees me and watches for a few seconds as I walk toward her before she turns back around. No smile or wave, but I suppose I wasn't expecting any.

When I reach the picnic table, I sit down across from her. There are dark circles, etched like shadows under her eyes. She looks like she's had as little sleep as I have.

"Hi," I say, trying to keep my voice steady.

"Hi Claire." She sounds dejected.

I look at her, waiting for her to start the conversation, but she says nothing.

"How are you doing?" I ask softly.

"Not great." I can see tears welling up in her eyes. "I've definitely been better."

"Yes. I'm sure it's been very difficult for you," I reply adding, "I can't even imagine."

"You know what the worst part is?" Her face takes on a certain hardness.

"No," I respond.

"I thought I knew him." She shakes her head. "All these years. I thought I knew him."

I can sympathize with that sentiment but say nothing.

"How long were you seeing him?" she asks.

Her question takes me by surprise. Although I was expecting that she might ask something along those lines at some point during our conversation, it seems so abrupt. I'm pretty sure she already knows about our affair, so there's no point in denying it.

"Not that long," I respond.

She looks at me and I can see she expects me to continue. "A few months," I add.

Karen nods. "He'd been distant lately. I suppose I should have figured it out. But every day he would tell me he loved me and I believed him." Her expression hardens as she asks, "Did you have sex with him?"

That's a strange question. Isn't that what most people do when they have an affair? I would go so far as to say that that's the whole purpose of an affair for most people. I look at her not sure what to say. The easy answer would be for me to say no. Maybe she'd have fonder memories of Brad if that was my response. But I'm tired of lying, and I'm not sure if she'll find out that Brad was with me in a hotel room on the night he disappeared, so I decide to tell her the truth.

"Yes," I say quietly.

Her face darkens, and I add, "I'm really sorry. I feel awful about it. I didn't plan to. It just happened."

She looks at me, her face tense. "Where did you have sex?"

Why does she want to know this? "Hotels," I reluctantly respond.

"Who paid?"

I'm finding these questions rather strange and intrusive. I wonder if I should even answer, but decide it can't hurt. "Brad used a credit card."

She appears more angry than upset.

Looking over at the tennis courts she says, "That's where you and Brad played tennis," almost to herself.

I wonder how she knows this. How did this become common knowledge? "Yes," I reply.

She sits there for a moment, saying nothing. Then she takes a deep breath. "Did he tell you he loved you?"

I don't want to answer this. I look down wondering how to respond. But before I have a chance to say anything, she asks, "Did you love him?"

I consider the question for a moment. "I thought I did," I reply honestly.

Her lips move slightly, caught between a sympathetic smile and a frown. Then there's an awkward pause in the conversation. After a moment, I say, "Looking back, I feel really ashamed about what I did. I was having a difficult time with my marriage, but that's no excuse. If it's any consolation, Brad always told me he loved you and that he'd never leave you."

She snorts and shakes her head, then looks off into the distance. When she turns back, she says, "He doesn't love me, and he never loved you either. He only cares about himself."

And with that, she gets up and starts walking toward the road at the other end of the park. I watch her until she disappears behind some trees. She never looks back.

Sitting there at the empty picnic table, I reflect on my conversation with her, but I can't make sense of it. A crow lands on the ground beside the table and looks up at me with a tilted head.

"Sorry buddy. I don't have any food."

It stares at me for a few seconds longer and then flies away as if understanding what I said.

Off in the distance, kids are playing soccer on the field, running here and there, yelling at each other to pass the ball. They look so innocent, without a care in the world. For a moment I wish it were me out there, running around with happy thoughts. But as I glance over at the tennis courts, my reality returns.

Getting up from the table, I start walking toward my car. When I'm halfway there, I stop and email Jenna. I want her to look into Karen. I get the feeling she knows more than she let on. I feel like something I said triggered her.

It's a couple of hours later when I drive to Carley's Cafe to meet Shelley. I get there first and find a table at the back. When Shelley shows up a few minutes later she rushes up to me and hugs me.

"Claire! I've been so worried about you. How are you?"

"I'm fine," I say, and attempt a smile that doesn't fully form.

"I can't believe you were arrested for Brad's murder," she whispers. "What the hell happened?"

I'm not sure how much to tell her, so I keep it short. "Someone planted some stuff in my car."

"Planted stuff? Like what?" she asks wide-eyed. The media reported that evidence was found in my car and that Brad's cell phone was located in the alley behind my office, but didn't release any further details.

"A ripped hoodie with his blood on it," I reply.

"Really? Who would do that? Do you think it was his wife?"

"I don't know. I can't picture Karen murdering Brad. I don't think she knew about our affair until recently, but it's hard to say. She was acting kind of strange."

I proceed to tell Shelley about my meeting with her.

"That does sound weird. It could have been her. Or maybe it's someone you don't know. Maybe someone was following Brad and saw the two of you together and thought you'd make the perfect suspect."

"Yes. It could have been anyone," I reply.

Not wanting to discuss Brad anymore, I say, "There's something else weird that happened."

"What?" she asks.

"Do you remember Cassie's brother Jeff?"

The colour drains from Shelley's face before she answers. "Yes."

"He showed up at my office on Monday."

"What?" Her eyebrows fly to the top of her head like startled birds.

"I think he'd been drinking. He seemed angry. It was scary."

"What did he say?" she asks, leaning partway across the table.

"He basically accused me of killing Cassie. He seemed to think I pushed her."

Shelley's eyebrows furrow and she shakes her head. "Why would he think that?"

"I don't know. Apparently someone told him I argued with her in the washroom that night. I examine Shelley's face to see her reaction.

"I didn't say that," she responds in a defensive tone. "I haven't even seen Jeff for years. I think the last time I saw him was when I dated Ethan for a bit after that boat cruise."

"Maybe Cassie said something to him that night," I suggest. "Who knows."

"Yes. It must have been Cassie," she says. But as she does, I see a flicker of nervousness dart across her face and I question if she's telling the truth.

It's two days later when I finally schedule an appointment with Steve. I'm not looking forward to our meeting, but I can't avoid him forever. When he walks in, he seems different. Not his usual happy self.

"Hi Claire."

"Steve. How are you?"

"I'm fine. How are *you*?" He looks at me with concern in his eyes.

"I've been better."

"Yes. I'm sure. It must have been quite traumatic." He seems unsure whether to continue. Then adds, "The arrest and everything."

"Yes," I respond. "It was but I'd rather not talk about it. Let's talk about something more upbeat." I try to smile and Steve looks away.

"How's everything with you?" I ask.

"Pretty good," he replies, but his voice still sounds somber.

"Well, why don't you go get changed?" I suggest in what I hope is a chipper tone.

A few minutes later, Steve is lying on his stomach as I'm treating his back. Our conversation is fairly mundane until he somehow steers it back to me.

"I know you don't want to talk about your arrest and I understand. But I was just wondering how you're doing. I mean, in general. It must be difficult at home with your husband. He must have seen the speculation on the news about you and Brad."

It takes me a moment to digest what Steve has just said. I can't believe he brought that up and it annoys me.

"Things are OK with Jon. He's been very supportive," I add somewhat sharply.

"Really?" His tone raises a level as he jerks his head up to look at me.

"Yes. Really," I respond. "I appreciate your concern, but I'd rather not talk about any of this. I find it upsetting."

"Yes. Of course," he says placing his head back in the massage cradle. There's an uncomfortable silence for a minute or so before I ask him how he's making out with his boat. We talk for a few minutes about that before our conversation tapers off.

When Steve finally leaves, he looks at me and says, "You can call me if you ever need someone to talk to Claire."

"Thanks," I respond.

He examines me for a moment longer and then says, "Really. I mean it."

I nod, and he turns around and walks out the door. As soon as the door shuts behind him, I walk over to the window to see what car he gets into. It's a dark coloured SUV. But as he drives by, I can see clearly through its windows. I feel a sense of relief as I realize that it likely wasn't Steve who was following me. The SUV that I saw earlier had tinted windows. It was probably a police vehicle.

Exhausted by the events of the day, I sit down at my desk and lean back in my chair. I just want to move on with my life and forget about everything that's happened with Brad. But I think it will be a long time before I'll be able to get through a day without having him on my mind in some form or another.

CHAPTER 24

It's a few days later when I receive Jenna's report on Karen. It reads:

Karen Carleton grew up in Surrey, B.C. Her mother, Kimberley, became pregnant at the young age of 18. Karen never met her father, who was apparently someone Kimberley had become romantically involved with while on a vacation in Thailand with her family.

Kimberley was mentally and financially unprepared for a child, and her parents, who were both working at the time, were unable to help. When Karen was 11 years old, her mother had a mental breakdown and was later diagnosed with paranoid schizophrenia. Kimberley was ultimately committed to a mental health center and spent the rest of her life in and out of hospitals. She was rarely in contact with Karen, who became a permanent ward of the government. Karen spent the rest of her childhood in foster homes. Although she alleged that she was sexually abused by one of her foster parents, these allegations were never proven.

Karen married at the age of 21 but divorced only five months later. The grounds for divorce were listed as her husband's infidelity. When Karen turned 22, she began working as a nurse at the Surrey Memorial Hospital. She kept that position for four years, after which she transferred to the Vancouver General Hospital. Karen left her job shortly after marrying Brad. The rumour is that she was fired after a disagreement with one of the doctors, but this could not be verified. Karen has remained unemployed since her marriage.

I feel bad for Karen. It sounds like she's had a rough life. It's sad that both of her husbands cheated on her. I'm sure it doesn't do much for her ego. It might explain our strange conversation.

Jenna reports that she did some surveillance of Karen but was unable to find any unusual activity. It did not appear that Karen was seeing another man. She visited with family but for the most part, she has been staying at home by herself.

When I asked Cole about Karen a couple of weeks ago, he told me that the police did question her as a person of interest in Brad's disappearance. She allowed them to search her house and car but nothing was found. The only incriminating evidence was that she was the beneficiary of Brad's life insurance policy. But this policy was purchased years before his disappearance, and he was also the beneficiary of her life insurance.

I sigh as I close the report. It doesn't look like I will find anything implicating Karen or anyone else for that matter.

Over the next few weeks, things start to return to normal. I'm back working full time and Jon has also found a full-time job. Steve has finally met someone who he's been dating, and he seems happy. His visits with me have tapered off.

Shelley and I have had a few lunches and we've managed to get off the topic of Brad and carry on with regular conversation. I'm finally starting to feel like I'm back to my old self again.

Jon and I have also been getting along well. Strangely this whole thing with Brad ended up improving our marriage. Maybe it made us realize that we had serious issues that we needed to address. I'm sure in the back of his mind he still has trust issues with me, and if I'm honest, there's still a small part of me that questions if he had anything to do with Brad's disappearance. But both of us have managed to push our doubts aside.

There haven't been any new developments in Brad's disappearance, and I'm starting to wonder if there ever will be. I still check my secret email every few days, just in case. I don't expect to find anything, but I don't want to lose hope.

Today as I log in, I brace myself for my usual disappointment. But to my surprise, I see an unread email. Its subject line is, *Miss you.* Confused, I look more closely. It was sent from Brad's account!

My heart surges. Could this really be from Brad? I click on the email. The words dance before my eyes.

It's me. I hope you're still checking this email. I'm sorry I couldn't contact you sooner, and I apologize for the pain and confusion it must have caused you. I need to see you. Can you meet me at our secret spot outside? I will explain everything.

Please don't tell anyone I'm alive. Not the police, not our families, not anyone. We have to keep this between us. I can't risk anyone finding out. It's the only way I can stay safe.

I'll be waiting for you at our secret spot on Thursday at 10 am. Please come alone. Love you. xo

I stare at the screen, my mind racing with a thousand questions. Did Brad really write this? Could it be the police who wrote it? Or Karen? It can't be Brad. He's dead. His blood is all over my car. My insides twist at the thought.

But whoever wrote this said they wanted to meet at our secret spot outside. I know where that is. We used to drive to a nearby park that has hiking trails, and we'd walk partway up a trail and veer off the path into the woods where there was a clearing. We'd put a picnic blanket down and have a drink and some snacks and then make love in the sun. We called it our secret spot. No one else could have known about this, unless Brad told someone. But even then, it would be hard to find the location if you hadn't been there before. Is it possible that Brad really did send the email? Or did someone follow us?

After thinking about it for a few minutes, I type a reply.

Brad? Is this really you? I can't believe you're still alive. I hope everything's OK. I've been so worried about you. I will see you on Thursday.

I pause before sending it. Do I really believe this is Brad? I so desperately want to. I push send.

I know I'm crazy to agree to go into the middle of the forest to meet whoever wrote this but if it is Brad, I need to see him. If it's not him, then at least I'll find out who's behind all of this. Obviously, I will need to take some safety precautions.

I look at the email again. It was written this morning. My gaze shifts to my calendar. I have three days until the meeting. It gives me some time to prepare. As I log off, I take a long, slow breath, centering myself. I'm still in shock at the possibility that Brad may be alive. But I don't want to get too excited in case it isn't him.

I'm starting to think that I should tell someone about the email. But who would I tell? The only person I can think of is Cole. He would have to keep solicitor-client privilege. But I know he will try to talk me out of going to the meeting or he'll try to convince me to tell the police. I pace back and forth across my office. It feels suffocating despite the open window. I ultimately decide not to tell anyone.

The days leading up to the meeting loom like an eternity. Each day feels like a labyrinth of emotions, a battle between hope and doubt. I try to distract myself with mundane tasks to mask the relentless anticipation. But a million questions claw at my mind and grate on my frayed nerves.

Thursday finally arrives. I've cancelled all of my appointments for the day, and I can feel the weight of anticipation. As I peer into the bathroom mirror, my tired eyes lock with their reflection. Dark circles lay like storm clouds beneath my weary gaze. I sigh and pick up a foundation brush. Layer after layer, I carefully apply powder hoping to hide the shadows under my eyes.

Next, I uncap a sleek, black tube of mascara. With a steady hand, I guide the wand upward over my lashes. With each stroke, my eyes start to awaken. Finally, I choose a vibrant tube of lipstick and trace the smooth bullet along the curve of my upper lip. Then I purse my lips together, carefully blending the hues.

After I'm finished with my face, I meticulously work my hair into an arrangement of sleek waves and gentle curls. When I'm done, I stand before the mirror, my transformation complete. I can't help but feel a surge of satisfaction. I know it's silly to spend so much time on my appearance, but if it truly is Brad whom I'm meeting, I want to look nice.

I leave my house at the same time that I usually leave for work so that I won't make Jon suspicious. Having a couple of hours to kill, I drive to my office. As I do, I frequently glance in my rear-view mirror in case anyone is following me. It's possible the police were monitoring my secret email account. However, I don't see any sign of them.

When I arrive at my office, I sit down at my desk, but I immediately stand up again. I'm too wound up to stay idle. What if someone murdered Brad and they're now luring me out into the woods to off me as well? I double check that I have my pepper spray with me. My cell phone should work out there as well.

Walking over to the window, I peer out to see if I can spot an undercover police officer staking me out, but I don't see anything unusual. In an effort to keep my mind occupied, I start organizing things in my office. But my thoughts keep wandering back to Brad. Unable to distract myself, I decide to drive to the park early. If I'm being set up, it's probably best to get there first anyway. That way I can watch who enters the trail.

On the drive there, I take a number of side roads and wrong turns just in case someone is following me. I also check my rear-view mirror many times to make sure no one has. It's 9:20 a.m. when I arrive at my destination. There are several parking lots to choose from and I choose the second closest to the hiking trail. It provides me with a view of the trail entrance, but I am far enough away that no one will see me.

I sit and watch and fidget and wait. The first person to enter the trail is a man with his dog. Next is a group of three women. Then a couple in hiking gear. I don't see Brad or anyone else that I recognize.

As time ticks by, I continue to stare out the front windshield watching the trail with eagle eyes. But I only see random people heading in or out. The sun is beating down through my windshield and I start to sweat. I check my watch for the hundredth time, willing the time to move faster but it seems to have slowed to a crawl, refusing to grant me any relief from my anxiety.

Should I leave now and arrive first and have my cell phone out ready to call 911 if necessary? Or will I be a target standing in the middle of the forest by myself? Then again, it's not like anyone could sneak up on me. It's impossible to be quiet when you have to step on sticks and push through branches to reach the clearing.

Ultimately, I decide that it's safer to wait in my car. The minutes continue to tick by as if trapped in a never-ending loop. I'm so lost in thought constructing scenarios for the meeting to come, that I'm surprised when I check my watch and find that it's 9:55 a.m.

As I get out of my car, I look around once again. There's no one in sight, so I quickly make my way across the road to the trail, looking back before I enter. Satisfied that no one is following me, I walk at a fast pace for about five minutes until I reach the landmark where Brad and I used to veer off into the forest. As I do, I stand there for a moment listening but I don't hear anything other than the birds chirping in the forest. Taking a deep breath, I start my walk into the woods. It's not too far off the trail, but far enough that no one on the trail could see me.

The branches snap as I walk on them and push them aside. I step over a fallen tree and know I'm almost there. I can see the area through the trees and I strain to catch any colours other than the yellows, greens and browns of the forest.

Then I see it. A dark figure that appears to be sitting in the cleared area. It's a person sitting down. I slow my pace as I approach. The person is turned with their back to me, and I can't make out if it is a man or a woman. There's a hood covering the back of their head. I pause when I'm about ten feet away. I know they hear me. Why won't they turn and look? Breathing heavily, I pull my cell phone out of my pocket in case I might need it. Then I call out.

"Brad?"

CHAPTER 25

The figure turns. I catch my breath and freeze. It's him. Brad. He stands up and removes his hood. He looks fine. Healthy. I'm not sure what I was expecting, but I thought he might at least have some cuts or bruises.

He smiles that gorgeous smile and my anxiety instantly lessens.

"Claire. You came."

I walk forward into the clearing, legs shaking. I don't know what to say.

"Are you OK?" I ask, my voice trembling. "What happened?" I still can't believe it's really him.

"Yes. I'm fine," he replies. "Come sit down."

It's then that I notice the brown and white plaid blanket that he has spread on the ground. I walk forward and he sits down. I join him. He reaches toward me and I stiffen, but he only gives me a brief hug.

"Did you come alone?" he asks.

"Yes," I reply. "No one knows I'm here." As I say it, I instantly regret it. Maybe I shouldn't have admitted that.

"Good. I knew I could trust you," he says looking at me with his deep blue eyes. I had forgotten how he could make my heart melt in an instant. I thought all my feelings for him had faded, but it only took a few minutes in his proximity to see that I was wrong.

"Where have you been?" I ask, anxious to know what happened.

"It's a long story, and you're not going to like it, but I want to you listen until I'm finished and don't judge me."

"OK," I respond, bracing myself for what's to come.

"But first," he grabs my hand, "I want to know how you're doing. Are you alright? I've been so worried about you."

His touch sends tingles through my body. "Yes. I'm doing fine," I reply.

He studies me as if he is trying to figure out if I'm being honest.

"Good," he responds, squeezing my hand and smiling awkwardly. "Anyway, I'm sure you're anxious to know what happened."

Brad looks up at the sky. "I don't really know where to begin. I'm still trying to figure out how this all happened myself."

He looks back at me. "It was about 6 months ago that I met Shelley at a company party."

I flinch at the mention of her name. I wasn't expecting his story to start out with *her*.

Seemingly unaware of my reaction, he continues. "She was there with her friend Ethan, who is also an acquaintance of mine. We talked and we both had too much to drink. Later in the evening, we ended up sneaking off to one of the empty rooms and having sex."

He pauses and looks at me, searching for my reaction. I already knew that the two of them had hooked up, but hearing him say it still causes my gut to clench. I look back at him trying not to show any emotion, and he proceeds with his story.

"I'm not proud of it," he says, "and I should have told you as soon as I realized that Shelley was your friend. But I was afraid of losing you and I was a coward, so I said nothing."

"Yes. I'm aware. Shelley told me," I respond, and it comes out sounding a bit bitter.

His cheeks flush slightly. He clearly wasn't expecting that. "Oh. I didn't know."

"She only told me recently," I add.

"I see. Well, in any event, Shelley and I saw each other for a short while after that, and then Karen found out about us. She saw a text message that Shelley had sent me that left no mistake about the nature of our relationship."

I nod hoping this part of the story ends soon.

"I told Karen that it was just a fling, that it meant nothing to me, which was true. Karen asked a ton of questions about Shelley—where I met her, how many times we hooked up and where we would meet. I don't know if she figured out who Shelley was, but someone emailed Shelley's husband at work and told him about our affair. After that, Shelley and I never saw each other again until you introduced us. I guess, as it turns out, that was the end of her marriage."

"Yes," I reply. Peter left her." Brad looks down as if ashamed before continuing.

"After that, Karen became very possessive, calling me throughout the day with excuses to check up on me. I even caught her following me once when I went to a business meeting." Brad pauses and takes a deep breath.

"One day she followed me to the park when I met you for a tennis match and she watched us. I don't know if we were affectionate or not, but she questioned me about it. I told her that you were just a friend who I played tennis with occasionally, but she didn't believe me. After that, she started booking treatments with you. I didn't know this until later."

"Yes. She did," I say. "I had no idea she was your wife."

He nods. "Anyway, at this point, things were going badly for us financially. I'm ashamed to admit that I falsified some of my business expense reports and I played around with the financial statements to make it look like my business was doing better than it actually was. I needed to do this to get a loan. I was having trouble making the rent payments for our condo, and eventually I had to tell Karen what was going on. I suggested that she may have to go back to work."

Brad looks off into the forest.

"Covid hit my business hard, and it began to fail. During the time that I was with you, I learned that some of my creditors were planning on petitioning my business into insolvency. I didn't know what to do. I was afraid of being caught for the fraud that I had committed, which could result in up to 14 years in prison, and I didn't want to go bankrupt and lose everything. I felt like such a failure. Everything was falling apart."

I already knew from Jenna's report that Brad was having financial issues, so this part of the story doesn't come as a surprise.

Brad turns toward me and looks into my eyes. "It was around this time that Karen came up with the idea of me faking my death so that we could get the life insurance proceeds."

I sit there frozen as the words sink in. *He faked his death?* For a moment I can't find my voice. Shock and disbelief take over and all I can do is stare at him with wide eyes. Is this some kind of a twisted joke? But his face is dead serious, and I know it's not.

Brad carries on talking. "We had a good life insurance plan that would pay out $800,000. I thought Karen was crazy when she first mentioned it, but she pressured me, saying that if I didn't agree to do it, my business fraud would end up being exposed and I'd wind up in jail. She didn't come right out and say that she, herself, would expose me, but I believed that she might. She was still hurt from my infidelity with Shelley, and whatever she knew about my relationship with you. She wanted us to move back to Montreal with new identities and live off the insurance money."

His words hang heavy in the air, and I feel a knot of unease in my stomach.

Tears start to form in Brad's eyes. "I know it was stupid to agree to go along with her plan, but I felt like I had no other option. She was on to my relationship with you and my business was failing. I had nothing left here in Vancouver. I couldn't leave Karen, because I was worried about what she might do to me. I was also worried that she might tell your husband about us. I felt trapped."

It does sound like a bad situation, but I still can't get over his plan to fake his death. There had to have been other options. And if he faked his death, did he also frame me for it?

As if reading my mind he says, "I know what you're thinking and I didn't set you up. I would never do that."

I look into his deep blue eyes and I want so badly to believe him.

"Karen had apparently researched the issue and she told me we needed to make it look like I was murdered. If I just disappeared and there was no body, the insurance company wouldn't issue a death certificate for at least seven years. There had to be some proof of my death.

"We started planning it. We decided I would go out with my friends one night and then disappear. Karen would say I never made it home and would leave evidence making it look like I'd been murdered. Being a former nurse, she took vials of my blood in the weeks leading up to my disappearance and we stored them in our fridge. She was supposed to plant the blood with my ID and cell phone at the park near our house. It would look like I was walking home and got jumped.

"Meanwhile, I would find a back alley and change into different clothes, put on a disguise and then catch a bus out of town. The plan was that I'd sleep overnight in an Airbnb that I rented under a fake name and pay for it in cash. The next day, I would catch a train to Montreal and assume my new identity. Crazy, I know. But my options were limited."

I can't believe what I'm hearing. All this time I thought Brad had been murdered or kidnapped or at the very least badly injured, and all along he had faked it? I'm still waiting for him to get to the part where he *didn't* set me up.

"I knew I was going to pull my disappearing act the week that I went missing," he says, "but I hadn't planned to do it that night. It was supposed to happen the following night. That Saturday evening was meant to be my last night with you. I told Karen I wanted to have one last night with my friends and she agreed.

"After our night out together, we walked back to your office and then you called a cab and I waited until you left. You were quite drunk and I wanted to make sure you got in the cab safely."

"Wait," I say, interrupting him. "Why were we at my office?"

"You don't remember? You were going to wait outside the hotel for a taxi, but I thought I saw someone that I knew so we decided to walk a couple of blocks and call a cab from there, but you had had quite a lot to drink and you fell while we were walking."

"Oh," I say, feeling my cheeks redden. "I don't remember that."

"Yeah. You were pretty loaded. You cut your knee. We went back to your office and cleaned you up, and I gave you some water to sober you up a bit. Then you called a cab and I waited to make sure you got into it safely."

So that explains my cut knee and bruised arm.

"Anyway," Brad continues, "after you left in the cab, I started walking back to my place. But the next thing I knew, Karen had pulled up beside me in her car and she was telling me to get in. She must have followed us. When I got in the car, she told me that tonight was the night I would disappear. I was pretty drunk at the time and was shocked to see her. She was acting strange. I could tell she was angry.

"She told me she had packed my disguise and money and had put them in a backpack that was sitting in the back seat of the car. She pulled into an alley, and I changed and left my clothes and cell phone in the car so she could plant them in the park. She had booked an Airbnb under a fake name for that Saturday night. She told me it had a smart lock with a code that I could use to let myself in. It all happened so fast. I wasn't expecting to leave right then, but I did what she said. The next day I caught a train to Montreal. Four days later, I arrived and found another place to stay that accepted cash."

"So, you were alive and well this whole time," I say. The hurt cuts deep.

Brad looks at me affectionately and rubs my hand. "You don't know how sorry I am for all this. I never meant to hurt you."

When I don't respond, he says, "I guess after I left, rather than planting my blood and everything else in the park, Karen went to work on setting you up. I had no idea she was going to do this. It wasn't until I saw it on the news that I knew what she had done. When I confronted her—we had burner phones that we used to communicate—she said we needed someone to be convicted for my murder. That way the courts would have made the finding that I was dead and it would be easy to get a death certificate issued to collect the insurance money."

Anger starts to bubble up inside me as I process Brad's words. He must have known for a while that he was going to pull this disappearing act and he never let on. Then he disappears knowing I'd think he was dead. And finally, he knew Karen set me up to be convicted for his murder but did nothing about it.

"So you let Karen frame me? You were just going to let me rot in jail?" I ask, voice rising.

"I wanted to do something, but the only way I could help you would be to turn myself in. If I did that, I'd be guilty of insurance fraud, and Karen would probably report me for my business fraud."

Tears prickle at the corners of my eyes as I struggle to make sense of everything.

"I wouldn't have let you go down for my murder," he says gently, looking into my eyes. "I didn't think they'd be able to prove you did it. If it came down to it, I would have turned myself in. But they let you go shortly after you were arrested so I didn't have to."

I'm not sure I'm convinced he'd have turned himself in, but I don't bother to argue. "Actually, it was Jon who got me out of prison," I say, hoping that he'd feel guilty that my husband had to fix the damage he'd caused."

Brad looks genuinely surprised. "Jon? How?"

"He had a tracking device on my car. It turns out he knew about our affair. He turned the device in to the police. It had a history that showed my car never left my office parking lot that night."

Brad is silent for a moment and I can see he's thinking. Then, with a half smile he says, "It's nice that Jon stepped up for you, despite how hurt he must have been about our affair."

"Yes. It was," I respond.

Neither of us says anything and the silence starts to become awkward.

"So why are you here?" I ask.

"Karen applied for a death certificate while you were in jail. But now that they've let you out, it will be difficult to get one. In any event, I don't think that Karen has any intention of sharing the insurance money with me if she ever collects it, and there's nothing I can do about it. She's stopped all communication with me. I think she was planning all along to keep my life insurance payout for herself."

I have to admit that Karen has taken me by surprise. I didn't think she had it in her.

Brad has a desperate look on his face. "I don't know what to do. I can't make any withdrawals from my bank account without getting caught. Karen has probably moved all our money anyway. I have no way of contacting her. She won't answer my calls. I had to risk coming back to Vancouver so that I could attempt to talk to her face-to-face. I went by our condo in the middle of the night last night, but when I tried my key in the door, it didn't work. She's changed the lock!"

"So what are you going to do now?" I ask.

"I don't know. I need to get Karen to talk to me. But I can't stay here in Vancouver without someone recognizing me. I also can't stay in Montreal indefinitely living off the little money I have. I'm sure I could get a fake ID and a minimum-wage job to get by for a while, but I don't want to live the rest of my life like that. I need your help."

Brad looks at me, his eyes searching my face. My heart breaks into a thousand pieces. After all the pain he's caused me, he shows up now and wants a favour from me? But as I look at him, I can't help but feel sorry for him.

"I don't know what I could do to help," I say, because I really don't.

"You mentioned before that you and Jon have a vacation cabin in Lions Bay that's empty. Porteau Cove, wasn't it?"

I'm surprised he remembers this. I mentioned it to him once a long time ago. "You want to stay at my cabin?" I ask incredulously.

"Yes. Just for a short time. I can't risk renting an Airbnb here. I'm all over the news. Someone might recognize me."

"Where have you been staying?" I ask confused.

"I just got here. I sent you that email from the train."

He looks pretty fresh for someone who had no sleep.

"I'm going to try to find a way to speak with Karen" he continues. "I need to catch her when she leaves our condo. But I have to be very careful that no one sees me. I know if I meet with her in person, we can work things out. Then you'll never have to see me again."

I'm starting to feel quite uncomfortable. I'm not a lawyer, but I'm pretty sure if I help Brad hide out, I'm going to become an accessory to him faking his death. This whole thing is crazy and I'm starting to feel used.

"I'm sorry Brad. I don't think I can let you stay at my cabin. I don't want to become an accessory in all this."

A shadow washes over Brad's face. "I thought you loved me," he says, eyes pleading.

I feel a stabbing pain in my heart.

"I thought I did too," I respond. "But now I'm starting to wonder if I even know you."

"Come on Claire. We've all made mistakes, done things we regret, things we're ashamed to admit." He pauses. "Even you."

I look at him with raised eyebrows. What is he referring to? Our affair?

"I'm friends with Ethan," he says. "I've actually known him since I first moved to Vancouver. He dated Shelley a month or so before I did. Anyway, I guess one night he and Shelley had been drinking quite a bit and she told him about what happened on that party boat that you were all on years ago."

I literally can't speak. I'm in complete shock. Why in the world would Shelley tell Ethan about that? And what exactly did she say?

"I'm not sure I know what you're talking about," I reply.

"She told him that the two of you were in the washroom with his ex-girlfriend, Casey or something—"

"Cassie," I correct him.

"Yes. Cassie. And you were arguing with her and she came at you and as you were defending yourself, she fell and hit her head and ended up dying."

Oh my God. Shelley really did tell Ethan. This is absolutely unbelievable. And she said that Cassie fell when *I* was defending myself? Why would she lie?

I look at Brad and say, "I didn't push Cassie. Shelley was the one defending herself when Cassie came at her, and Cassie slipped. The only thing we did wrong was to not get help. But who knows if getting help would have made a difference anyway."

"Well, either way, it doesn't look good, does it? When Ethan found out I was seeing Shelley, he confided in me about his relationship with her, and this story came up."

Is this a veiled threat? That if I don't help him, he can tell the police what Shelley and I did years ago? "So why are you mentioning all of this?" I ask.

"I'm just pointing out that you've also made mistakes in your past and I didn't judge you for it. If the situation were reversed and you came to me today asking for help, I would help you."

He looks at me with his big blue eyes. "I love you, Claire. I never meant to hurt you. I just got in over my head. Will you help me?" He reaches for my hand again and I pull it away.

His lips twitch and I see a flash in his eyes before they soften and he continues. "If I ever get caught at your cabin, I'll say I broke in. I won't implicate you. I just need somewhere safe to stay, and your cabin is vacant. I won't stay long. It will just be for a couple of days. I only need enough time to find a way to speak to Karen. Then I'll go back to Montreal. You'll never hear from me again."

His eyes grow misty. "I really do love you, Claire. I always did. I would have left Karen for you if I could have. I always wanted to have a child with you."

This last statement softens me. It's almost as if he knew that I thought I was pregnant with his child. He seems genuine.

"OK," I say reluctantly, and then realize he'll need my help getting to the cabin. "I can take you to the cabin now. I have the key on my keychain. But I don't want anyone to see you with me. There's a parking lot further up the road that's usually empty. I'll pick you up there."

"Thanks," he says, face beaming, while he stands up. I stand as well and he moves towards me as if to hug me. But then he sees my expression and stops.

"I'll meet you in a few minutes," he says, and then he bends down and starts folding the blanket.

About ten minutes later, I pull into the parking lot and wait. Brad shows up with a hood pulled over his head and a pair of sunglasses on. Shortly into the drive up to the cabin, Brad rests his head against the window and closes his eyes.

Pretty soon he's asleep, or he's pretending to be because he doesn't want to talk. I'm not sure which.

When we arrive, about forty minutes later, I let Brad into the cabin. Jon and I usually spend a few weeks of our summer here, but this year it has remained empty.

We walk in and Brad looks around. "Nice place," he says while shutting the blinds.

Then he looks at me romantically. The way he used to, and I'm not sure if he is thinking we're going to hook up. I look away and ask, "How long do you think you'll be here?"

"I don't think I'll be any longer than a few days," he responds. "I'll leave the key under the front doormat when I leave."

"OK," I reply, taking the key off my keychain and handing it to him.

"Could I ask one last favour?" he asks with his charismatic smile.

My heart sinks. What does he want now?

"Is there a store around here where you could pick up a few groceries for me? I don't want to be recognized by anyone."

I reluctantly agree. "There's a corner store a few blocks away. I could grab something for you."

"Sure. That would be great if you don't mind. I'm starving. I haven't eaten since yesterday."

As I leave, I wonder why I agreed to pick up groceries for him. It's amazing the spell he has over me. Somehow he always manages to weave his tendrils into my heart. I should hate him for everything that's happened, and instead I'm setting up room and board for him. Oh well. I guess it benefits me too, since I don't want him wandering around and getting recognized. The last thing I need is for the police to catch him staying at my cabin.

There's a corner store a few blocks away where I pick up some milk, juice, tea, bread, eggs, cheese, a premade sandwich and a couple of frozen meals. When I arrive back at the cabin and open the door, I see Brad standing there in his royal blue T-shirt and jeans. He looks good. It occurs to me that he always wears blue. Probably to emphasize the colour of his eyes. Then it dawns on me. Is Brad the blue rose in my dreams?

Brad steps toward me and takes the bags out of my hands, snapping me out of my thoughts. "Thanks, Claire. I really appreciate this," he says while smiling his infectious smile. That smile always had the power to chase away all the clouds and bring a little bit of sunshine into the day. But today is different. The room is heavy with the weight of goodbye.

I look at him a moment longer, knowing it will probably be the last time I see him.

"I hope everything works out for you," I say. "I honestly do."

"Thanks," he responds, smile disappearing. "I'm so sorry for everything that's happened. Take care of yourself, Claire, and know that I'll always love you."

I take one last long look at him, and then I turn around and leave. As I step outside onto the weathered porch and the cabin door shuts behind me, I drink in the memories of laughter and stolen kisses. The scent of wildflowers mingles with the distant promise of rain, adding to the bittersweetness of the moment.

CHAPTER 26

By the time I make it to the highway, the bitter taste of regret has started to form on my tongue. I can't help the feeling that I've made a grave mistake. I should never have helped Brad. For some reason, I don't think clearly when I'm in his presence. It's those damn eyes!

I don't know why I agreed to let Brad stay at my cabin. Now that I've had a chance to process everything that's happened, I realize that throughout all this he had no consideration for me whatsoever. Everything he did was for himself. He didn't care that I've been worried sick thinking he was dead, that I've been a complete wreck trying to figure out who was setting me up for his murder and that I went through the extremely traumatic experience of being arrested and thrown in jail. I was even questioning whether Jon was somehow involved, which I feel horrible about now.

If Brad gets caught, I'm not so sure that he'll pretend to have broken into my cabin like he promised. I hope I made the right decision in helping him. I feel like I'm walking on a tightrope, one misstep away from disaster.

Jon is home when I arrive and I can hardly look him in the eye, I feel so guilty.

"How was work?" he asks.

"It was fine. It wasn't that busy today," I reply as I take my shoes off.

"Is everything OK?" he asks.

"Yes. I'm just feeling a bit under the weather," I respond. "I think I'll have a bath." I pass by him, eyes looking downward, as I walk to the bedroom to get changed.

"OK. I hope you feel better," he calls out behind me.

After my bath, I try to push any thoughts of Brad out of my mind as Jon and I order take-out and sit down to watch a movie. But as we wait for our dinner to arrive, I find myself fidgeting and unable to focus on the show we selected. I keep glancing at my watch, wondering if I can come up with an excuse to go to bed early.

Finally, the doorbell rings and I jump up to answer it, relieved to have a moment to myself. I pay the delivery driver and bring our take-out back into the living room for us to eat while watching the movie. When it's finished, I tell Jon that I'm still feeling unwell and that I will go to bed early.

Not surprisingly, I can't sleep. I toss and turn worrying about what's going to happen with Brad. My body is wound tight, my nerves on edge. I need to talk to someone before I go crazy, but I definitely can't say anything to Jon. The topic of Brad is very touchy and he'd be furious if he knew I helped hide him in our cabin.

I also can't talk to Shelley, as she's proving to be untrustworthy. Cole is the only person who I can trust.

I wake up early, despite only having had a few hours of sleep. Knowing that there is no hope of going back to sleep, I get out of bed and get ready for work. When I arrive at my office, I call Cole right away. Luckily, he's available and answers the phone.

"Claire! It's nice to hear from you. How are you doing?" he asks in a cheerful voice.

"Fine," I say out of habit. Then I correct myself. "Actually, I'm not doing that great. I think I may have done something stupid."

"Oh?" he asks, and his voice changes to a more serious tone.

"Yes. I wanted to talk to you about it. But I want to make sure that everything I say to you is privileged. I mean, you can't repeat anything I say to anyone no matter what, right?"

"Yes," he answers. "I wouldn't be able to tell anyone what you say to me unless there is an imminent risk of death or serious bodily harm and I need to disclose the information to protect someone."

I breathe a sigh of relief. "So, even if I've somehow participated in a crime, you can't tell anyone?"

"No. What's going on Claire?"

"Brad's alive."

"What? How do you know?"

I tell him everything that's happened. He stops me to ask a few questions as I'm telling the story.

"Claire, I'm happy to hear that Brad is alive, but I think you made a mistake in helping him to hide out in your cabin. There's no actual crime for faking your own death, but it would be fraud, obstruction of justice and possibly public mischief and now you have become a participant in all that."

"So what should I do?" I ask.

"Well, I'm not sure there's anything you can do now. It would be best if Brad left your cabin as soon as possible. You also have the option of telling the police so that you can clear your name."

"I don't feel comfortable with that second option," I say. "I feel like Brad may have made a veiled threat. Unfortunately, he learned what happened with Cassie, the girl I told you about that died on the boat many years ago. The version he heard was that I pushed her. I don't think I could handle dealing with a second arrest for murder."

"I see. I don't think there would be any chance of you getting convicted for Cassie's murder or even manslaughter, but I understand your concern."

"Brad said he'd only stay at the cabin for a couple of days. I will check if he's gone the day after tomorrow and if not, I will tell him to leave."

"Be careful Claire. It sounds like Brad is pretty desperate right now. I wouldn't want to see anything bad happen to you."

"Oh, I don't think he'd ever hurt me," I say. "But I'll be careful.

After ending my conversation with Cole, I feel a bit better. It was nice to have someone to talk to. However, my good mood quickly changes in the afternoon when I receive an alarming message through my work email. All it says is:

Nothing will happen to you. But if you say anything about my transgressions, I will say something about yours.

What the hell does that mean, and who sent this? The email address isn't one I recognize. It's just a bunch of numbers and letters. The only person who could have sent this is Brad. But why? Is he worried I'll report him for his insurance fraud? Is he threatening to tell the police about Cassie if I do? I can't believe he'd do this. He had better be out of my cabin by tomorrow or I'm going to kick him out.

It's an hour later when I spot a police car pulling into the parking lot. I watch as José gets out and walks toward my office with another officer. I have a sinking feeling that something bad has happened.

I open my office door before they reach it and watch as José approaches.

"Claire, we are going to need to bring you in for questioning regarding Brad Carleton."

My jaw drops. "What?" *Did something happen to him?*

"If you come with us, we will explain more when we get to the station."

"Is he OK?" I ask.

"Yes. We've found him alive," José responds. "Please come with us."

My stomach turns. Brad got caught. Great. I wonder if I'm now implicated in all this because he stayed at my cabin. Did he keep his word and tell them that he broke in?

I tell José I need to cancel my last appointment for the day and grab my things. A few minutes later, I follow José to the station in my car. Sweat beads on my forehead as I make my way through traffic, trying to shake the feeling of impending doom.

When I arrive, José formally escorts me into the same room where he and Dianna previously interviewed me. Dianna is sitting there waiting. I seat myself across from her. She looks at me, and I think I detect amusement in her eyes.

"Claire, do you know why you are here?" she asks.

"No. Not really," I say. "José says Brad was found alive."

"Does that surprise you?" she asks.

"Yes," I respond. I am actually surprised that they have found him so soon.

"You didn't know he was alive?"

"Why did you bring me here?" I ask, avoiding the question.

"Well," Dianna says staring at me with icy eyes, "Brad came into the station this morning quite distraught. He says that you have been holding him against his will in your cabin up in Porteau Cove since the night he went missing. He says he was finally able to escape today. He's wearing the same clothes he was wearing when he went missing and he has a number of cuts and bruises.

As soon as the words leave her mouth, I know I've been duped. A surge of anger and betrayal washes over me. How could Brad do this?

I sit there staring a Dianna in shock and disbelief. All the pieces of the puzzle are finally falling into place, and the truth is a painful realization.

"What?" I finally ask in a raised voice. "That's insane! I did not kidnap Brad or hold him against his will."

"We went up to your cabin this morning, Claire, and found a pair of handcuffs with some of Brad's dried blood on them. He has bruising on his left wrist consistent with being restrained. He also has some old wounds that are healing."

I look at Dianna still trying to comprehend what's happening. Is Brad really doing this to me? I think of the email I received this afternoon.

Nothing will happen to you. But if you say anything about my transgressions, I will say something about yours.

Was it a warning not to tell the police about his insurance fraud? It's all coming together now. His attempt to defraud the insurance company fell through when the police dropped the charges against me and he didn't want to stay in hiding for the rest of his life so he set it up to make it look like I kidnapped him. It's the only explanation for his disappearance that would be consistent with the evidence the police already had. But his email also said nothing would happen to me. What did that mean?

Dianna's voice snaps me away from my thoughts.

"We also questioned the teller at the corner store a couple blocks away from your cabin, and he says you were just in there buying some groceries yesterday. Are you denying that you were keeping Brad at your cabin against his will?"

"Yes," I say. "I am denying it." I think for a moment. Then I ask, "How could I possibly have kidnapped Brad and driven him there when Jon had a tracking device on my car? You've already looked at the tracking history on the device and you've seen that my car was at my office the night Brad went missing. How could I have taken him to my cabin?"

"Brad told us that you knew about the tracking device and that you would take it off your car and leave it at your office when you met with him. He suspected you did the same on the night he disappeared."

Asshole.

I let out a long breath. I'm so pissed off right now. I can't believe this is happening. "This is ridiculous," I say, my voice seething with rage. "Am I under arrest? Because if I am, I would like to speak to my lawyer."

Dianna takes a moment to respond. "Not at this point."

"Then I'm leaving." I stand up and push my chair strongly back across the floor making a screeching noise.

"We'll be in touch," Dianna says, a small smile playing on her lips.

I glare at her and walk out.

As soon as I get back to my car, I call Cole, hand shaking, and tell him what happened.

"Next time call me before allowing them to question you. Did you advise them about your meeting with Brad?" he asks.

"No," I say, and then I tell him about the email I received. "I'm hoping Brad isn't intending on pursuing this absurd kidnapping story and he's just using it as a way to get around his insurance fraud. I didn't want to say too much, but I guess I'll have to tell them everything if I'm arrested."

"Yes," Cole responds. "I think you will. It's a good sign that they didn't arrest you, though. It means they don't have enough evidence on you. Let me see what I can find out."

I wait patiently in my office for Cole to get back to me. He calls about 40 minutes later.

"Good news Claire. Brad is refusing to press charges against you. The police could still charge you with a crime but it would be very hard to get a conviction given that he has advised them that he refuses to testify. He told them that he fell and cut himself and that you didn't intentionally hurt him. He claims you are mentally unstable and he just wants to see that you get the help you need."

Nice. "So, as suspected, he used me as a front so that he could re-appear alive without any consequences. What's going to happen now?"

"I would advise you not to speak to the police any further. If you are arrested, we will discuss what you should say."

"OK," I respond. "But now that Brad has shown up alive, won't it be all over the news? What's he going to tell them? I don't want people to think that I kidnapped him or that I'm mentally unstable."

"Brad can't do that, and neither can the police. You've denied the allegations and if either of them tells the media that you kidnapped Brad, you'd have a very strong defamation lawsuit against them. I've already spoken to José about this, and I have asked them to make this clear to Brad as well."

"Thank you. Brad has no money so there wouldn't be much point in suing him, but I don't think he'll say anything anyway because he knows I'll expose what he did. His kidnapping story would never hold up."

As soon as I hang up the phone, I know I'm going to have to tell Jon what has happened, and I need to do it before he finds out through the press that Brad is alive. I grab my jacket and lock up my office.

As I pull into my driveway beside Jon's car, I feel sick. I sit there for a moment before summoning the courage to get out of the car.

The front door creaks as I push it open. As I unclasp my jacket and hang it neatly on the hook, the sound of keys clattering against the wall echoes like an admission of guilt. I can hear Jon's footsteps coming from the living room and a few seconds later, my gaze meets his.

"Claire, you're home," he says with a smile, but as he looks more closely at me, the lines etched on his forehead deepen. "Is something wrong?" he asks.

I take a deep breath, knowing the disappointment and hurt that I'm about to cause him. I can feel the tension in the air, a silent judge waiting for my confession.

"Brad's alive," I say, my voice trembling.

Jon tilts his head in confusion. "What?" he asks as if he misheard me.

"He faked his death to collect life insurance," I say.

"He—How do you know?"

I swallow what little saliva is left in my mouth. "I saw him."

Jon stands there, his face a canvas of emotions. Confusion battled with hurt and anger simmering beneath the surface.

I tell him everything that happened.

"Unbelievable," he says. "This guy is really something. He sleeps with another man's wife, then he fakes his own death, and now he's faking a kidnapping? I think he needs some serious help. And it looks like he's trying to set you up for all of this!"

"Yes. It looks that way," I say, feeling embarrassed.

"Are you going to let him get away with this? Did you tell the police that he faked his own death for the insurance money?"

"No," I say, wondering how to explain it. "Brad is refusing to provide any evidence against me, so there won't be any charges, and I don't want to get involved with his insurance scam. He basically threatened to take me down with him, if I did that."

"But you had nothing to do with that," he says, and it sounds like more of a question than a statement.

"I know, but he'll make it look like I did," I respond.

Jon nods. "That guy is a real asshole. He deserves to be locked up. I don't know what you ever saw in him."

He's right. I was naïve, to say the least. "I don't either," I reply, tears forming in my eyes.

Jon seems to consider it for a moment, his lips drawn into a tight taut line. Then he turns toward the kitchen and says, "The pizza's here. I was just getting the plates out when you walked in."

I follow him into the kitchen as he opens the pizza box and serves us both a couple of slices.

"Looks like you could use a glass of wine," he says, walking over to the wine rack and pulling a bottle out.

I take it and smile realizing that Jon is going to drop this. He's not going to hold a grudge. I know the foundation of trust that we've been rebuilding has been shaken, but I think Jon realizes that Brad is no longer a threat.

I uncork the bottle of wine. "Can I ask you something?"

"Yes," he responds grabbing some napkins from the drawer.

"How did you find out about me and Brad?"

He pauses, seemingly surprised by the question. "Someone sent me an email telling me you were having an affair with him."

149

"Who?" I ask.

"I don't know. It was anonymous. The email address was something like, *yourfriend101.*"

I furrow my brow. "That's strange," I say. "Maybe it was his wife."

"Maybe," Jon responds and I can tell he doesn't want to talk about Brad anymore.

"Can I ask you one more thing?"

"What?" he responds in an annoyed tone.

"Did you follow me downtown that night that Brad disappeared?"

Jon hesitates before answering. "Yes. I hired a private detective after receiving that email and I placed a tracking device on your car. When you left, I tracked your car to your office, but I didn't know where you went after that. I did drop by JJ's and saw that you weren't there with Shelley, so I figured you were meeting him. But I didn't want to wait around all night at your office, so I returned home."

Jon takes his plate of pizza and walks into the living room. "Let's not talk about this anymore. I would like to have a relaxing evening and not have to think about Brad."

I pour myself a glass of wine, grab my pizza and join him in the living room. "Shall we watch a movie?" I ask.

The next morning, I wake up early and after getting ready for work, I turn on the morning news to see if there are any stories about Brad. It only takes a few minutes before a reporter comes on to announce that Brad has been found alive, he was being held somewhere against his will but he refused to reveal by whom. He would only say that the person who did it was someone known to him who had mental health issues, he is unharmed and he is not laying charges.

I roll my eyes. *I don't think I'm the person with the mental health issues Brad.*

Then Karen makes an appearance. Her eyes brimming with tears as she addresses a cluster of news reporters gathered outside her apartment building.

"I can't express how grateful I am that my husband has been found alive and well," she says, her voice trembling with emotion. "I was so worried, not knowing where he was or what had happened to him. It's been a nightmare. But by some miracle, he's back home safe and sound now. We're just so thankful to everyone who helped look for him while he was missing."

She pauses and takes a deep breath, then continues. "He's been through a terrible ordeal, held against his will. But he's a strong man and he will recover. We just hope that the person who did this gets the help they need. Thank you." She wipes her eyes before walking back into her apartment building.

What a joke! Those two deserve each other. I pick up the remote and turn the TV off.

Grabbing my jacket, I step out the front door to leave for an early appointment at work. I stop abruptly on the doorstep as I'm met with a small group of reporters stationed on my driveway. I wasn't expecting to see them so soon, but I'd prepared myself for the possibility that they might show up. With a

150

deep breath, I square my shoulders and face the small crowd. The warmth of the sun on my face contrasts with the cool apprehension coursing through my veins.

Microphones are raised and a few cameras flash sporadically. The reporters, sensing the opportunity to uncover a sensational story, start firing questions at me.

"Claire, were you holding Brad Carleton against his will?"

"Did you kidnap Brad?"

One reporter with a determined expression etched on his face, pushes past the others and blocks me as I try to get to my car. "Claire, there are allegations circulating that you held Brad Carleton against his will. Can you clarify your involvement in this matter?" A microphone is shoved into my face.

"Yes," I respond in a steady voice. "I had nothing to do with Brad's disappearance. I didn't know he was alive until yesterday."

I meet each reporter's gaze hoping to convey the sincerity of my words. But the simplicity of my answer is met with skeptical glances and raised eyebrows.

"I was working at my office throughout many of the days that Mr. Carleton was missing," I continue. "I spent every night here at home with my husband."

A brief silence settles over the scene, punctuated only by the rustling of paper and the shuffling of feet.

"Please let me through," I say, as I push past them and get into my car. As I do, I see Jon peeking out through the blinds in the living room. The commotion outside must have woken him up. I really hope the reporters don't bother him as well.

When I arrive at my office, I text Jon to see if the reporters are still there. Thankfully they've left. They don't return. The story dies soon after that.

CHAPTER 27

A week later, I receive another email from an unknown address. As soon as I see it, I know it's from Brad. The subject line is *Sorry*. My mind starts to race, thoughts colliding like cars in a chaotic intersection. I squeeze my eyes shut, willing the onslaught of emotions to subside, but they cling to me like a relentless vine. I click on the email, heart pounding against my ribcage. The screen flickers and my gaze locks onto the first sentence. I start to read.

I'm so sorry for everything that's happened. I know what I did was hurtful and caused you pain. I had no choice. It was the only way out for me, but I tried to protect you the best I could. I know you'll never forgive me and I don't expect you to. But just know that I never meant to hurt you.

Karen and I have separated and I plan to move back to Montreal, so you don't need to worry about ever running into me again. I wish you all the best in life. I still love you. You will always have a piece of my heart. xo

I begin typing a response, and it goes something like this, *Fuck you Brad.* But then I change my mind and delete it. I also delete his email. *I don't want your heart. You can keep it.*

I feel like a fool for ever allowing Brad into my life. To say that he turned my life upside down would be an understatement. But I've started taking steps to repair all the damage that was caused by that relationship.

Yesterday I suggested that Jon and I go to couples therapy. Things have been going well between us, but I think we need to learn how to communicate better. I was happy when Jon agreed to go. It means he feels the relationship is worth saving, despite my betrayal. I will make sure he doesn't regret it.

Although some people might think he's weak for forgiving me, I see it as a strength because forgiveness is not always easy. It takes a strong person to be able to set aside their ego and let go of the grudges and negative feelings they have toward someone who has wronged them. It's a strength to embrace understanding and compassion. I'm working through the same process, trying to let go of my negative feelings toward Brad and Karen.

As part of my healing process, I contact Karen and ask if we can meet again in the park. I have some questions that need answers. Surprisingly, she agrees. We have plans to meet tomorrow morning.

I also reached out to Shelley after not seeing or talking to her for a week. I have plans to meet her for a coffee this morning. As I walk to the café, I think about what Brad told me and I can't shake the feeling of betrayal. I don't understand why she would have told Ethan her distorted view on what happened with Cassie. I thought it was our secret. We vowed never to tell anyone, and I kept my word on that.

When I arrive at the café, I glance around but don't see Shelley, so I order a chai tea latté and find a seat at the back. Shelley arrives a few minutes later with a worried look on her face.

"Hi. Is everything OK?" she asks. "I haven't heard from you in a while. I've been trying to get a hold of you. I can't believe Brad is alive!"

"Everything is fine," I respond. But she knows something's up. I've been ignoring her phone calls and texts.

"Actually, there's something that's been bothering me," I say, my expression serious.

"What?" she asks, looking at me intently while readjusting herself in her seat.

I get right to the point. "I spoke to Brad and he said that you told Ethan that we were in the washroom with Cassie when she fell."

Shelley's eyes dart around the room as if desperately seeking an escape route. Then she looks back at me, her face contorted with guilt. "I'm sorry. I should have told you, but I thought you'd be mad."

"Why would you tell him that?" I ask, trying to control my anger.

She sighs. "Ethan and I were talking about the night we first met, and of course, Cassie came up. Ethan was saying how sad it was that she had fallen and passed away. But while we were talking about it, he mentioned that she had died almost instantly. I asked how he knew, and he said she was dead when they found her and the coroner reported that she likely died within minutes of hitting her head on the counter."

My breath catches, held captive by this unexpected revelation.

"I was so relieved when he said that," Shelly continues. "I realized that it wouldn't have mattered if we got help. She would have died anyway."

Shelley's face is beaming. "I was so happy, I started crying tears of joy. Ethan was asking what was wrong, and I ended up telling him what happened."

A sense of relief floods through me, dispelling the heaviness I had carried for so many years. My mood is instantly lifted. But there's still something that's troubling me. I look across the table at Shelley. "Brad said you told Ethan that Cassie fell into me and that I pushed her into the counter."

Shelley's brow furrows and she pulls her chin in. "No. I didn't say that. I said I pushed her away from me, and she slipped and fell into you before hitting the counter. You didn't push her, you just put your hands out to stop her from hitting you."

Good. At least she didn't say I pushed her. "I don't remember touching her at all," I say a bit defensively.

"Oh. I thought you did. It's all a blur. Anyway, it doesn't matter. She fell. It was an accident, and there was nothing we could have done to help her."

I consider what she's said. "You're right," I respond. And she is. But she still betrayed me. Although she only shared the story of what happened after she learned that we couldn't have done anything to save Cassie, she still lied about it, just like she lied about her meeting with Brad. I've learned a lot about Shelley since Brad went missing, and now I think I see why Jon never liked her. Although we've been friends for almost 20 years, this experience has changed things.

It's 10:00 a.m. the next morning as my car pulls into the familiar parking lot of the park. When I turn off the ignition, I look toward the picnic table and see that this time I have arrived first. As I get out of the car, I feel the warm sun on my skin. I walk up to the picnic table where Karen and I met last time and lower myself onto the worn wooden bench, feeling its familiar texture against my legs.

As I await Karen's arrival, my mind races through a litany of uncomfortable scenarios. I can already hear the strained conversation, the forced pleasantries and the painful silences stretching between us like an unbridgeable chasm.

As I sit there, my apprehension grows, tightening its hold on my senses. The chirping of the birds, once a source of solace now sounds like a cacophony of discordant sounds. The warmth of the sun is starting to feel oppressive, intensifying the discomfort brewing within me.

Moments later, Karen arrives. She seats herself across from me, face tight. No smile or hello. An awkward silence passes between us.

"Thanks for meeting with me," I finally say.

She nods, breathing out heavily. I can see she is as uncomfortable as I am. "I'm glad you contacted me," she says. "I've been wanting to apologize, but felt uncomfortable reaching out to you after everything that's happened."

"You mean after you framed me for Brad's murder?" I ask, and it comes out a bit more sharply than I intended.

"For participating in it all. It was Brad's idea, but I take responsibility for my part."

Brad's idea? I feel a lump in my throat.

"Why did you do it?" I ask.

She takes a deep breath. "I had caught Brad with another woman before he was with you. He claimed they were just friends and denied having sex with her."

Shelley.

"He promised me he wouldn't see her again."

I interrupt before she continues. "Did you tell her husband they were having an affair?"

"Yes," she responds with a puzzled look on her face, probably wondering how I knew. "But only after Brad told me that he had stopped seeing her and I realized he was lying. I saw her text messages to him, and I was able to track her down through her phone number at work and figure out who her husband was through her social media account. I thought he had a right to know."

Probably, but I suspect she did it more out of vengeance than out of concern for Peter's rights.

"Anyway, I didn't believe that Brad had stopped seeing this woman. That's how I ended up finding out about you. I followed him because he was acting suspicious and I thought maybe he was meeting her again. But he was meeting with you to play tennis."

I nod. This is consistent with what Brad told me.

"When I asked him about you, he got defensive and said you were just a friend, his massage therapist, and he should be allowed to have female friends. He said you were happily married. I looked you up, and decided to come in for some treatments thinking that maybe I could figure out if he was telling the truth."

She picks at her fingernail, then continues. "I followed Brad one day and watched the two of you check into a hotel. That's when I decided to tell your husband."

As she says this, she has a look of quiet triumph, an unspoken declaration of having shared something of significance. "I'm sorry," she says, "but I thought if you found it appropriate to ruin my marriage, then I would ruin yours as well."

I feel a surge of anger, but then realize she has a point. At least I know now how Jon found out. I suspected it was Karen, but wasn't sure.

There's something else that I've been wanting to ask her. "Did you put a note through the mail slot at my office?"

"No." Her face twists in confusion. "I didn't put any notes through your door. Why?"

"Oh, someone delivered a threatening note. I just thought it might have been you."

She snorts. "No. It definitely wasn't me."

After I heard Brad's story, I was convinced it was Karen, but now that I'm speaking with her, I no longer think so. I asked Jon, too, and he (angrily) denied it as well. I'm pretty sure it was Jeff. He's the only person who was unstable enough to have done that. It makes sense. Ethan probably told Richard that Shelley and I were in the bathroom when Cassie fell.

"Anyway," Karen continues, pulling me away from my thoughts. "Brad's business had been failing for a while and he told me that it may become insolvent. He wanted to move back to Montreal. He said we'd have to start over with nothing, and that he also might be in some trouble for doctoring his financial statements. He told me that he could even end up in jail, but that he had a plan to fix it all."

This story doesn't sound at all like the story Brad told me.

Karen continues. "I was shocked when he told me that he wanted to fake his death and have me collect the life insurance, then move back to Montreal and live under new identities. I thought the idea was ludicrous at first, but he kept chipping away at me and eventually convinced me that it would be exciting and we'd have a fresh start together. He'd done a bunch of research on collecting life insurance when there was no body and he said we'd have to set it up to make it look like he was murdered."

I can feel my jaw tightening as Karen speaks. It's sounding like it was Brad, not Karen, who came up with the scheme to fake his death.

"Brad asked me to get some syringes and take vials of his blood so he could set up a murder scene. I had no idea he was going to frame you. I believed he was out with his friends the night he disappeared. He took a disguise and the vials of blood in a backpack and he was supposed to leave his ID, cell phone, ripped clothing and blood in the park near our condo. I didn't learn until after he disappeared that he had decided to frame you."

Her gaze shifts toward me as if trying to measure the impact her words had upon me. I say nothing, keeping my expression neutral, and she carries on with her story.

"Brad told me that he needed to make it look like you murdered him because if you were convicted for his murder, then it would be easy to get a death certificate. He said he had made it look like the two of you were having an affair by drugging you and taking you up to a hotel room."

In that suspended moment, my mind scrambles to make sense of the new reality before me. My thoughts collide, pieces of the puzzle snapping into place with jarring force.

"He drugged me?" I ask incredulously.

"Yes. He put some roofie in your wine so you wouldn't remember the end of the night with him. That way you couldn't believably deny anything."

The world around me fades into the background, my focus narrowing to the weight of this new revelation. The whole time he was setting me up. I want the ground to swallow me whole, a chance to re-write my story with a wiser, more discerning hand. But for now, I'm left with this lingering feeling of being a complete fool.

Karen regards me with a hint of sympathy. "His plan fell through though, when your husband gave the tracking device to the police. Once they let you off, we realized we would probably have to wait a long time to get a death certificate if we could get one at all. Brad didn't want to hide out for the rest of his life under a fake identity with no money, so he came up with the plan of saying that you were holding him against his will at your cabin the whole time. That way he could re-appear without any consequences. I told him not to do it."

Well, Karen's version of events is in stark contrast to Brad's.

"That's not what Brad told me," I say. "He said that you stopped all contact with him and you were planning on keeping the insurance money for yourself."

Karen shakes her head. "That's a lie. I was in contact with Brad the whole time. But I stopped taking his calls when he suggested framing you for his kidnapping so that he could come out of hiding. I didn't want to have any part in it. I didn't even want him to frame you in the first place."

"I could have spent my life in prison," I say, anger rising.

Karen looks down at a small twig that she's picked up off the table, her fingers nervously twirling it in circles. "Yes, I know. Like I said, it was never my intention to frame you. But once Brad set you up, there wasn't much I could do without admitting my role in everything."

She puts the twig back down on the table and looks at me. "I made an appointment with a lawyer to see if there was some way I could tell the police the truth without any consequences, but when you were released from jail, I cancelled it."

I study her face, and it looks like she's is telling the truth.

"Claire, before you contacted me, I was going to get in touch with you. I've decided to make a deal to testify against Brad in exchange for immunity. You might be interested in providing evidence."

I'm not surprised to hear this. The police have been asking to interview me again, but I've refused for now. However, I did cooperate in providing my business records, which confirmed that I was working on most of the days that Brad was missing. They also questioned Jon who verified that I was home every night, apart from the nights I spent in jail. Cole said the police had quickly figured out that Brad had made up the story about being held against his will. They suspected that he'd faked his death to avoid paying his debts and to collect the life insurance money. I suppose all this brought them to Karen.

"I will definitely consider providing evidence against Brad," I respond. "Especially now that I know what really happened."

A small smile starts to form on her lips but never reaches fruition. "I think it's time for him to take some responsibility for his actions. It's his turn to suffer."

She's right, and I can't say I feel sorry for whatever ends up happening to him. But I don't want to waste any more negative energy on Brad. I would rather concentrate on my own life.

Karen stands up and glances over at the tennis courts before looking back at me with a distant look in her eyes. "Brad is a pathological liar. He used both of us, but I think in the end we will both be happier now that he's out of our lives. I wish you all the best Claire."

"Thanks," I respond. "You too."

Karen nods. Then I watch as she walks off across the park. It wasn't that long ago that I was sitting here watching her walk away under entirely different circumstances. I feel like I've changed a lot in that short period of time.

As I reflect on my past, I realize that although I've always valued trust, honesty and loyalty, every compromise that I made from my list of values took me further and further away from the person I thought I was, until I reached a point where I didn't even recognize myself anymore. And if I'm honest about who I was, I'd have to admit that I was a liar, a cheat and a coward. I did things to make myself feel good at the expense of others. I lacked the courage to have an honest conversation with Jon about the issues in our relationship. Instead, I chose the easier path of seeking fulfillment elsewhere. I wish I'd learned how to be happy on my own—that I'd known that you can't rely on someone else to make you happy. But I can't undo the past, and dwelling on it isn't going to change anything.

So, who am I? This is a question that has plagued me for as long as I can remember. Am I the person society tells me to be? Or am I someone else entirely, something deeper and more true to myself? As I sit here watching Karen walk away, I realize I may never fully know the answer. But that's OK because in this moment, I am content in simply being myself, flaws and all. And as I close my eyes and take a deep breath, I can't help but feel grateful for the journey that has brought me to this point. Who knows what the future holds, but for now, I am exactly where I'm meant to be.

AUTHOR'S NOTE

Thank you for joining me on this thrilling journey through the pages of my new novel. Crafting this psychological thriller has been an exhilarating and rewarding experience, and I sincerely hope that you have enjoyed reading it as much as I have enjoyed writing it.

As a new author, I understand the vital role your feedback plays in shaping my growth as a writer. You opinions and insights are invaluable to me, and I would be immensely grateful if you could take a moment to share your thoughts by leaving a review. If you liked this book, your review will improve the probability of others finding it. Thanks again for being part of this thrilling adventure.

ABOUT THE AUTHOR

Marley Quinn is an exciting new voice in the world of psychological thrillers. By day, she navigates the intricate twists and turns of the legal world, but by night, she weaves captivating stories that keep readers on the edge of their seats. A lover of literature from a young age, Marley's voracious appetite for books eventually led her to pen her own thrilling narratives.

When she's not immersing herself in the world of her characters, Marley can often be found savouring a glass of rich red wine. She also enjoys the simplicity and tranquility of long walks, as well as unleashing her energy in the boxing ring. But above all, Marley cherishes spending time with her loving family, who provide the support and inspiration necessary for her creative endeavors.

Made in the USA
Columbia, SC
11 October 2024

44210251R00102